LOV
YOU
GON

ALSO BY RONA HALSALL

Keep You Safe

LOVE YOU GONE

RONA HALSALL

bookouture

Published by Bookouture in 2018

An imprint of StoryFire Ltd.

Carmelite House
50 Victoria Embankment
London EC4Y 0DZ

www.bookouture.com

ISBN: 978-1-78681-685-6
eBook ISBN: 978-1-78681-684-9

For the men in my life:
David, Big John, Little John, Oscar and Robin

PART ONE: NOW

CHAPTER ONE

Friday

'When will you ever learn?' Luke said to the boy sitting beside him, his frustration apparent in every syllable. 'Didn't that black eye teach you anything?'

Callum stared at him, his bottom lip quivering slightly, the blue and yellow haze around his right eye all that was left of his injury. Defiance shone in his eyes, but he wouldn't speak, just sat there, a smouldering presence in the passenger seat. He was only nine, but had a teenager's attitude and reminded Luke of himself at that age, with his mess of sandy curls, earnest blue eyes and a tendency to bottle everything up. Except Luke's eyes hadn't been masked by fear, and his body hadn't scrunched in on itself like Callum's did, his shoulders pulled up to his ears. Luke's fingernails hadn't been bitten so much that the skin around them bled.

Rain drummed on the windscreen, the monotonous sound of the wipers getting on Luke's nerves. He turned the heater up a notch, aware that Callum was shivering.

'We are going and that is it.' Luke tried to make his voice calmer than he felt. 'No arguments. Okay?'

Luke sighed. It was all his fault, wasn't it? His fault that his child had started wetting the bed, that he cried himself to sleep, that he hardly spoke to him anymore, wouldn't even look at him most of the time. So much anger in that little heart. So much pain.

It has to stop. Luke knew that, and this trip seemed like the only option open to him now. But could he bring himself to do it? Could he really end this life that he'd made for them all?

What a responsibility children are, he thought. *Their little lives in our hands.* And he'd managed to mess up his children's lives good and proper.

Luke's hands gripped the steering wheel a little tighter. This was so much harder than he'd imagined. He stared ahead at the four lanes of cars, stuck in a stationary queue on the Thelwall Viaduct, just outside Manchester; the M6 at its finest. He checked his watch, an excuse to not look at his son, who he knew was still glowering. Luke could feel the waves of anger flowing from Callum, reverberating through the air, and being sucked into Luke's body with every breath he took.

He looked in his rear-view mirror, the car behind almost resting on his bumper. He caught a glimpse of his dark-haired daughter, head bent over her tablet; another reminder that this decision was not just about him. This was about his children. About taking the pain and fear and worries away. He nodded to himself. He could do that for them, couldn't he? However hard this was going to be, it was an act of mercy that had to be done. There really was no choice now. He inched forwards as the queue started to move.

Luke flicked a glance at Callum. 'Sorry, fella, I didn't mean to get cross.' He ruffled his son's hair. 'I know this is scary, but let's just stick with it for a little while longer, okay? You've got to trust me.'

Callum pressed his lips together, a frown making a groove between his eyebrows, his expression so like his mother's that it made Luke's breath hitch in his throat. Callum nodded before turning his face away, such a familiar expression of defeat that it squeezed Luke's heart. The beep of a horn made him look up. The cars in front had moved on and he accelerated, shifted the car into second gear, his jaw clamped shut. They were on their way again. On their way to peace.

CHAPTER TWO

Sunday

Mel squinted against the explosion of light in her rear-view mirror.

'Dip your flipping lights, would you?' she muttered as she cautiously negotiated her way round a tight bend. The car behind was large and chunky, its headlights as bright as searchlights in the black of the February night, and was tailing her so closely she hardly dared brake for fear that the driver would end up on the back seat. She looked at the clock on the dashboard. This damned thing had been behind her for almost a quarter of an hour and she could feel the tension dragging at her shoulders.

She knew she was driving slowly, but the road was narrow and twisty – and everything would have been so much easier if she'd arrived here in the daylight as she'd originally intended, but... *Well, the delay was worth it*, she thought, with a wry smile. Finally, she had the promise of a new contract with a company she'd recently started doing a bit of work with, and that wouldn't have happened if she hadn't stayed and put in the extra effort. Occasionally, when you were a working mum, business had to come before family. She nodded to herself. That was the unfortunate truth of it.

Branches clawed at the passenger door as she navigated yet another tight bend, her teeth gritted so hard her jaw was starting to ache. It was a mystery why they were coming here for a holiday, given that they lived on the edge of Snowdonia in North Wales. You'd think that was wilderness enough to explore, but apparently not. Apparently, this area had other things to offer. That's what Luke had said when he'd told her where they would be spending the half-term holidays.

'Why couldn't he just have booked Center Parcs like any normal person?' she asked the empty passenger seat, like she had an invisible friend sitting there. She swung the wheel round a sudden corner, almost running up the grass bank, and her heart flipped for a second, sensing she was going to crash. It was no good, she was going to have to stop and let this idiot get past. Thankfully, the road widened a little and she pulled into a gateway, allowing the car to get round her and speed on its way. She sat for a moment after it was gone, trying to return herself to the sense of calm she'd felt earlier. When she'd thought she had everything nicely organised in her mind.

'Should have booked it myself,' she huffed. 'Daft letting a man make holiday arrangements.' But she knew in her heart that she'd been pleased when he'd surprised her with it, even though it had clashed with a work event, because it meant some quality time together as a family. Something they'd been missing in recent months. What did it matter where he'd booked? *It's the thought that counts*, she told herself, smiling at the mental image of her big, handsome husband with his wavy blond hair and rugged features; a nose that had been broken playing rugby and was now a little crooked, a scar on his right cheek from a rock-climbing accident, his square chin with a little dink on one side from a childhood mishap. And those crystal blue eyes that still made her stop when he gazed at her.

A whole uninterrupted week on holiday. How long since that had happened? She felt her annoyance evaporate, to be replaced by a small buzz of excitement. The children were going to love it, being at an age where they could handle an adventure, and that's exactly what this holiday was going to be.

'It'll be great,' Luke had said. 'Honestly, wait until you see the website. All these activities right on the doorstep.'

She'd leant over Luke's shoulder as he scrolled through the pictures, his enthusiasm infectious.

'See. We can hire mountain bikes and go for rides in the forest. Have picnics. You know the kids love a picnic. Loads of walks. Look, there's a sculpture trail. You'd like that, wouldn't you? We could even go up one of the fells if the weather's good. And look at this…' he'd scrolled down, 'A high ropes course!' He'd looked up at her, his face alight, and her heart had melted. He was as excited as the children would be. Not that she would be going near the thing, but she'd happily take pictures and enjoy seeing them having a good time.

She'd wrapped her arms around him and snuggled her face into his neck.

'What a lovely surprise,' she'd said. 'That'll be perfect.'

And it would be, she thought now, if only she could find the place.

She clicked on the inside light and checked the directions, looked at the map he'd printed for her, not wanting to rely on her satnav, because he'd warned her it might not work too well on these little lanes. She seemed to have been on this road for an awfully long time and she wondered if she'd gone wrong again. *Surely I should be there by now?* She traced the road with her finger and realised with a sigh of relief that she was only a couple of miles away.

'Hallelujah! Hallelujah! Hallelu-jah!' She sang the words, then jazzed it up with a gospel rhythm, adding a few Praise the Lords for good measure. Singing always cheered her up, but there was no doubt that she felt a little confused. New possibilities had presented themselves over the weekend, another option that she wasn't sure what to do with.

Mum and wife. That was all she'd ever wanted to be and now her life was a twisted knot of conflicting priorities. She squared her shoulders, pushed any thoughts of work out of her mind and focused instead on getting to her family. That's what was important.

The village was a mere blip on the map, just a collection of cottages on the edge of Grizedale Forest in the Lake District, and as she got nearer she slowed down, hunched forwards over the steering wheel, checking for road signs. *My god, these roads are awful.* Spooky as well, surrounded by trees for miles and miles. Anyone could be hidden in these woods. Or anything. She gave an involuntary shiver.

Despite Luke's enthusiasm, she still felt that a week of getting cold and wet would not do their tempers much good, cooped up in a little cottage with unpredictable February weather hurtling around them. She shivered at the thought, unsure why he hadn't booked them a holiday in a warmer destination. Clearly her hints about Tenerife being a nice place for a family break had been too subtle, and she decided that she'd have to try and be a little bit clearer next time.

No heated swimming pool. No childminders. No lovely coffee shops and restaurants. Nope. All those amenities are miles and miles away. Down these tortuous roads. And don't get me started on the fact it's self-catering!

But then, the holiday wasn't about her, it was, as Luke had said, all about the kids. She smiled to herself and put a hand on her stomach. Wondered if, by some miracle, it had worked this time, if one of her aging eggs had actually succumbed and was, at this very moment, growing inside her into a new being. *Positive thoughts, positive thoughts*, she told herself, as she willed a baby into existence.

A sign loomed out of the gloom in front of her. Satterthwaite.

'Yes! At last.' She breathed a sigh of relief that seemed to start at her toes and work its way up through her body, leaving her sagging in her seat as she peered over the steering wheel. On the left, the instructions had said. And there it was, a wooden sign on a gatepost, the lights of the house visible behind a tall privet hedge. And Luke's mud-splattered 4x4 parked in the drive, next to the house.

Mel swung off the road, parked up and wriggled her feet, uncomfortable in her smart shoes, which really weren't the best design for driving. Six o'clock, that's when she'd told Luke she'd be here in her last text, promising to set off after the morning workshop, which she'd told him she was running. As a management consultant, she usually stayed to do a bit of networking after every event she organised, cementing her place as a professional they could rely on. However, this weekend had not really gone according to plan and now she was two hours late.

Mel was Mrs Punctual, always on time, early rather than late. Always. Her heart gave a little jerk. Manchester to the Lakes. How could it have taken her the best part of eight hours? She took a deep breath. Obviously, she'd had to stop for something to eat, and that had taken longer than planned. Then she'd decided to avoid the motorway because she hated the M62 and there had been an accident on the M6. Nobody could predict the traffic, could they? Plus, the last bit of the journey had resembled a rally track more than a road. She couldn't be blamed for being careful. Better that she got here late than ending up in a crash somewhere because she was rushing to make up time.

Anyway.

She took a deep breath and stopped her mental gabbling, picked up her handbag, rested it on her lap and rummaged inside until she found her make-up bag, then tilted the rear-view mirror so she could see her reflection. She tutted and tried to tidy her hair, which was misbehaving on one side, as if she'd slept on it when it was wet. Her mouth twitched. She found her comb and persuaded her hair back into some sort of shape. Normally it was a sleek shoulder-length bob, a shiny black curtain that swung round her face; a style which looked simple, but had cost a fortune to create. Still, it was worth it, giving her the right professional image, and she looked a lot younger than her forty years. Everyone said so. Wide-set brown eyes sparkled back at her as she tidied up the smudged mascara with a face wipe, swiped a new covering of powder on her cheeks, nose and brow, then touched up her lipstick.

She zipped up her make-up bag, gathered her reading glasses and phone, put everything into her handbag and sat for a moment, taking a few calming breaths. *You're here now.* She wondered if they'd eaten or whether she'd have to start cooking. She hoped he'd done the shopping, and got some easy dinner in; the thought of slipping straight into catering mode after a long and emotionally exhausting day was not something she wanted to contemplate.

'Don't worry about the cooking,' he'd told her, when he'd seen her face fall at the idea of a holiday cottage instead of a hotel or the resort that she'd favoured. 'We'll all share the jobs. Make sure it's a holiday for everyone.'

Hmm.

She made her mind change tack, her eyes scanning the cottage, which looked like it was a decent size and much smarter than it had appeared in the pictures. This looked like it had potential for a bit of comfort. And she really, really hoped he'd bought wine. She closed her eyes for a moment, aware of her exhaustion now that the adrenaline of the weekend was starting to fade.

Running the workshops always got her hyped up. It was like being on stage, putting on a performance, but she had to be alert, watch all the interactions between attendees and pick up on the different personalities. She allowed herself a glow of pride; the success of the event was all down to her and the clients had been delighted with the way everything had gone.

'We'll definitely want you to do some more work with us. And I'll recommend you to Head Office,' the Regional Manager had said. It was a big company, with branches all over the UK, and it could turn out to be a real money-spinner, not to mention the fact that it would look good on her company website and social media profiles.

Yes, there was no doubt that she was good at her job, but it did keep her away from her family at times, and she'd started to wonder if she needed to balance things better. That's why this week was so important; a bit of time for bonding and not thinking about work at all.

'Get out of the car,' she told herself, her energy levels on empty, making such a simple action seem like a Herculean effort. The lights glowed from the windows and she imagined Tessa and Callum, all excited about being in a new place, planning what they were going to do during the week, Luke getting the house organised. She smiled to herself, and climbed out. It would be fine. Fun. They were going to have a great time, a holiday to remember.

She started to drag her case up the gravel drive, the little wheels bumping and sticking, making it feel like she was wrestling with the damned thing. Her stomach gave a gurgle, a reminder of hunger, or possibly nerves? Was Luke going to be cross that she was so late?

Although the glow of the lights made the house look warm and welcoming, when she opened the front door, it was as chilly inside as out. *Does the place even have central heating?* she wondered, a nugget of dread settling in her mind. *Imagine what it's going to be like if it doesn't.* She shivered and closed the door behind her.

'Luke,' she called. 'Luke?' She stopped and listened; the air felt still and undisturbed.

She left her bags in the hallway and went from room to room, taking in all the details, possessions scattered everywhere. The lounge ran across the front of the house, with a huge picture window looking out onto the front garden. It was nicely furnished with a red, squishy sofa in front of an inglenook fireplace, equipped with a large wood-burning stove, and two matching armchairs on either side. A blue patterned rug sat in front of the hearth, a pile of logs stacked on one side of the stove, a basket of newspapers and kindling on the other. Pictures of landscapes hung on the walls, and a series of downlights gave the room a cosy glow. *Nice.*

She went back out into the hall and opened the door on the opposite side, walking into a spacious dining kitchen, which was surprisingly sleek and contemporary, with a U-shaped worktop and an enormous American-style fridge-freezer on the far wall. The dining table was a large slab of oak, all wavy round the edges, sitting on stainless steel legs. A laptop was open on top of it. A pink fleece hung over the back of a chair, Luke's jumper lay in a heap on the floor and shoes were scattered by the back door.

Mel clacked through the kitchen, Her heels slipping on the tiles. The back door was unlocked, just as the front door had been, and she peered outside, the kitchen lights casting a glow across a paved patio area. Beyond that was a wall of rustling blackness. She closed the door and walked back to the hall, noticing the row of wellingtons. She frowned and glanced around. *How strange. Maybe they're hiding?* It was just the sort of practical joke they'd play on her. Callum thought it was hilarious every time he made her jump out of her skin. She nodded to herself, a smile on her lips.

She slipped off her shoes and crept up the stairs, stopping to listen at every creak of the floorboards. But all was quiet. She held her breath as she sneaked into the first room, the master bedroom with an en suite bathroom by the door. She checked inside. Nobody there. Luke's pyjamas lay on the floor. A T-shirt and underpants had been discarded on a chair by the bed. She threw open the wardrobe doors to find Luke's clothes hung up, all neat and tidy, a pair of shoes sitting underneath, but nothing else. No child waiting to spring out and scare the bejesus out of her. Her eyes swung round the rest of the room and she walked over to pull the curtains closed. There was something eerie about a black pane of glass, something she really didn't like, but as she glanced out she wondered if they might be hiding outside in the bushes somewhere.

She crept out of the room.

Back down the hallway, she peered into the children's bedrooms, tutting at the mess they'd managed to create in the space of two days. A jigsaw puzzle had been started on a dressing table in the room that Tessa had claimed, the box tipped up on the floor, pieces everywhere. Clothes were scattered all over the unmade bed, sheets rumpled as though caught in a whirlpool. In the next room, Callum's tablet lay on his pillow. She tapped it and a frenzied battle scene emerged on the screen, Transformer robots made out of cars, the sound deafening, making her scrabble to turn the thing off again. She listened. Surely there would be a giggle, a rustle of clothing, the sound of breathing?

Silence filled her ears, stuffing them full of the absence of her family. A shiver ran through her, making her teeth chatter, and she wrapped her arms around herself.

They're not here.

She straightened, deflated by the lack of a welcome, and went back downstairs, no effort to be quiet now, her teeth nipping at her bottom lip and annoyance furrowing her brow. They were going to make her go outside. In the freezing cold. While they were probably all wrapped up in coats and scarves and not cold at all.

Well, they could wait a bit longer. In fact, she'd let them come and find her, while she worked out how to get some heat on. She sighed, disappointed that her imagination had been so wrong, her expectations of happy smiles and hugs so wide of the mark.

She hurried back into the kitchen to see if she could find a boiler of some sort. She had no idea what sort of heating arrangements there were, but she could see radiators, so that was encouraging. A search of the kitchen and utility room found no sign of anything resembling a heat source. Then she remembered the log burner in the lounge and wondered if it heated the house as well. It seemed the only option. She put a hand on the black metal. Cold. It was when she straightened up again that her eyes caught the note propped on the mantelpiece.

Gone for a hike. Weren't sure when you'd be here. Luke

The note was scrawled on a scrappy bit of paper torn from a note-book. She went to put it back, then stopped, frowning. *Shouldn't they be back by now?* It had been dark for a couple of hours, and knowing how meticulous Luke was when he planned his outings with the kids, she knew he would have made sure that he got his timings right. Then it dawned on her. *A night hike! Why am I not surprised?* It's just the sort of adventure he'd decide to do with the kids, to make the holiday a little more special. They were probably out looking for badgers or bats or some other nocturnal creature.

She stared at the cold fire. So, they'd gone out and forgotten to stoke it up before they left. An easy oversight, she told herself, when you were used to a boiler on a timer that switched itself on and off, with no need to even think about it. Still, she could get the fire going and let the house warm up for their return. In the meantime, she had a little bit of space to grab something to eat and relax.

She sent him a quick text telling him she was at the house, and headed to the kitchen. She pulled the fridge door open then stopped when her hand grasped a bottle of wine. *Wait a minute there. We need to think about this.* She put a hand to her stomach. *Can't take risks. Not at my age. This could be my last chance. My very last chance.*

She pulled out a carton of milk and flicked the kettle on. 'Let's make do with a nice cup of tea,' she said into the silence. The fridge was well stocked and she was pleased to see bags of fresh pasta and ready-made sauce. Nice and simple. Things were looking up, she decided, delighted that she wasn't going to have to start creating a meal from scratch.

Humming to herself, she took her mug through to the lounge and perched it on the mantelpiece while she started to get the fire going, looking forward to being there to welcome her tired and bedraggled family back home again.

On the whole, Luke hadn't done too badly, she decided. It was a nice house. No, it was a lovely house. Plenty of space, homely, nicely decorated with a lovely bathroom and an en suite. There was even a utility room, she'd noticed, where all the wet and muddy clothes could go. Yes, it would do very nicely.

An hour, two cups of tea and a bowl of pasta later, Mel sat in front of the fire, watching the logs glow red, while she pulled the blanket she'd found in the bedroom tighter round her shoulders. She'd changed into her joggers and sweatshirt, with a fleece over the top and thermal socks on her feet, just until she'd properly thawed out. At least she could feel some heat from the fire now, but the rest of the house was taking a while to warm up. She checked her watch again and frowned.

They should be back by now.

She glanced at her phone, but there was still no answer to her text. Mind you, reception was a bit intermittent, she'd noticed, better at the front of the house than the back.

Slowly, she uncurled herself and straightened, feeling like she'd been frozen into place, all her joints stiff as she walked to the window, glad to see the reception change from one bar to two. *Maybe that's the problem?* She rang his number, but his phone went to voicemail. She tutted and peeped through the crack in the curtains, not able to see much for the rivulets of rain trickling down the window panes.

Fancy taking those poor kids out in this weather. She was starting to feel a bit annoyed now. He must have checked the forecast, because he always did, and would have known there was a weather front coming in.

Going outside was not something she relished, but she decided she had to go and have a look, see if there was any sign of them coming up the road. She shuffled into the hall, slipped her feet into her wellies, pulled on her waterproof and opened the door, shivering in the wind that rattled branches and murmured through the hedges that bordered the garden.

She walked to the road, the glimmer of lights from the house shining on the wet tarmac, but beyond that, an oppressive darkness. A loud swooshing heralded a sudden burst of hailstones, which bounced on the road, off the cars, the trees, finding their way down her neck, icy rivulets melting down her back, making her gasp and run inside, slamming the door behind her.

She wrapped a strand of hair round her finger and tugged.

Although Luke had taken the kids out in the dark plenty of times, it was now nine o'clock on a cold, wet February night and pitch-black outside. She'd been here for over an hour and the fire had been stone cold when she'd first arrived, so she had to assume they'd been out for several hours.

They should be back by now.

CHAPTER THREE

Sunday

Mel went to the mantelpiece and looked at the note again. No time on it. No clue as to which direction they'd gone. She checked her watch. Ten past nine. Her jaw worked from side to side as she stared at the note, wondering what to do; unwilling to just sit there, waiting. She tried ringing Luke again, but when it went to voicemail, panic started to whisper in her ear that something was very wrong. Snatching up her car keys, she headed outside, her wellingtons slapping against her legs, in too much of a rush to find any other shoes to change into.

She backed out of the drive and decided she'd head left, towards Hawkshead, given that she'd driven in from the other direction and if they'd been walking that way she would have passed them. She drove slowly, her headlights on full beam, scanning the sides of the road. There was no pavement, just stone walls and trees and she followed the road through Hawkshead, all the way to Windermere. Then she turned around and retraced her route until the road branched, taking her to Coniston. She passed very few other vehicles and definitely no people walking. The wind had whipped up now, thrashing through the trees, splattering squally showers against the windscreen with a sudden force that made her clutch at the steering wheel as she struggled to see the road through the deluge.

The knot of nerves tightened in her belly.

Luke wouldn't let them be out in this.

He was an accomplished outdoors person, having grown up on a farm in the mountains of Snowdonia and then, when he'd been in the forces, been trained in survival techniques. He would never put the children at risk. Of that she was sure.

They'll be safe and warm somewhere, she decided, and headed back to the house. Maybe they'd crossed paths and had already returned. Her heart was racing now, her palms clammy as she hurried down unfamiliar roads.

She dashed inside, but could feel by the stillness, the eerie silence, that they weren't there. It didn't stop her calling their names, hoping to hear a reply. She left another message on his phone, desperation in her voice as she asked him to ring her.

Her hand went to her forehead as she paced in front of the fire. If they'd been caught out by the weather, or got lost even, maybe they were in a pub somewhere? That was a possibility, wasn't it? She looked on her phone and located the pubs within a ten-mile radius, then started ringing them one by one, her heart pounding in her chest as each person she spoke to said they definitely hadn't seen them and apologised for not being helpful, taking her number just in case.

She sat on the sofa, rocking backwards and forwards, chewing her lip so hard she could taste the blood. Her mind was crammed to bursting with possibilities, all of them worrying, making her uncertain what to do next.

Perhaps they'd had an accident and were in hospital? Her heart squeezed at the thought, but it made perfect sense. He'd have his phone switched off in hospital, wouldn't he? Holding her breath, her fingers flashed over her screen as she found the nearest hospital, and waited while somebody answered. No, they hadn't been admitted and weren't waiting in A & E, she was told. Which was a relief in one way, but not in another; at least if they'd been there they would have been safe.

Rain lashed against the windows, the wind humming down the chimney, making the flames flutter in the stove as the storm raged outside.

She closed her eyes, unable to imagine what might happen if they'd been caught outside in this weather. They'd be hypothermic in no time.

Mountain Rescue. Her eyes snapped open. *That's it!*

She dialled the emergency services, her heart galloping, sure now that this was her only hope.

'Hello? Police? My husband and our children. They're gone,' she said as soon as the phone was answered. 'Please help me. I don't know where they are.' Her voice cracked and the tears she'd been holding at bay shook through her body.

The operator soothed her until she was able to speak again and then took the basic details.

'I understand that you're worried,' she said when Mel had finished. 'But the kids are with their dad. Hopefully he's just not got a signal, and they're all okay.'

'This is an emergency,' Mel said, disbelief rattling round her head. *Is nobody going to help me find them?* She swallowed the fear that bubbled up her throat and tried to tone down the shrillness in her voice. 'We're talking about people who've gone out hiking and not come back. That's what we're talking about.'

'I appreciate that, and what I'm going to do now is put you through to Mountain Rescue. They'll ask you for more information.'

Mel waited while the call was transferred. Her fingers drummed on the arm of the sofa. She looked at her watch again. Five past ten. Had she left it too late? Should she have rung straight away and then gone out looking for them?

A voice answered, jerking her from her thoughts, and she gabbled her story to the woman on the line in one long, turbulent sentence.

'Can you be as precise as you can with the location, please?' the woman said.

'I'm in Satterthwaite. Grizedale Forest area. I can't think of the names of the other villages near here. I'm sorry. It's all new...' Mel stopped herself and took a deep breath, panic snatching at her words. 'We're staying in Dove Cottage.' Mel's body was trembling now, although the house had warmed up nicely. Things were getting serious. 'I arrived today. This evening. And I found a note saying my family had gone out hiking. I've tried ringing my husband, but it just goes to voicemail.'

'Can you give me a grid reference?'

'A what?'

'A grid reference, for the trail they're on. Or do you know the name of the trail or what time they set off?'

'What? No...' Mel tugged at her hair. 'No, the note didn't say. I honestly have no idea where they went.' Mel was silent for a moment, her brain frozen with the idea that nothing was going to happen if she couldn't come up with a grid reference. She barely even knew what that was, never mind how to produce it. 'Can't you just come and look round here? Round the cottage?'

She could hear the clicking of keys on a keyboard before the woman came back on the line. 'Yes, that's no problem, we can use the cottage as a start point. It's just the more information we have the better.' She heard the woman take a breath. 'Now, I'm sure you've thought of this, but could they have gone to a pub and are going to be late back? Could it be something like that?'

'I've rung all the ones in a ten-mile radius and nobody has seen them.' Mel started chewing a nail, then stopped when she remembered it was acrylic. No more nail chewing for her. It didn't go with her profession. You couldn't have people who chewed their nails telling you how to keep calm in difficult situations. She grabbed a lock of hair instead, curled it round her finger. 'I've just got here. I told you. And there's a note.' Mel's voice was rising, getting more strident. 'And they aren't back and it's been dark for hours.'

'And they didn't take a car?'

'No, the car's still in the driveway.'

'So, they're probably within a four- to five-mile radius of Satterthwaite, given the ages of the children. Ten and nine you say?'

'Yes, yes, that's right.'

'And this is out of character, would you say? To not be back on time?'

Mel had to think about that. 'Totally out of character,' she said, which was possibly a lie.

'Okay, the team are on their way. It'll take half an hour or so to get them together. And if your family turn up in the meantime, then you will let me know, won't you? All these people are volunteers, you see. Most of them have got work in the morning.'

'Yes, yes, I'll definitely do that.' There was a quiver in Mel's voice. 'Please hurry.'

She put the phone down on the sofa and wiped her hands over her face, not sure what to think because one of the woman's questions had touched a raw place in Mel's heart. This was not such an unusual occurrence. Luke and the kids did go out and not come back when she expected them. She'd given up trying to ring him on these occasions, because, as he'd told her several times, if they were nature watching he had to turn off his phone so the noise didn't cause a disturbance. And then there were the times when he went up to the farm to see his family, when he would ring her at ten o'clock and say they were staying over, having left her fretting at home on her own.

She hated being left on her own, not knowing what was going on.

Mind you, it wasn't that she was bothered about going to see his family, because they were an odd bunch up at that huge old farmhouse. Freezing, it was, at this time of year, and everyone wore several layers of clothing indoors, even hats and scarves. Smelly, too. Quite a strange mixture of aromas; herbal incense and a whole range of different sorts of shit. Cows, sheep, pigs, horses and chickens. They kept them all and inevitably muck came in on the boots, which were kicked off in the hallway. She shuddered at the memory and remembered gagging the first time she'd walked into the house. So… grubby. Yes, she'd have to say the place was grubby. Nobody did any dusting, that was for sure; the windows were practically opaque and the floors always looked like they could do with a good mop. But then they would, with a pack of dogs and several pairs of muddy boots in and out all the time.

The family farmhouse was way up in the mountains, miles away from anywhere, at the end of a valley between Caernarfon and Porthmadog. A difficult place to grow up, Luke had said, especially when he reached his teenage years. She could only try to imagine how frustrated he must have been, not being able to meet up with his mates when he wanted to, always reliant on someone giving him a lift. You'd feel powerless in that situation, she thought, and she'd often wondered if that was the root of his troubles, where all the anger came from.

His family unnerved her, with their silences and sideways glances, so she was happy not to have to be anywhere near them. No, it was the fact that Luke just abandoned her at times that hurt.

But he always let her know. Always.

A knock at the door brought her back to the present.

They're missing.

My family.

CHAPTER FOUR

Sunday

Four men stood at the door, an assortment of shapes and sizes, wrapped up in red waterproof jackets and dark trousers. A couple of dogs on leads sniffed round their feet. The tallest man stood at the front, the others standing one step back. He was thin and gangly, with a prominent pointed chin and a livid starburst of a scar on his left cheek. His dark hair was greying at the temples and in need of a cut. Raindrops pattered on their clothing, tapping out a steady rhythm, plastering the man's hair to his head, dripping down his face.

Mel gasped with relief, her hand going to her chest.

'Mrs Roberts? Mike Brown, Mountain Rescue.' He held out a hand and shook hers with a firm grip.

'Oh, thank God. Come in. Please, come in.' She held the door wide and moved back to allow them through, but Mike shook his head.

'No, no, don't want to make a mess. We just need to know where we're looking and who we're looking for.'

Mel frowned, having hoped this would all have been sorted out. She really didn't know anything about grid references or where to start searching for missing people.

'I told the woman on the phone.' She realised her disappointment made her sound a bit snippy and she forced a desperate smile. 'I think it might be better if you came in. Look, it's a tiled floor. I can mop up any mess.' She opened the door as wide as it would go, and after a moment's hesitation, they traipsed inside, leaving the dogs sitting in the rain.

The men stood in an awkward huddle in the hallway, their clothes creaking and rustling as they all tried to fit in, puddles forming around their feet as the water dripped off them.

Mel plastered a smile on her face, telling herself the mess wasn't a problem. It really wasn't.

'Come into the kitchen. I'll make a cup of tea, shall I?'

The men looked at each other. Out of the corner of her eye, she caught Mike shaking his head. 'No, you're alright. We'd rather get on. It's going to be a long night as it is.'

'Oh, okay. Yes. Well…' Mel stuck her hands in her pockets, fidgety now that she was the centre of attention and four pairs of eyes were staring at her. 'I just got here at eight o'clock. Tonight. I was working today, you see.' She could feel the colour rising up her neck, burning her cheeks. 'I got delayed getting here. Anyway, the lights were on all over the house, as if Luke and the kids had just popped out. But the fire was cold.' She frowned, wondering why the two things hadn't connected in her mind before now. 'So, I suppose they can't have just gone out. Luke left a note, saying they'd gone for a hike and would be back later.'

'That's it? No clue as to which direction they went?' The men looked at each other, and she caught one rolling his eyes. Her hands clasped the material of her pockets. *Is it me he thinks is stupid, or Luke for not telling anyone where they were going?* 'So, where have you looked?'

'Well, I drove to Windermere and then back over to Coniston. I didn't go the other way because that's the way I came and I would have seen them if they'd been on the road. And I didn't pass any houses, so there's really no neighbours in that direction that they might have taken shelter with. And before you ask, yes, I have rung all the pubs.' She was getting frustrated at having to repeat herself while her family were out there in the freezing cold. Wet and hungry. They needed to be found, but she had no idea how to help the men narrow down their search area.

Mike frowned. The men glanced at each other. Mel squirmed.

'Well, they didn't go in the car,' she said. 'That's still in the drive. So, I'm assuming they've walked from here.'

'There are so many trails through the forest. Needle in a haystack,' Mike said with a sigh. He ran a hand over his forehead, smoothing wet hair out of his eyes. 'Right, so we'll see if the dogs can pick up anything.' He turned to Mel. 'Can we have an item of clothing for each of them, just to give the dogs a scent?'

'Yes, yes. Of course. Yes.' Mel hurried upstairs, snatching up pyjamas from where they'd been dropped on bedroom floors, her heart racing. She'd gone about this whole thing all wrong, should have called these people straight away. But now she'd lost over two and a half hours, and when it came to hypothermia, that could be the difference between life and death. Her stomach roiled as her mind spelt out her worst fears. That they were dead. Her husband, her children. Lying dead in the rain somewhere. Her chest heaved and she screwed her eyes shut, not wanting to think about it, not wanting to imagine this was even a possibility.

She ran back downstairs and fluttered the clothes at Mike, her voice cracking as she tried to keep control. 'Here you go. Will these do?'

'Great, thanks.' He took the clothes off her and his face softened at her obvious distress. 'Right, we'll just see what the dogs can do, okay? If your family are in the forest, well, they could be anywhere and it's a big space to search at night. I'll ring in and see if they'll put up the helicopter. They might pick up something on thermal imaging.'

Mel nodded, her hands wrapping themselves around each other. 'Yes, yes, that sounds great. Thank you.' Her chin quivered. 'Thank you so much.'

Mike's gaze searched her face, his voice gentle.

'Don't you worry, now. Most times people have just got lost, or plans have changed, or the phone battery has gone dead.'

She nodded, trying to make herself believe that there was nothing to worry about. 'Straight to voicemail,' she said, looking at Mike. 'Maybe you're right. Flat battery.' She let out a sigh. That could be it. Nothing sinister at all, just a flat battery. Which would mean he couldn't ring her or text even if he wanted to.

The men left and she went into the kitchen, found the mop and cleaned the hall, wiped round the work surfaces, and washed up her plate and mug. Then she put the kettle on, just for something to do. She hadn't really taken to Mike Brown, assessing her with those eyes. She got out a clean mug. *The truth is rarely straightforward, is it?* she thought as she tipped a slug of brandy into her tea, then realised what she'd done and threw it down the sink. She took a deep breath, in lieu of alcoholic fortification, as the idea of a baby fluttered in her stomach. *Not worth the risk.*

She filled a glass with water, went into the lounge and stood by the fire, warming the backs of her legs while she thought through the possibilities, trying to make a mental list of the things she could be doing to try and find her family.

An accident was still the most obvious possibility and she checked again to make sure she'd called everyone she could. She tried the nearest A & E department again, and ten minutes later, she knew they still weren't there. Then she discovered that there were two other hospitals in Cumbria, so she tried them, and found out they weren't there either. But then she'd known in her heart that they wouldn't be.

Luke had been roaming the mountains all his life and it seemed impossible to her that he would have gone on a hike that was in any way dangerous, not when he knew how worried she'd be about the children. And even if one or both of them had been hurt, then surely Luke would still be standing to raise the alarm?

The only other option was… was what?

Somebody kidnapped them? Even as the idea popped into her mind she knew it was fanciful.

Her hand went to her mouth as another possibility slunk into her thoughts. One that, although terrifying, she could imagine being feasible. She sagged onto the settee, her legs suddenly weak.

'Please find them, please find them, please find them,' she muttered under her breath, her face in her hands as she rocked away the horrible ideas that were circling like vultures, heralding death.

There was nothing to do but wait.

A couple of hours later, she was staring at the flames of the wood burner, her mind numb with fear, when a knock on the door startled her.

She jumped up and flung the door wide, watching the men traipse inside, wet and obviously weary.

'Well,' Mike said, 'the good news is the dogs picked up the scent straight away. Looks like your family walked up the road to Hawkshead. Then we lost the scent. So, what we think is they got on a bus. Could have gone to Coniston, Ambleside or Windermere. Take your pick.'

'A bus,' Mel repeated, as though he'd said they'd been beamed into a UFO by aliens.

'That's right.' Mike sighed and ran his hand through his wet hair, smearing it back from his brow. 'Thing is, I'm really sorry, but there's nothing more we can do tonight. Not when we've no idea which direction they went. The helicopter has had a good look round with the thermal imaging – they've circled over a wider radius and they can't see anything, so we don't think they're out in the forest. Not within walking distance of here anyway. And there'll be nobody at the bus company at this time, so there's nothing we can do on that score.' He gave her that steady stare again, and said gently: 'Most times, in these situations, it's a simple explanation and everyone turns up safe. But if they're still missing tomorrow

–' Mel looked away, unwilling to think that far ahead – 'then I think it's probably a job for the police, rather than us lot. We'll update them on what we've found.' He gave her a smile, firm and brief. 'But, listen, let's not jump to conclusions. Let's not think the worst. You try to get some rest tonight. I'm sure it'll be fine.'

Mel's mind skimmed over his reassurances and settled on just one word. *Police?* That suggested they thought something bad had happened, didn't it? Her heart hammered in her chest.

'Maybe they took a bus to Windermere or Coniston and got stuck there? Why don't you try ringing a few more pubs, widen the net a bit? And try some hotels. Maybe they decided to stay over for the night?' He shrugged. 'Is that possible?'

Mel stared at him. 'Even if his phone battery is flat, don't you think he would have rung me if he was staying over somewhere?'

Mike pursed his lips. 'I suppose he would. If he knows your number off by heart. Not many of us do these days, do we?' He looked as tired as she felt, dead on his feet, and she realised what he said made sense, igniting the faintest glimmer of hope.

She nodded at him as they turned to leave, barely able to mouth her thanks, tiredness dragging at her body as the adrenaline started to ebb away.

CHAPTER FIVE

Monday

Once the mountain rescue team had disappeared out of the drive and down the road, Mel slumped on the sofa, elbows on her knees, hands anchored in her hair.

What would Luke do? If they'd been caught out somehow, what would he do?

He'd get a message to her somehow. He would have rung the police himself and told them his predicament, wouldn't he? If he was in a pub or a hotel and didn't have his phone, couldn't remember her number, he would have found a computer, asked to borrow a phone and messaged her. She was sure of this. Absolutely sure.

If Luke was okay, he would have found a way to let me know and stop me worrying.

She scrolled through her phone, checking and re-checking, walking over to the window where the signal was stronger and refreshing her screen, but there was nothing.

Her body was limp with exhaustion and she leant against the windowsill. It was well after midnight now and she couldn't imagine that anyone would be manning reception desks in hotels. Pubs would be closed. There really was nothing more she could do tonight.

She wandered back over to the sofa, despondency adding weight to her limbs, heaviness to her heart. She curled up in a corner, the blanket draped over her. She couldn't go to bed. Not with her family out there. She tried the hospitals again, but she got the same reply. Re-checked her messages and still there was nothing.

Her screensaver photo caught her eye and she scrolled through her pictures; her life, her favourite memories right there in front of her. The Christmas play, the sponsored walk they'd done up Snowdon to raise money for the school, Callum on his scooter, Tessa on a pony, Luke all smart in a suit for an event. She smiled when she came to the picture of them all at the Greenwood Centre, an eco theme park in Snowdonia where they'd enjoyed a wonderful day out. They were all smiling at the stranger who Luke had asked to take the photo, genuine happiness on their faces. Tears pricked at her eyes. Would they ever be that happy again? Would she even see them again?

She found another picture, her and Luke on their wedding day, a picture taken by one of the witnesses, a man who they'd practically dragged off the street. She smiled to herself as she remembered the happiest day of her life.

It had been a whirlwind romance. Eight months after she met him they were married, and when all was said and done she'd have to take responsibility for that. She'd organised a surprise holiday. A break in Scotland, a whole week just the two of them, to wander on romantic walks, explore ancient castles and become enchanted by the Scottish wilderness. Exactly the sort of holiday she knew Luke would love. And if he was happy, then she was too.

Of course, she'd always had a plan, even though it seemed a little far-fetched, more of a fantasy really, but it was a leap year, so how could she not take advantage of it? Especially when Luke was so cautious. It was obvious he was madly in love with her, devouring her with his eyes, his mouth and his body whenever he had the chance. Oh yes, Luke was a very physical man, the strong, silent type, letting her chatter on, as she liked to do. He was perfect in every way, she'd thought, but she'd soon realised it was going to be up to her to make the move. And if things didn't go according to plan, well, it would have been money well spent setting the whole thing up, because the idea of it was thrilling enough.

'Luke,' she'd murmured to him on Valentine's Day, looking up at him from under her lashes as they sipped wine in the hotel dining room after a day exploring the beautiful Loch Lomond. 'I have a question I want to ask you.'

He'd smiled at her, his eyes crinkling at the edges, his face smoothed free of worry. She'd never seen him looking so relaxed and handsome and knew in her heart that this was right. She put a small red box on the table and he looked at it, puzzled. Her heart raced.

'Go on, it's a present,' she'd said, pushing the box closer to him, excitement pulling at her insides, tugging at the corners of her mouth.

He picked it up like it was an eggshell that could break any minute and snapped the lid open to reveal a gold ring inset with a ruby. Red being his favourite colour.

She'd licked her lips, her voice wavering with nerves as she took the boldest step of her life. 'Luke, will you marry me?'

His eyes had widened and he was silent for a moment. A waiter hovered in the background with the bottle of champagne she'd ordered, just in case. The air stilled, the silence thickened, filling her ears. Her skin had felt a sudden chill as she'd gazed at his bowed head. And just when she thought she might have misjudged the whole thing, he'd taken her hand and gazed into her eyes, a look so full of meaning she felt a delicious shiver run through her. Nobody had ever looked at her like that before.

'Yes,' he'd said, a smile on his face, his voice thick with emotion. 'Yes, I'd love to marry you.'

She'd laughed, relief washing over her in waves that made her light-headed as she put the ring on his finger. A perfect fit. Of course it was. She wasn't going to spoil the moment by getting that one wrong.

Later, as they'd lain in bed, sweating and tangled in the bed covers, she'd said, 'We could get married here, in Scotland, Luke. No fuss. Gretna Green is on our way home, you know.' She stroked his chest.

He looked away, and she could feel his heart thumping beneath her hand, making her wonder if he was having second thoughts. If she was pushing him too fast.

'No need to wait, is there?' She'd drawn a finger down towards his belly button and felt a shudder run through him. 'If this is what we want.' She sighed. 'And I know that you are everything I have ever wanted and more. I love you so much, Luke. So very, very much.'

He'd turned his head and kissed her in lieu of a reply, and they'd made love all over again. But he didn't give her a definite answer until the following morning, when they were sitting at the breakfast table.

'We'd better go shopping today,' he'd said, wiping his mouth with his napkin, a smile in his eyes. 'If we're getting married tomorrow.' He'd reached for her hand, his fingers interlaced with hers, the ruby glowing as if it was his beating heart. 'We need to look the part, don't we? And there's a ring to buy for you.'

Honestly, she'd almost exploded with happiness. At last she'd found her man, the one who would father her children, the partner who would be by her side for the rest of her days.

And now he was gone, and the children with him.

She curled into a ball, her heart aching for him, for the children, the family she had waited so long to cherish, knowing from the lack of contact, the futile search, that something was terribly, horribly wrong.

CHAPTER SIX

Monday

Mel woke stiff and bleary-eyed, shivering under the blanket in the lounge. She'd fallen asleep on the sofa and had a crick in her neck. But that was the least of her worries, she realised, as the events of the previous evening flooded into her mind, pouncing on her now that she was awake. Light filtered through a crack in the curtains and she sat up, rubbing her neck as she checked her phone, noticing the time was just after eight.

Her teeth chattered and she pulled the blanket around her, gazed at the blackness of the wood burner while she tried to pull her thoughts together. She checked again for calls and messages but there was nothing, and Luke's phone went straight to voicemail, making her throw her phone down in frustration. She slid her hands over her face, rubbing her temples as she tried to massage her brain into action. *What to do next?*

Her head ached, her tongue stuck to the roof of her mouth and she felt grubby. Inspiration was going to be elusive, she decided, until she'd got herself cleaned up.

She made up the fire and re-lit it before heading upstairs for a shower. As she stood under the pounding stream of hot water, she ran through the list of things she could do now that it was morning.

Having accepted that Luke and the children weren't going to magically reappear, it was up to her to hustle things along, and make a nuisance of herself so people would take things seriously.

The mountain rescue man seemed to think there was nothing to worry about, but Mike Brown didn't know Luke like she did. And she knew that the lack of contact signalled a possibility she hardly dared to think about. *Do not give up*, she told herself as she took a deep breath and rang the police.

Finally, after being bounced around several people, she was told by an efficient-sounding woman that the matter was in hand; two police officers were already on their way and should be with her within the next half hour, traffic permitting.

Mel put the phone down, unsure how traffic could possibly be a problem in such a remote area, but at least she knew now that something was happening. She stoked the fire and went into the kitchen, nerves tugging at every sinew as she wondered if there was any news.

Did she even want to hear any news? Would it be better if there wasn't any? *No news is good news, isn't that the saying?*

She clicked on the kettle, fumbled some bread out of the packet and dropped it in the toaster, more for something to do than from any burning desire to eat. *Feed your brain*, she told herself as nausea threatened at the very thought of eating. How could she eat when her children and husband were out there somewhere?

The worst possible scenarios lit up her mind and her hands flew to her mouth.

No, no, don't you dare think that. Don't you dare.

Bile burned up her throat and she leant over the sink as her stomach threatened to empty itself. The toast popped up, the kettle clicked off and she concentrated on the act of making tea and buttering the toast until her nerves settled.

She functioned on autopilot, going through the motions of the morning, getting herself ready for the day, munching her way through the toast without tasting it, scalding her mouth on her tea as she gulped it down. She stared at her phone, willing it to ping into life; a new message, a text, the trill of a call, but it lay stubbornly silent on the table.

As she waited for the police to arrive, she scrolled through her recent photos and found one she'd taken of Luke just a week or so ago. A candlelit dinner she'd made for him, a selfie she'd taken of the two of them, heads pressed together. She was grinning, but Luke... She studied his face. Was there something in his eyes she should have seen? A sign, a clue that everything was not as it should be?

A knock on the door startled her so much she dropped her phone on the table with a clatter. She snatched it up and reassured herself that it was still working before pushing her chair back and hurrying to the door. A man and a woman stood on the doorstep.

The man was tall and broad with a big belly hanging over the belt of his trousers, his shirt buttons straining to accommodate his girth and his jacket clearly not large enough to fasten anymore. His cheeks were ruddy, hair thinning on top to a sparse fuzz. He surveyed her with earnest brown eyes. His companion was small and slight, with a plain oval face devoid of any make-up, her thick brown hair tied in a short ponytail. She looked matter-of-fact and competent.

'Oh, thank God you're here,' Mel said before they could speak. 'Have you found them?'

He held out a hand. 'Inspector John Stevens, Cumbria Police, and this is Sergeant Ailsa Lockett and no, I'm sorry to say that we haven't found them yet, but there's plenty going on behind the scenes.' His voice was brisk and assured, friendly in an 'I know what I'm doing' sort of way, his handshake firm as he grasped Mel's clammy hand. 'We'd like to get a bit more information, and if you have some photos we could use, then that would be very helpful.'

They haven't found them.

Her brain froze at the thought, scalp prickling as though it was shrinking, tightening round her skull.

'Come in, come in,' she said, holding the door open, already walking down the hallway as they were wiping their feet on the doormat, wanting to get things moving. She led them into the kitchen and seated them at the table while she put the kettle on. 'Can I get you a drink?'

'Tea would be lovely, thank you,' Sergeant Lockett said, giving her companion a sideward glance. Mel scuttled around, placing mugs on the table along with a carton of milk and a bag of sugar. 'I'm sorry, not very refined,' she said, impatient to get started, 'but we're basically camping here and I can't find a milk jug or sugar bowl anywhere.'

'Just like my house.' The sergeant smiled and loaded a couple of heaped teaspoons of sugar into her mug. Mel gazed at her for a moment, then picked up her own mug in both hands and took a sip, holding it in front of her face as she fought back tears. In her mind, she'd willed them to have news. Good news.

'We'd like to start at the beginning, if you don't mind?' Inspector Stevens said. Mel nodded and blinked a couple of times while she got her thoughts straight. 'I know you've told Mountain Rescue but we'd like to hear for ourselves.' Lockett got out her notepad and the inspector gazed at Mel, nodding his encouragement as she started to speak.

'Well, I had to work this weekend.' Mel's eyes were restless, flicking between the inspector and the sergeant, then looking down at her drink. 'And I was delayed so I was late getting here. They came on Friday, and should have been here when I arrived, but the house was unlocked, all the lights on and they...' She bit her lip to stop the tears from coming, and took a deep breath before carrying on. 'They weren't here, just a note saying they'd gone hiking.'

The inspector nodded. 'And what is it that you do, Mrs Roberts?'

'I'm a management consultant. I help organisations with change management and run workshops and training weekends to help them to work out how to do things differently. More effectively.'

He nodded and gave her an encouraging smile. 'Right. So, you have to work weekends?'

'Not often. But this was a new client. And there was some… urgency, let's say. I can't say too much, but financial problems were forcing a bit of a radical restructuring. So we arranged an event to work through the suggestions and weed out the most promising ideas.'

'And the family came up here before you?'

'Yes, that's right. They arrived on Friday sometime. That's changeover day, apparently.' Mel put her mug down, her hands still cupped round it. 'My husband booked it.'

'Okay. So, they've been here all weekend?'

'Yes, yes. As far as I know, anyway.'

Lockett frowned. 'As far as you know? You mean you haven't spoken to them?' Mel caught the glance she sent to her boss and chewed on her lip.

'Friday. I know they got here on Friday. Luke sent me a text to say they'd arrived safely.'

'But nothing since?'

Mel picked up her mug and took a sip of tea. 'He didn't want to disturb me. I have to stay focused when I'm working, you see. We agreed that's how we'd do it, unless there were problems.' Mel put her mug down again, drew a pattern in the wet ring that it had left on the table. 'He's a very capable man, you know. Ex-forces. He doesn't need me babying him, or bothering him about whether they're coping. He's in his element outdoors, it's his natural habitat.'

'So, when did you arrive?' Stevens asked.

'I think it was about eight last night. Something like that.'

'Quite late then?'

'Yes. Well, I… I should have been here sooner, but the traffic…'
Mel's voice tailed off.

'And then…?'

'Well, when I got here, all the lights were on and the door was
unlocked, like they'd just gone out for ten minutes or so.'

'The place was unlocked?' Stevens looked at his sergeant, who
underlined the word in her notes.

'Yes. But then if they'd locked it I wouldn't have been able to get in.'

'They could have hidden a key and told you where it was.'

Stevens looked Mel in the eye and she glanced away, wriggled
in her chair. 'Yes, I suppose they could have done that, but it's
not what we agreed. We agreed that they'd be here when I arrived.
Simpler that way.'

He frowned. 'You didn't think it was strange, then, for the
house to be empty?'

Mel was quiet for a moment. 'Well… no, not really. I thought
they'd just gone out for a bit of fresh air, you know. Up and down
the road a little way, or something.'

'In the dark?'

'Well, they could have been looking for bats or… or, I don't
know, a creature that only comes out at night.' She shrugged, a
little impatient at the speed of progress, but told herself she had
to keep calm. *Just answer the questions.* This was the police she was
dealing with now. They knew what they were doing.

'And your husband does that sort of thing often?'

'Sometimes, yes. He was brought up on a farm, you see. He
likes nature and Tessa loves it.' Mel picked up her mug again, hid
behind it.

'Ah yes, the children.'

Mel nodded, eyes widening as she thought about them, out
there all night somewhere. 'Tessa and Callum.' She took a sip of
tea and swallowed down the surge of worries that saying their
names unleashed.

Lockett checked her notes and looked up at Mel. 'Can you confirm their ages for me?'

'Tessa's almost eleven and Callum's nine.'

The inspector nodded and gave her an encouraging smile 'So, let's go back to yesterday evening shall we?'

Mel put her mug down and started fiddling with a teaspoon. 'Well, I got here at eight. I thought they were hiding at first, playing a trick.'

'And do they do that often?' the sergeant butted in, and the inspector's mouth tightened as his line of questioning was interrupted.

Mel gave a rueful laugh. 'Oh yes, they like their practical jokes.'

'And after you got here?'

'Well, I looked all over the place, but there was no sign of them. The fire was cold, and I realised later that meant they must have been out a while. Maybe they went out in the morning? But then the lights were on, so perhaps it was early evening?' Her chin wobbled and her voice cracked. 'I honestly don't know. There were no clues as to how long they'd been out. Just the note on the mantelpiece.'

Stevens nodded. 'Ah yes, the note. Can we have a look at that please?'

Mel got up, glad of an excuse to wrestle her emotions under control. She left the room, snatched the note off the mantelpiece and hurried back into the kitchen, passing it to the inspector, who read it and handed it to his colleague. Mel noticed now that the writing was a slanting scrawl, like it had been written in a hurry, an afterthought.

'Hmm.' The inspector's mouth moved from side to side. 'Not very enlightening. But it shows that they intended to be back last night.'

Mel nodded.

'And when did you start to get worried?'

'Well, it was ten o'clock when I rang 999.'

'Two hours?' said Lockett. 'That's quite some hike. In the dark. And it got dark before six p.m. yesterday, probably earlier given the bad weather.' There was a slightly caustic note to the sergeant's voice, Mel thought, as she watched her flick back through her notes. 'And remind me, what time were you supposed to be here? You said you were later than you'd intended.'

'I was aiming for… for six. Six o'clock I said I'd be here.'

'So, when you arrived, you were two hours later than you should have been? And you waited until four hours after your husband thought you were going to arrive to notify anyone that they weren't here?' The sergeant's voice made it clear what she thought and the inspector visibly winced.

'Yes, well, I went out looking for them in the car, then I rang round pubs and the hospitals. And when none of that worked, I rang Mountain Rescue.'

Mel's cheeks were glowing and she was feeling increasingly flustered, as she wondered why the spotlight was on her when they should be out there looking for her family. A tear tracked down her cheek and she wiped it away with the back of her hand.

'Don't you worry, Mrs Roberts,' the inspector said, his face softening at her obvious distress. 'There's plenty of reasons why he might not have come back from a walk. Let's not think the worst just yet.'

'We could do with a photo though, to help with—' Lockett stopped mid-sentence, then started again, 'We need to ask around, see if anyone has seen them.'

'Does he have any friends in the area? Might he have gone to visit someone and forgot to tell you?' Mel turned to look at the inspector, frowning as she thought about it, annoyed that she hadn't asked herself the question the previous night. *Is there anyone?* She didn't know a lot about Luke's friends, if she was being perfectly honest. In fact, there were whole swathes of Luke's life, things that happened before they met, that she knew nothing about.

She shook her head. 'I don't think so. But there may be ex-forces people...' Her chin quivered. 'Did I tell you he was in the air force? He doesn't really talk about that period in his life.' Mel buried her face in her hands to hide the onset of tears, gulping them back as she spoke. 'I'm so worried now. Luke's at home in the outdoors, so competent, I can't imagine what would have happened to stop them coming home. Please find them. Please.'

The inspector's phone rang and he excused himself while he walked into the hallway to take the call.

'Try not to worry too much, Mrs Roberts.' Lockett gave her a reassuring smile. 'Missing people normally turn up safe and well. It's probably a misunderstanding of some sort.'

Mel closed her eyes as her emotions swelled inside her, filling her chest and threatening to burst out in a fit of sobbing.

'That was our colleague,' the inspector said when he came back into the room.

Mel took her hands away from her face and looked at him, hope flickering in her heart. *Tell me they've found them. Tell me they're okay.*

'It seems we've located your husband's phone. In Grizedale Forest.'

Mel's eyes widened. 'Just up the road?'

'That's right, we'll just pop up there and see what's happening. If you could give us your phone number –' he nodded to his sergeant – 'we'll keep you up to date.' Mel dashed into the lounge to find her handbag and one of her business cards, all the while wondering what this new development might mean. *That's not good, is it? In the forest?* She handed her card to the sergeant, who put it back in her pocket, along with her notebook.

'I'm coming. I'm coming with you.' Mel hurried into the hall and slipped her feet into her wellingtons, the only footwear she had to hand.

'It might be better if you just wait here, Mrs Roberts.' The inspector glanced at his colleague, who frowned, just for a moment, before her face cleared. 'Sergeant Lockett will stay with you and finish getting all the details.'

'No!' Mel's voice was louder than she'd intended, magnified by her desperation to do something. 'No, I want to come. Please.'

'But it might be a mistake,' the inspector said. 'It'll be better if you stay here and let me deal with this. We need to expand our enquiries and to do that we need you to give us contact names and numbers. Honestly, it'll speed up the operation if you talk to Sergeant Lockett.' He gave them both a firm nod, signalling the end to any arguments. 'I won't be long.'

Mel watched him as he walked down the driveway, saw him take a quick peek through the windows of Luke's 4x4, then her Audi TT parked behind it. She frowned and wondered what he might be looking for.

'Let's have another cup of tea, shall we?' Lockett said, when they were back in the kitchen. She filled the kettle and clicked it on, taking charge in a way that made Mel bristle. 'You can tell me about any family or friends who might know something.' Mel was aware that she was being studied, every move of her face noted and analysed. 'Does Luke have family?'

Mel turned and sat back down at the table. 'Yes. His parents still live on their farm, in Cwm Pennant. That's in Snowdonia, near Porthmadog. His sister Ceri lives with them. And her two little children. And then there's Luke's cousin, Ted. They all run the farm together.'

'And their full names?'

Mel chewed on her lip as she looked at the sergeant, having a little debate with herself. *Is now the right time?* She ran her tongue round dry lips. 'There's something I need to tell you.' The sergeant stared at her and the look in her eye told Mel it was exactly the right thing to do. 'I'm not...' She took a deep breath. 'I'm not the children's mother.'

CHAPTER SEVEN

Monday

The sergeant's eyes widened and her lips compressed into a thin line as she waited for Mel to fill in the obvious blanks.

Mel gathered her thoughts, rounding them up like errant sheep. She hated this – telling people that the children weren't hers – because it made her feel inferior in some way, as if only a biological mother had the power to love a child. But that was wrong, so very, very wrong. She'd always treated the children as if they were hers and if anything, she believed she treasured them far more than a biological mother would have done. Because, to her, they were precious, giving her a role that she'd almost given up hope of ever fulfilling.

'Their mother died. An aneurysm. All very sudden. I'm not sure how much of it has registered with them. Anyway, I'm their mum now and I love them like they're my own.'

The sergeant gazed at her and Mel wondered what more she was supposed to say.

'They're everything to me. Them and their dad.' She leant over and grasped the sergeant's hand, her voice pleading. 'We can't waste any more time. Please find them.'

Lockett nodded and Mel realised what she'd done. She snatched her hand away, letting it fall to her lap, where restless fingers nipped at the fabric of her joggers. 'What else do you need to know? Tell me how I can help.'

It took quite a while, Lockett noting everything down in a small, neat script. So many questions, little details that, to Mel, seemed unimportant. *Just get out there and find my bloody family*, she wanted to shout. But she accepted there were procedures, that there were other people at work, behind the scenes, following up leads.

Things are being done, she assured herself, but the tension in her shoulders refused to budge, and the feeling of loss that settled in her heart refused to lift. She looked up contact details and rattled off names as they worked through the network of people that knitted their family and work lives together. She found pictures and they decided which would be best for identification. And all the while she was listening for the phone. For the call that would tell her that her family had been found.

It wasn't a phone call but a knock at the door that finally interrupted the endless stream of information that the sergeant seemed to need. But although the exercise was mundane and annoying, it had been a welcome distraction and had helped to fill the time, stopping Mel's mind from travelling to the darkest of places.

She jumped to her feet and dashed into the hallway, throwing the door open just as the inspector was about to let himself in.

'Have you found them?' She clung to the door frame, waiting for him to put her out of her misery, Lockett hovering behind her.

Stevens looked thoughtful and sighed before he spoke, which made Mel's heart skip a beat – a sigh was never a good way to start answering a question. *Bad news?* She held her breath, waiting for the words she had been dreading.

'Well, a mountain biker found the phone, apparently. On one of the trails. Handed it in to the information desk. But they didn't think to keep him there for us to talk to.' He shrugged, his mouth pinched round the edges. 'So he's gone. But we have a good idea where the phone was found and the search and rescue team are out now, combing the area.'

'But you haven't found them?'

The inspector shook his head. 'No. Not yet.'

'I can help.' Mel grabbed her jacket. 'I can help them look.'

Stevens put his hand on her arm, stopping her from dashing out of the door. 'No, it's best to let them get on with it. They know what they're doing and we don't want to get in their way.'

Mel leant against the wall, a pained expression on her face. 'But I can't just wait here. It's killing me.' She looked at him, eyes brimming with unshed tears, hoping he'd understand. 'I can't.'

Lockett took her gently by the arm and led her into the lounge, settling her on the sofa. 'We'll stay here with you,' she said as she put a couple of logs on the dwindling fire. 'And we'll work through these people we've got listed to contact. See where that gets us while they do the search.'

Mel could feel the panic flapping in her chest, making it hard to breathe. But what could she do? Realistically, what on earth could she do to end this nightmare?

The inspector stood in front of her with his back to the fire, a puzzled expression on his face.

'It's all a bit odd, really.' His steady gaze unnerved her and a surge of heat flushed up her neck. 'It's quite a hike from here to Hawkshead, where they'd have to go to get on any bus, either the one going west to Coniston or east to Windermere.' He pursed his lips and looked at his sergeant. 'Must be about four miles?'

Lockett nodded. 'Somewhere around that.'

He tapped his phone and scrolled through it for a few moments. 'I'm just looking at the bus timetable. The last buses on a Sunday would set them down at six thirty p.m. if they'd gone to Coniston or five fifty p.m., if they'd gone to Ambleside or Windermere. By which time it would be dark. So they'd walk back on the road, not through the forest, which would be nigh on impossible to walk through at that time of day. But they didn't come back. So that means the dogs picked up their scent going from the house to the bus stop, not coming the other way.'

He looked back at Mel, his eyes seeming to bore right through her. 'In which case, how was the phone in the forest?'

Mel's mouth opened. And closed again. Silence filled the room, just the gentle ticking of the fire as the metal expanded with the heat. 'Maybe someone stole his phone?' It was the only thing she could think of, but given the lack of people in this part of the world, it seemed like a long shot.

The sergeant frowned at her, then at the inspector, and Mel saw a glance pass between them. 'I've got a list of people to work through,' Lockett said to him. 'Shall we get on with this in the kitchen?'

'We'll get the team organised,' Stevens said to Mel. 'If you could have a think, see if you can remember anything else that might help our search?'

They left her then, went into the kitchen and shut the door. She could hear the murmur of voices and wondered if they were talking about her. She wondered what they knew, what they'd find out. What she should tell them.

Her pulse quickened as the implications of things unsaid revealed themselves in her mind. She stared at the fire, her vision clouded by the swirl of what ifs and maybes that played themselves out in her head.

She was startled out of her trance by the buzz of her phone. A text. Her breath hitched in her throat as she snatched it up and looked at the screen. Then she sighed, deflated. It was Annabelle, the mum of one of Tessa's friends, wanting to know dates for the next fundraising meeting at the school. Mel was the chairperson and had been instrumental in a couple of successful events that she was hoping they could replicate in the summer term. Annabelle was her biggest fan and probably her closest friend among the school mums. She fired off a quick text and put the phone down.

She thought about the new friends she'd made through school, the mums who looked up to her, relied on her to organise the fundraisers that had brought so much new money into the school's coffers. She was something now, somebody important. Queen bee in her mumsy world, and it was a role she revelled in. Before Luke she'd just been a single working woman, living alone, with little social life apart from the choir. It was a lonely existence being self-employed, no work colleagues to socialise with and a need to keep a professional distance from her clients. For so long, she'd yearned for a family to call her own. And now... now, they were gone.

Her hands clasped together in her lap, squeezing tighter and tighter as she held on to the images of the people she loved, as if they would disappear if she let go. But this was no good, this sitting here, doing nothing. No good at all.

Mel paced round the house, a bundle of nervous energy, her mind unable to focus on any part of the situation she now found herself in, and unsure what to do next. She tidied the bedrooms, straightened duvets, carefully folded clothes and put them in drawers, picked up the children's tablets and turned them off. She hadn't been too happy when she'd spotted them, not when she thought they'd agreed that the kids should have a break from tech devices for a while. Seems Luke had made a different decision, but maybe he'd thought it would be something for them to do if the weather was bad. A holiday treat. He was all for treating the kids, was Luke.

She sighed as she remembered the discussions they'd had about that. Heated discussions, if she was being perfectly honest. He spoilt them, of that there was no doubt, and the last thing she wanted was spoilt kids. She put their last argument out of her mind and went downstairs to carry on her tidying, an activity that she'd always found therapeutic. But her pulse refused to calm down, her heart banging away in her chest as if she'd run a half marathon. How her family lived like this, she didn't know; their messiness was a constant bone of contention and they never seemed to learn. She put books back in the bookcase, a DVD back in its case, hung jackets on coat pegs, straightened the pile of wellingtons in the hallway, then walked round the house again, wanting it to be nice and tidy for when they came back. Because they would, wouldn't they?

The place was so quiet, so empty, just the low murmur of voices from behind the closed kitchen door. She inched closer, trying to listen, but the words didn't carry through the solid pine and she walked away a few steps. She hugged herself, needing the comfort of arms around her as her eyes focused on the row of wellingtons she'd just tidied, going down in size from Luke's size tens to Callum's size twos.

Her family, right there in the hallway.

But the tears wouldn't come. It wasn't sadness that she felt, it was… apprehension? No, worse than that. Fear. It jabbered in her head, all the possibilities piling themselves up into a mountain of worries. Her life, as she knew it, had come to an abrupt end, a halt, an impasse. And Luke was to blame. Her hands tightened round her ribs, fingernails digging in. She'd trusted him to come up here on his own with the kids, trusted that they'd be okay. *And look what he's done!*

She gripped herself tighter as she looked at the wellingtons again, their shapes still remembering the feet that owned them. Callum's hand-me-downs worn through at the toes. Tessa's leaning inwards due to her flat feet. Luke's still plastered in mud from helping out on the farm.

She was still standing next to the kitchen door when it opened and Lockett burst out, almost walking into her.

'Oh, I was just coming to find you. To give you an update.' She held open the kitchen door, her face a closed mask, expressionless. 'Why don't you join us.'

The sergeant looked at her a little differently, Mel thought, a look that sent a shiver of nerves up her spine. *What do they know?*

CHAPTER EIGHT

Monday

Mel sat at the table, opposite the police officers, sensing a distinct change in their manner. The inspector didn't look quite so friendly and sympathetic. Neither did the sergeant, although, to be honest, she hadn't been that friendly to begin with. Mel's heart squeezed in her chest and she could almost feel it struggling to pump the blood round her body, making her feel light-headed. She clung on to her chair, worried that she might faint.

'We've got a bit of a puzzle on our hands here,' Stevens said. 'And we're going to need a bit more clarity on a few points if we're going to sort it out.'

Mel nodded and ran her tongue round dry lips.

'You see, the bus drivers do the same routes all the time. They know the regulars and notice new people. And the driver on the route that goes through Hawkshead swears that your husband and children got on the bus on Friday, and he hasn't seen them since. He didn't bring them back that day or Saturday. And neither did the other driver who covers the route on a Sunday. So, can you tell us again when he last contacted you?'

Mel couldn't think, his words filling her mind. 'Friday? No, they can't have been missing since Friday.'

'But when did you last hear from him?' Lockett stared at her and Mel looked down at her hands, words stuck in her head as if glued there.

'Do you want to check your phone?' Stevens asked.

Mel felt hot now, uncomfortable under their gaze.

'I don't need to check. It was Friday. I think I told you that before. That's when he sent me a message to say they'd arrived safely.'

She twiddled her wedding ring round her finger.

'And you haven't heard anything since?' The inspector's voice was neutral, but there was a challenge in the question. They obviously thought she was lying and her cheeks burned.

When she finally spoke, her voice sounded shrill, defensive. 'I told you, we had an agreement when I was working that we didn't contact each other unless there was an emergency.'

Mel looked up to see two pairs of eyes studying her.

'Anyway, I thought…' She sighed. 'I thought he was still cross with me. I thought that was why he wasn't replying to my messages.'

'And why would you think that?' Lockett asked. 'You'd had an argument?'

Mel sighed again. 'Look. The thing is… my husband, he's not… he's not well. He's been having a few problems and…' She stopped, trying to work out how to phrase it. In the last six months, things between them had become… difficult. She thought back to a night that changed everything and a situation she should have handled differently. More carefully.

'Daddy, can I come into bed?' Callum's voice was shaky, punctuated with little sobs.

'Hey, course you can, son.' Luke's voice was a sleepy murmur as he took his arm from around Mel's waist and shuffled her over the bed a bit to make more space. 'Hop in.'

A draught wafted over her back as he lifted the covers. Her lips pursed and her body tensed as Luke turned his back on her so he could cuddle his son, leaving Mel hanging on to the edge of the bed.

'Another nightmare, was it?'

'I thought you'd left me, Dad. I was all on my own in this dark place and something was chasing me and you weren't there.'

'Just a nightmare, son.' Luke's voice was soft and warm. 'Nothing to worry about. I'm here.'

'I've got that meeting in the morning,' Mel said, jaw clenched. It was a pitch for her first major customer, her big break, the thing she'd worked five years to achieve. 'I've got to be up at half five. New client, remember?'

'Oh, yeah,' Luke mumbled, already drifting back into sleep.

'Daddy?' Callum's voice was a stage whisper.

'Yeah?'

'Can we go fishing tomorrow?'

'Fishing?'

Mel's hands curled into fists under the pillow, her teeth grinding.

'The river by Pops'. I saw a great big fish in there on Saturday.'

'Did you?'

'It was this big.'

Mel elbowed Luke in the kidneys. 'Shift up, will you, I'm falling out here.'

'I can't shift up.'

'Well, can Callum shift up?'

'He's on the edge.'

'Well, it's not going to work then, is it?'

'Course it will. You're okay, aren't you, Cal?'

She didn't hear him respond. Maybe he nodded. Wide awake now, tension bunched her shoulders as she looked at the digital display of the alarm clock: 2.53. 2.54. 2.55. She took a deep, calming breath and her eyes started to close.

'Can we, Dad?' Her eyes flicked open. Luke shifted, nudging her further towards the edge, and she could feel herself slipping.

'For Christ's sake!' Mel jumped out of bed. 'Please, I need to sleep!' She lowered her voice, spread out the words so the meaning was absolutely clear. 'I've got a really important meeting tomorrow.' Her nails dug into her palms, frustration coiling insider her like a spring as the pressure built. 'I do not want to hear about fucking fish!' That came out louder than she'd intended and sounded harsh, making her instantly regret her outburst. The bedclothes rustled, feet thumped on the floor, accompanied by the sound of snuffling sobs as Callum ran from the room.

'Did you have to?' Luke snapped. He put on the bedside light and she squinted in the sudden brightness. He glared at her, his eyes narrowed in an angry frown.

'I've got a—'

'I know what you've got,' he said, clearly annoyed, as he got out of bed. 'But we've got a son and he's more important than any frigging meeting.' She watched him march out of the bedroom and winced as he slammed the door behind him, a hollow feeling swelling inside her.

He hadn't come back to bed and, after a little while, she had gone to find him, wanting to put things right between them all.

Looking back now, that had been a mistake. It would have been better to let things cool down. But instead, things had been said and done, the memories of which still festered underneath the skin of their relationship like a boil.

'He can flare up,' she said now, aware of the police officers watching her. 'He has these little trigger points.' She chewed at her lip, wondering if she was making sense. 'He's easily stressed and it was all a bit of a rush getting ready for the holiday.'

'So, what do you think has happened?' Lockett asked.

Mel sighed again, not really wanting to air their problems in public. But she had to now, didn't she? If she wanted them to be found. She opened her mouth to speak, then stopped herself as she tried to find the right words, but there was nothing in her mind to

soften what she had to say, nothing to make it easier. She blurted
it out, her fingers bunching her joggers in her lap.

'I've got to be honest with you. The fact is, things haven't been
easy. This holiday was a "start again" sort of thing. We were putting
it all behind us and he was making a real effort.' She looked at
them and nodded as if to reassure herself. 'He was.' Her eyes shone
and a tear tracked down her cheek. She wiped it away with the
back of her hand and took a deep breath. 'He's not been well. He
was in the forces, you see; did I say that?' Stevens nodded and
Mel stared at him, not wanting to put her worst fears into words,
but she had to try, had to make herself face up to the truth of the
situation. 'He gets these… these depressions and I just hope…' She
covered her face with her hands. 'I hope he hasn't done anything
to himself and the children.'

Now that she'd said it, it seemed the only feasible option. If
they hadn't been found by now, with all the people searching, had
he hidden himself away and done what he'd threatened to do?

Lockett pushed back her chair, walked over to Mel and put
an arm around her as the tears streamed down Mel's face. 'I just
pray he hasn't hurt them. Please find them. Find my kids. Please.'

'Don't you worry, Mrs Roberts,' the inspector said. 'There's
lots of lines of enquiry for us to follow. Let's not think the worst
just yet.'

Lockett rubbed Mel's shoulder; an empty reassurance, Mel
thought, just like the inspector's words.

CHAPTER NINE

Monday

Mel couldn't hold back her tears any longer, a flash of panic burning through her once she'd voiced her worst fears. That Luke would kill himself and the children. Had things been that bad between them? She thought they'd sorted it all out, thought they'd talked through their problems and were coming out the other side. He'd seemed a bit more upbeat in the last few days, their household a little calmer, and she'd thought it had signalled an end to the sniper war that had raged in their household. It had exhausted them all, but neither of them had seemed able to stop the downward momentum, which had gone on for months, ever since the Callum-in-the-bed incident.

It didn't mean she didn't love him, though. Because even now, especially now, he was everything she wanted. Him and the children. They just weren't used to living with a woman who stood up for herself and refused to be a doormat.

'We've only been married for a year,' she sobbed and she felt the atmosphere shift. The sergeant's hand stopped rubbing her shoulder and she looked up to see the inspector staring at her. A hard stare that held a whole host of questions. Mel chewed her lip.

Should I have told them earlier? Would it have made any difference?

'But together longer, presumably?'

Mel shook her head. 'Not really, we'd only been together six months or so when we got married.'

Lockett's mouth dropped open for a moment before she spoke. 'So, when did their mother die? I don't think you said. I was assuming it was some time ago, but did I get that wrong?'

Mel studied her hands, fingers knotted together. 'I'm sorry, I should have said. Their mother died nearly three years ago. They were living in Scotland then, but Luke wasn't coping on his own and moved back to Wales to be near his family.'

The sergeant's mouth pressed into a thin line of annoyance. 'We'll need details of where he used to live in Scotland, then. Where he worked, any friends he may have been in contact with, to add to the list. Is it possible he's hooked up with someone he used to know from up there?'

Mel shook her head, her face a picture of regret. 'I don't know. Honestly, I don't know any of his Scottish contacts. I'm so sorry I didn't make it clear earlier.' But she knew why she hadn't and recognised denial on her part. She wanted to be the children's mother. Their real mother, instead of a stand-in, a pale imitation of the wonderful Anna. 'I just thought they'd be back by now. I didn't think it was important. Thought you'd never need to know.'

They never wanted me.

She surprised herself with the words. Spoken in her head, thankfully, and not out loud. But the bitterness of her thoughts made her heart shrivel inside her chest.

But it's true, isn't it? Look what happened just a couple of weeks ago.

'Tessa, why don't we have a girls' day out?' she said when she went into Tessa's room. The girl hardly ever came out these days and Mel thought it was unhealthy, something she needed to try and address. Tessa always seemed angry with her at the moment and she put it down to a sudden flush of hormones. Maybe if they had a day out together, she could get to the root of the problem, because there was clearly something bothering the girl. She saw other mothers out with their daughters, having a lovely time, taking selfies and shopping together. Surely it was only normal for her to want that too?

Tessa, who had been lying on her bed, reading a book, stared at her for an uncomfortably long time, before saying, 'No thanks,' and turning over, so her back was to Mel.

Rude, Mel thought, recoiling as if she'd been slapped and with no idea what to do next to bridge the chasm between them.

Callum wasn't much better. He stuck to his father's side like a little limpet, doing anything to attract his father's attention. And Luke fell for it every time. Like last week. All that fuss about the bloody dog. In fact, they'd all been as bad as each other on that occasion.

Animals die. They do. Mel sighed. *It wasn't my fault. That was Luke as well, though he'd be the last person to admit it.*

There was no getting away from the fact the kids resented her. She'd been so excited to have a family after all this time, but she'd completely underestimated how hard being a stepmum would be. Especially when their biological mother appeared to have been a saint. Who could measure up to that?

No, they just hadn't taken to her and she could only see things getting worse as they became teenagers. She could see rebellion in their eyes when she asked them to tidy up, to help around the house, to switch off whatever damned device they happened to be on. It drove her mad, the way they ignored her in favour of technology, with its virtual friends and make-believe worlds. She'd taken steps to try and redress the balance but they never wanted to spend time with her, wouldn't let her be their mum, and Luke did nothing to help.

'Give them time,' he'd said, like a soundtrack on repeat. 'It's not easy for them to have a new mum.'

Well, it wasn't easy inheriting children either, when there was no biological tie, no natural bond of love to soften the necessary conflicts of parenting. She'd lost count of the number of times she'd said sorry. Sorry for what? For trying to be a decent human being and bring up someone else's kids to an acceptable standard? Sorry for trying to run the house and their finances properly? Sorry for being herself?

'So, there was a bit of tension in the family?' The inspector's voice broke into her thoughts.

Mel's fingers gripped each other more tightly, her mouth moving from side to side as she contemplated his question. 'The children are very close to their father. And he has one view of parenting and I have another.' She sighed. 'It's caused a few arguments, but then what family doesn't argue? We have a lot of fun as well, days out together, evenings in all snuggled on the sofa. I don't think we're different to any other family, to be honest.' She sat up straight and took a deep breath. 'I think as a stepmum you always feel a little insecure.' She gave the inspector a tight smile. 'It's still early days, still getting used to each other's little ways, you know.'

'But, in light of the fact that you're not getting on too well, we have another scenario we need to look into, don't we? Might he have left you?'

Mel's eyes widened, her heart jumping as if she'd had an electric shock. Never for a minute had she considered this to be a possibility. They were only just married. They'd said their vows and only a few days ago, he'd told her how much he loved her. That he was sorry. That they'd make it work.

She shook her head. 'No. No way would he leave me. Honestly, that really isn't an option.'

Lockett gave her a look, which she thought might be pity, and she glanced away. What did she know about Mel's life? About the depth of their love, the special bond they had? *She knows nothing*, she thought, and decided that she didn't particularly like the woman. *Judgemental, and anyone doing her job really shouldn't be judging.*

'I want to do an appeal,' Mel said, gabbling now. 'On the news. Can't we do that? Somebody must have seen them in Windermere. Maybe they hitched a lift back here on Friday, instead of catching the bus? That's a possibility, isn't it?'

Stevens pursed his lips and glanced at his sergeant, who shrugged.

'It's worth a try, isn't it?' He gave Mel a reassuring smile. 'Sergeant Lockett can record it for us, then I'll get it sent out to the PR people, see what they can do for us on social media, as a first step. To be honest that seems to work better than the news these days.'

Mel sat back in her chair, a lightness to her breathing, relieved that she could actually contribute something positive to the search. It felt better to have told them everything, warts and all. Nobody had a perfect relationship, or perfect children, did they? Not in real life. She hadn't thought about Luke's friends from Scotland, but talking to them was a good idea. She didn't know them, but she was sure the police would track them down. At least it would widen the net and an appeal would jog people's memories.

Almost an hour later, after a few tries at the appeal, with Lockett coaching her, Mel managed to control her emotions enough to beg people to phone the police if they had seen her family, or knew anything that might help them to be found.

'That was great,' Lockett said, when the final attempt was deemed to be acceptable. 'The PR team will add an introduction and slide in the photos, and we'll get that circulating as quick as we can.'

'Yes, well done,' Stevens added. 'Not everyone is as comfortable speaking to an audience as you seem to be.'

Mel swallowed. *What does he mean by that?* 'It's my job,' she said, defensively. 'As a management consultant, I run training events and speak to rooms full of people all the time. Thank goodness it's helped me to do a good job here.'

Lockett tapped away on a tablet and finally looked up. 'The PR team are on it now. They say it should be on the local six o'clock news tonight as well.'

Stevens nodded. 'Fingers crossed it leads us to them.' He looked at his sergeant. 'Okay, well, I think we'll just have another quick look around if that's okay, see if there's anything else in the bedrooms that might help.'

Mel nodded. 'Yes, yes, please help yourselves. I'll put the kettle on.'

It wasn't long before they came back downstairs with the children's tablets in their hands. 'Is it okay if we take these?'

Mel hesitated for a moment then nodded and pointed to the worktop. 'Luke's laptop is over there if that'll help.'

'We can check their search history, see if they've been looking at places, or walks, or transport. If you could make a note of the passwords.'

'Oh, I don't know.' Mel shook her head. 'I've no idea about passwords. I didn't even know the kids had these tablets until I got here and saw them in their rooms. Luke must have bought them as a holiday treat. And I've never used Luke's laptop.' She shrugged, feeling helpless, berating herself for not knowing. 'I'm sorry, I just have no idea.'

The inspector sighed. 'Right, well, we'll get them up to the techies, see what they can do, and if you think of anything they might have used as a password, then please will you let us know?'

Mel nodded, her heart thumping, aware that once again she was falling short.

CHAPTER TEN

Monday

When the police finally left her, after what seemed like days but was only a few hours, Mel's brain was exhausted, her emotions spent. She wasn't normally a crier, but this situation had brought out what felt like a lifetime's worth of tears. Now she was alone she was glad to finally stop, and as she sat curled up on the settee, she wiped her tear-stained face, gazing at the fire as if it held the answer.

Her stomach gurgled, but she didn't have the energy to go and make something to eat, a feeling of nausea rising up at the thought of food. How could she eat when they were gone? When her life was falling apart. How could she?

Her thoughts travelled back over the day and she shivered, pulled her fleece round her body.

It's my fault, she thought, *for being so impulsive.* It had always been a problem and had always got her into trouble. *I should have learnt by now. Good things come to those who wait. Isn't that the saying? So why do I always do the opposite? Why can't I just use my bloody head and think before I act?*

The TV blared out the music for the six o'clock news and dread threaded its way through every nerve in her body. Then, when the local news came on, there it was. A family have gone missing in the Lake District. The police need help finding them. The pictures flickered up on the screen and she studied Luke's face, her heart lurching as if it had forgotten how to beat, her love for him as strong as it had even been.

Where are you, sweetheart? Where the bloody hell are you?

The pictures of the children. So young and innocent.

Then there she was, her face blotchy, eyes red-rimmed, pleading for her family to get in touch or for anyone to phone who might have information. She was shocked by how ragged she looked, but almost pleased as well. Surely people would take pity, take notice and something useful would come in?

When the newsreader moved on to the next story, Mel sat back and wondered how she'd got it so wrong, how her hopes and dreams of a perfect family unit, complete with a new baby, had been so comprehensively shattered.

She thought back to the recent bout of trouble, which had started about two months ago. She'd been squeezed into a lacy basque that she'd bought at Ann Summers. She'd thought it might tempt him, pique his interest a bit, because activity in the bedroom had been intermittent to say the least, especially since the Callum-in-the-bed incident.

She'd been to the beauty parlour and had everything waxed to perfection. Then she'd made sure the kids were out on a sleepover with her new best friend Annabelle's kids, who were a similar age. And finally, she'd bought a dine-in-for-two from M&S, and in return for all her efforts, she'd hoped for a night of passion.

His expression said it all when he walked into the bedroom and found her stretched out on the bed, giving him her sexiest smile.

'It's the right time of the month, Luke. Come on, darling. Tonight's the night.'

His face reddened. 'I'm sorry, Mel, but I'm just… you look lovely, but…' Luke sighed and sat on the edge of the bed, head clasped in his hands.

Mel went over to him and wrapped an arm round his shoulder, pressed an ample breast against his arm.

'Aw, I know you're tired, sweetheart, but I don't mind doing all the work. You can just lie back and enjoy yourself.' She went to slip a hand down the waistband of his trousers, but he slapped it away. Then he looked shocked. Worried. He stood up and backed away from her. 'I'm sorry, I'm sorry, Mel. I didn't mean anything.' He tugged at his hair. 'It's just that… I can't.'

She stood too. 'What is it? What's wrong with me?' She indicated her body, which was toned and slim for a forty year old. Although she was six years older than Luke, she knew she looked young for her age, having the benefit of good genes, and she'd always kept herself in shape.

He shook his head. 'I just…' He let out a shuddering sigh. 'I don't think I want another baby.' He took a step closer to the door and she followed, teeth clenched.

'You… What did you just say?' Her voice was shaking, she could feel it right the way down through her legs.

He ran a hand through his hair, not looking at her, his eyes fixed on the floor. 'It's such a responsibility. And we have two great kids. I just don't feel that I can cope with any more.'

'But what about me?' she said, closing the gap between them. 'Where does what I want come into any of this?' She put a hand on her chest, could feel her heart racing, colour rising to her face. 'You know I want a baby. I want my own child, not…' She thought she'd stopped herself in time, but there was a hard glint in his eye now. She'd pressed the wrong button. He stalked out of the room, shutting the door behind him. This time, she didn't follow. Even though she wanted to with every fibre in her body. *Don't beg*, she told herself. *Do not beg. He'll come round. Just be a bit more subtle next time.*

He'd slept in the spare room after that night, locking the door. Whenever she tried to mention it to him, he said he wasn't sleeping well and didn't want to disturb her. There wasn't much she could say to that, after the Callum incident and the other little argument when he'd had a cold and had kept her awake. She hated going to work all fuzzy-headed and bleary-eyed. For one, it didn't look professional and for two, it was essential that she was on the ball. Looking back, she could see that she'd overreacted to him disturbing her sleep in the past, and she could understand why he might not want a repeat performance.

She shook her head sadly, the thoughts fading in her mind as she smothered them with regret. Somehow, she'd started something with Luke, a falling apart, a tearing at the seams, that she couldn't seem to stop.

Ten days ago, it had been time to revisit the 'let's have a baby' conversation, because she was at the peak of her cycle and the whole getting pregnant thing was taking far too long. Now she was almost forty, she was starting to worry that it would never happen. And that was an idea that she couldn't bear to think about, not when she'd already told all her mummy friends that they were trying and they kept asking her if she had any news yet. It had been going on so long it was getting to the point where it was embarrassing and their words of encouragement were tinged with pity.

She'd cooked his favourite meal for tea; a rich beef lasagne, with a nice rioja and tiramisu for dessert. She'd packed the kids off again and it was a little while until he worked out they weren't there.

'Oh, Annabelle invited them for a sleepover.' She beamed at him, buoyed up on the thoughts of how the evening would pan out. 'I think there's a little gang of them going.'

His mouth twitched at the corners as he studied the table, with the fancy tablecloth and a little vase of flowers. Napkins. Candles. He glanced at her, his mouth a thin line.

'I'm meeting Rob for a pint tonight, I'm not sure I'll have time for anything to eat.'

Mel frowned, her heart fluttering with alarm. 'After I've made all this effort? No! No, you're not.' She bit her lip, caught her temper and smoothed it down with a few soft words. 'I'm sorry, darling. It's just that I've been waiting for you.' She mustered her brightest smile, determined that her plans wouldn't be derailed, confident in her powers of persuasion. 'And it's all ready. Why don't you sit down and I'll dish up?'

She carried on smiling at him, while her mind whirred. It was only half past six. No way was he meeting anyone just yet. He never went out until after eight at the earliest. *He knows*, she thought. *Knows what I want to talk to him about.* Her heart clenched. The omens were not good, but she had to get to the bottom of this thing. How was she going to face all the other mums? They were popping babies out at regular intervals, and a couple of them were older than her. *Why can't it be me?*

She busied herself with plates while Luke sat, his hands crunched into fists on his thighs, his body language all wrong for the conversation. But once she'd put his plate in front of him and sat opposite, she ploughed ahead anyway.

'Luke, I don't know what's happened to us.'

'What do you mean?' He stuffed a large forkful of food in his mouth.

She sighed. This was going to take an awful lot of patience. She ate quietly for a moment and when she looked up, Luke was staring at her. She looked down at her plate. 'I mean, we don't even sleep together anymore.'

'It's probably better. I can't disturb you then, can I?' There was a sarcastic tone to his voice, a little snipe in his words that didn't bode well.

She winced. *Still harping on about that, are we?*

'I'm sorry, Luke. Honestly, I am. I don't know how many times I have to apologise.' She could hear her voice rising, going shrill and she stopped herself, took a sip of wine. 'It's just this piece of work I'm doing at the moment. Well, it's crucial I get it right and make a good impression. If I don't get all the management team on board, then we can't get any further. As it is, the company has restructured and they'll save half a million a year in overheads. But I can't do that stuff if I'm half asleep and not thinking straight.'

'Exactly.' Luke was speed eating, sucking it down rather than chewing, and was already halfway through his plate of food. 'That's why it's better if I sleep in the spare room.'

She put a hand across the table and grabbed his. 'Darling, please forgive me. Please?'

He gave her hand a fleeting squeeze, then carried on eating again without looking up. 'Okay.'

There was no emotion in his voice and she couldn't believe he really meant it, but she smiled at him and lifted her glass. 'Let's drink to that.'

He looked up, frowning. 'To what?'

'Forgiveness.'

The tic at the side of his mouth twitched again as he lifted his glass and chinked it against hers before taking a large swig.

'Luke, will you come back to our bed tonight?'

'I think it's better if I don't. Honestly, Mel, I don't want the arguments. It's not good for any of us. Not for you, or me, and especially not good for the kids.'

'Please, Luke. I'm not getting any younger and if we're…'

His frown deepened. 'If we're what?' He sounded suspicious. Nervous, maybe.

Her resolve snapped. 'I can't make a baby on my own, Luke. It's something we talked about before we got married. It was part of the deal. What we both wanted. You said… you said you'd like another child. I wouldn't have…'

He threw down his fork and sneered, leant towards her across the table. 'Wouldn't have what? That was a condition, was it? Part of the contract? Did you really want me, Mel, or was it just my sperm? Oh, and this lovely house of ours that took all my money to buy?' He leant back and pushed his plate away. 'And a ready-made family to get you in with the other mothers? It's all about image with you, Mel, isn't it?'

Mel gasped, so hurt by his words that she couldn't speak for a moment. He'd never spoken to her like that before. Something had changed. She started to tremble.

'I just want a baby,' she sobbed.

He stood up and threw his napkin on the table. 'Well, it won't be mine.' His gaze bored into her, his face twisted into a mask of pure vitriol. 'I had a vasectomy.'

She stared at him, open-mouthed, her heart skipping a beat. 'You did what?'

'You heard,' he said, before he grabbed his coat from where he'd dumped it over the back of a chair and walked out.

That's when she'd had to re-evaluate everything about their relationship.

CHAPTER ELEVEN

Monday

Later that evening, Mel tried to ring the police, to ask if anything useful had come up, if they were closer to finding her family, but the line was constantly engaged. *That's a good sign*, she thought, as she paced up and down in front of the fire, wondering what she could do to take her mind off things. The sound of tyres crunching on the gravel drive, accompanied by the purr of an engine, got her running to the front door. She flung it open to see the familiar police officers walking towards her.

'Have you found them?' Mel was talking as soon as she opened the door, gabbling to stop her mind from jumping to conclusions. 'I saw it on the news. I tried to ring but nobody was answering, but I suppose that's because everyone was busy taking calls?' She held the door wide. 'Come in, come in.'

'No, we haven't found them yet,' Stevens said as they walked down the hallway towards the kitchen. 'But the appeal has brought in some good leads, which we're in the process of following up.'

She scurried about getting tea as the police took their usual places, needing to settle her thoughts before they started to ask questions. Because they must know by now. They must know something. She brought everything over to the table and started talking as she stirred sugar into her tea.

'I didn't imagine they wouldn't have been found. Or not come back.' She stopped stirring, realising that she was creating a mini whirlpool in her mug that was slopping tea onto the table. She tucked her hair behind her ears and the sleeve of her sweatshirt fell away, revealing her lower arm. 'I'm scared they're really... really gone.'

The inspector leant forwards, frowning. 'Mrs Roberts, is that a bruise on your wrist?'

Mel gave a little gasp and dropped her hand, wriggling the sleeve back into place before she picked up her mug.

'Can I have a look, please?' Lockett said, gently.

Mel chewed her lip, then slowly held out her arm, a ring of blue and yellow bruises clearly visible, circling her wrist. The sergeant checked Mel's other wrist, pulling up her sleeve to reveal a matching set of bruises.

'It's nothing,' Mel said, taking her arms back and shrugging her sleeves down again. She shook her head, dismissively. 'I bruise easily.'

'He did these?' Lockett scowled. 'Your husband?'

Mel paused and looked at her for a moment, then her eyes filled with tears and she looked away, started fiddling with her teaspoon. A hush fell over the room before she put the teaspoon down, cleared her throat and started to speak.

'Okay. Okay. Like I said, Luke and I... well, we were having a few problems. Our last argument got a bit heated.' She wiped her tears away with the back of her hand, unwilling to look at either of the police officers. 'Six of one and half a dozen of the other. You know, just winding each other up.' She shuffled in her seat, her head bowed.

'Are you sure that's all it is, Mrs Roberts?' The inspector's voice was gentle. 'You see, we've had one of the children's teachers on the phone, responding to the appeal for information. She was quite upset. And according to her, the children have bruises as well. And their father is a drunk who gets into fights. So that's why we came back tonight. We need to know if she's right.'

Mel looked at him then, her lips quivering as she fought to control her emotions. 'I'm sorry... I should have...' She covered her face with her hands, shoulders shaking as she burst into tears.

'It's okay, Mrs Roberts,' Lockett said, softly. 'It's not your fault. We understand how hard it is in these situations. But we need you to be completely honest with us if we're to find your husband and children.'

After a few minutes, Mel managed to bring her tears under control, aware that she was in sympathetic company. Nobody was blaming her. How could they? She let out a long, shuddering sigh, her fingers fiddling with the material of her joggers, a comfort blanket of sorts.

'I'm sorry I haven't been completely honest with you.' She chewed her lip, unsure how to continue. 'He doesn't know his own strength. Flips when he's mad, you see, and then he lashes out. I just hope that...' She stopped as her chest heaved, her voice strangled. 'I hope he hasn't hurt them.'

The inspector shook his head, a deep frown on his face. 'Well, he seems to have fooled a lot of people. We checked with his work colleagues and everyone said that he was troubled, but not depressed.' He let his words settle for a moment before he continued. 'They said that you were having problems with your marriage and he was worried about the future. Then we spoke to his doctor, who confirmed that he isn't on medication and has never been treated for depression. Nobody thought he was suicidal.' He caught her eye. 'Or would do anything to harm the children.' He waited a beat. 'Everyone except the teacher saw him as a devoted father. So we're just wondering what's the truth of the situation.'

He doesn't believe me, Mel thought. Her fists clenched under the table, anger rising within her.

'Well, they don't live with him,' she snapped, sitting back in her chair, poking her chest with a finger. 'It's me who sees him day in, day out. Me and the kids who suffer his rantings. His drunken rages.'

Stevens raised his eyebrows, nodded his encouragement.

Her face crumpled and she wiped at her eyes with her hands, tears rolling down her cheeks. Lockett got up and fetched the box of tissues, handing it to Mel, who gulped back her tears. She dabbed at her face, blew her nose and took a deep breath.

'It's my fault,' she murmured, eyes fixed on the soggy tissue in her hand. 'I should have said no to this holiday. I should have taken them away from him. You know, acted sooner. But they're his kids. And he was always so sorry for what he'd done. Always promised it wouldn't happen again. And… and I believed him. Then, when…' She stuttered to a halt and it was a moment before she continued. 'When… he thumped Callum and gave him a black eye, and I said that was it, he had to leave, he threatened me. Said he'd rather the kids were dead than let me have them.' She looked at the police officers, her eyes flicking from one to the other. 'That's why I couldn't tell anyone. That's why I couldn't leave him. And that's why I agreed to try again. I did it for the children. And to be fair to Luke, he's been lovely to us ever since, seemed a different person, you know, much happier in himself. But it only takes a tiny thing to set him off and I just hope…'

She squeezed her eyes shut and there was silence for a moment before the inspector spoke.

'Well, thank you for being honest with us, Mrs Roberts.'

'I want you to find the children.' Her voice was wrought with fear. 'Please find them.'

'We're doing everything we can,' Stevens said. 'We've got officers searching for sightings of your husband and the children, following up the phone leads. But we just wanted to have a more thorough search round the house, if you don't mind, see if we missed anything. If you'll give us permission, we can do that now. Or we can wait and get a search warrant.'

Her eyes flicked open. 'Of course you can look around, whatever you need to do, it's fine.'

Mel took another tissue and wiped her face. *Is now the time to tell them?* she wondered. *Is it too much at once?* But she understood that it was better for everything to come out now. She'd probably waited too long to tell them the whole story, and she'd been too slow to call for help at the start of this whole thing.

It's got to be now.

She gathered herself before she spoke, trying to ignore the hammering of her heart, and looked up at the police officers.

'He got involved with... with drugs.' She fiddled with the damp tissue in her hands, ripping it into little shreds. 'I think he was selling the stuff.'

The inspector's eyes widened. 'He was a drug dealer?' He sounded incredulous, as if perhaps he didn't believe her.

Mel chewed her lip, nodded. 'Marijuana.' Her voice was a whisper, her eyes downcast.

'And how do you know this?'

Mel didn't look up, her cheeks reddening. 'I had him followed. I thought he was having an affair, you see. He went out and wouldn't tell me where he was going, or told me some lie. So I paid an investigator to follow him. He saw him dealing.'

'Okay.' The inspector scratched his head. 'Well, we'll add that to the list of things we're looking into. I don't suppose you have any photographic evidence we could use? Maybe help us find his supplier or customers?'

Mel shook her head. 'I did have, but I destroyed the pictures. It wasn't evidence that I was after, you see. I just wanted to know where he was going. And I couldn't let him know I'd had him followed.'

She reached out and grasped the inspector's hand. 'Please hurry, find them while they're still alive. I couldn't face it if Luke... did something. Or he's got them in trouble.'

'Well, with this new information, I think we need to cast the net a little wider, get alerts out to ports and airports. We've got a few more possibilities to look at if drugs are involved.'

Mel bowed her head, unable to look at them, her ears filled with the noise of blood pulsing through her body. She looked like a woman who was mentally exhausted, emotionally drained and just wanted the whole thing to end.

'We just need to go over your movements yesterday one more time, if you don't mind,' Lockett said, sounding apologetic. 'Just so we're clear about timings.'

Mel swallowed. 'I told you. I stayed overnight on Saturday and set off at about midday yesterday.' She blushed and fiddled with her ring. 'It might have been a bit later, I didn't really take much notice. The traffic was horrible. And I took my time. Got here about eight.'

'Eight hours from Manchester?' Stevens left a silence for his words to hit home. 'That's a long time for a relatively short journey.'

Mel swallowed again and put a hand to her forehead. 'I might… I might have got my timings wrong. I can't quite remember.'

'Well, if you could just have a think for us that would be very helpful,' Stevens said, his voice tinged with impatience.

They think I'm lying. What to do? What to do? Her mind fluttered around her options, like a trapped bird. She swallowed and looked up, her eyes flicking from Stevens to Lockett and back again.

That's when it all became very clear. This was make or break. She had to do everything she could, say whatever she had to say, to make sure the police believed her version of events, if she was going to get her children back.

PART TWO:
TWO YEARS EARLIER

CHAPTER TWELVE

Two years ago

Luke looked around the house, making sure it was perfectly empty. No toys lurking in corners, nothing left in cupboards or on shelves, the carpets clean, the kitchen and bathroom spotless. Clearing the place out had been quite an effort after living there for ten years. The kids had been born there, both of them home births, so the house held such precious memories; it had been a tough decision to leave. He looked in the living room, could almost see the birthing pool in the middle of the carpet; Anna, red-faced and straining as a new life made its way into the world. Twice he'd been blessed with that experience. He felt his chest tighten and squeezed his eyes shut, pinching the bridge of his nose to try and hold back his tears. They'd been so hopeful then, so full of plans, and now that life was gone.

He closed the door and walked to the car, wiping his face with his hands as he told himself to man up and get a grip. *Be strong for the kids.* He took a deep breath, shooed Bernie the cocker spaniel off the driver's seat, and got in the car, then turned to smile at his children, who were buckled into their seats in the back, both of them looking so serious and unsure. This corner of Scotland was the only world they knew and now he was dragging them hundreds of miles away to North Wales; somewhere the locals spoke another language and where they'd never been, to live with people they didn't know. *What am I thinking?*

He swallowed his doubts. He was thinking about his children's future, that's what. Their quality of life. He'd been blessed with a close family as a child and he wanted that for his kids. This was the only way it was going to happen, and just as important, it would give him a bit of space to catch his breath, steady himself, and somehow find the energy to start again. He couldn't do that here, not with the house and neighbourhood so ingrained with reminders of Anna and his loss, sending him deeper into his trough of despair.

'Okay, ready to roll.' He turned the ignition and looked at his children. 'Who wants to go on an adventure?'

'Me,' Tessa said, although he could see the apprehension in her eyes. His heart melted for her and the brave face she had learnt to put on things since her mother's death. At almost nine years old, she'd already taken on the role of looking after her little brother when Luke was struggling.

'And me,' Callum said, his seven-year-old face covered with chocolate.

'Bye-bye, house,' Luke said, giving it one last look.

'Bye-bye, house,' Callum echoed.

'Bye, Mummy,' Tessa mumbled, her bottom lip quivering.

'Mum's coming with us,' Luke said, trying to make his voice bright. 'She's always with us. Wherever we go, she's watching us.'

'But she's buried over there in the graveyard,' Tessa said, pointing across the road to the little church where the funeral had been held, just a small gathering of close friends, given that Anna's parents were both dead and her Irish grandparents, who she'd lived with during her teenage years, were now too infirm to travel. 'She's going to miss us when we go.' Tessa gave a little sob, her face crumpling. 'I don't want to leave Mummy all alone.'

Luke had to bite his lip to stop himself from crumpling too. He turned to her and put his hand on her knee, gave it a gentle rub. 'But Mummy's spirit is no longer in her body, sweetie. Remember?

We talked about this, didn't we?' He tapped his chest. 'Her spirit is in our hearts. Always.' There was a quiver in his voice. 'She'll always be there in our hearts.' He tried a smile, but knew that he wasn't fooling his daughter. She'd caught him sobbing on several occasions, creeping up with cat-like stealth, her little arms reaching round his neck and holding him tight. 'Wherever we go, she comes with us. You really don't have to worry about leaving her behind.'

'How can she be in all our hearts when there's only one of her and three of us?'

Tessa's logic was a difficult thing to deal with at the best of times and Luke sighed, closing his eyes for a moment while he gathered his thoughts. How hard it had been to explain death to the children. Especially when it had been so sudden, an aneurysm while Anna was doing the weekly shop in Tesco. More or less instant, the doctor had said, no suffering, which was the only thing about the whole incident that gave Luke any measure of comfort.

When he opened his eyes, both his children were gazing at him, waiting for an answer that would make sense to them, that would help to iron out this emotional bump; a bump that would catch them out whichever road they found themselves on. 'Because Mummy was very special,' he said, emphasising his words with a nod, hoping that he could stop his voice from cracking. 'And she had so much love in her heart that it's more than enough for all three of us. That's how.'

He handed his children a bag of sweets each, turned back to the steering wheel, and took a deep breath before he rolled out of the drive for the last time, not daring to look back in case his fragile resolve decided to break.

After Anna's death, Luke had soon discovered that grief was an all-absorbing emotion, and as hard as it was to manage his own feelings, he had to support his children through the experience as well. Not to mention holding down a job and organising everything that had to be done to run a household. Initially, life was a blur of activities that had to be done, something he just had to get through, day by difficult day; time, a concept that blurred into a meaningless continuum of tasks.

Months went by before he recognised that he was failing, letting standards slip to a point where the headmistress had pulled him aside at school and asked if there was anything they could do. Could she perhaps ask social services to help? Or was there a family member who could take the children for a little while? He saw it then. Tessa's tangled hair, full of knotted clumps that he couldn't seem to comb out. Her tights with holes in the knees, shoes that were obviously too small. Callum's jumper with baked bean stains and egg down the front, his clothes crumpled and smelly.

Luke had looked at the headmistress and nodded, forced a smile that he didn't feel and made a decision that he understood was inevitable, however much he hadn't wanted to see it. 'Thanks for your concern. It's good to know that you're looking out for us. But you don't need to worry. We'll be moving back to Wales shortly. My family are there.'

He'd seen the relief in her eyes and knew it was the right thing to do. He was letting Anna down and that was the very last thing he wanted. It was time to swallow his pride and mend the bridges that he'd broken with his parents all those years ago when, at eighteen, he'd chosen to join the armed forces.

His parents were staunch pacifists and they were furious and heartbroken at his choice of career, but Luke had believed the adverts. He was young and restless, wanted to see the world and get trained for a profession at the same time. To him, it made so much sense. And it wasn't like he'd chosen to actually kill people, he wasn't front line. He'd chosen to be an engineer and learnt how to look after helicopters, a profession he knew would keep him on the ground, in a base and away from danger. Which it had. And after five years, when he'd decided to bail out of the forces, his training had allowed him to get a good job in Aberdeen, looking after the helicopters that flew crew and supplies to the oil rigs.

There was no doubting that his decision had given him a good life and provided opportunities that just wouldn't have been there for him in rural Snowdonia. It had also led him to Anna, who he'd met in Cyprus, where she was a rep with a travel company. Yes, he had a lot to thank the armed forces for and he had no regrets, even though it had driven a wedge between himself and his family. It had been worth it to have those eleven years with Anna.

He blinked to clear his eyes, made himself concentrate on the road ahead of him.

Now he was going back to live on the family farm. *It'll be fine*, he reassured himself, clasping the steering wheel a little tighter. *Absolutely fine.*

Luke hadn't rung ahead, just in case he lost his nerve and ended up turning round before he got to the farm. So his mum wasn't technically expecting him. But she'd been fine on the phone a few weeks ago, when he'd first called, like they'd only spoken the other day instead of fifteen years ago.

'Luke! Luke, it's you, isn't it? Oh my God. Luke.' Her voice had been breathless, quivering with excitement and very different to the harsh tones she'd used when he'd told his parents of his decision to join the forces. 'I didn't bring you into the world to have you go off and get killed in some stupid bloody war that's about nothing more than sodding oil.' That was the tone of voice that he'd heard in his head for all those years, along with his father's final shouted words: 'You know how we feel about war, about mindless killing. Joining the armed forces goes against all our beliefs. And you know that! You leave here, son, then you don't come back.' His face had been red with rage, his fists twitching as if he'd wanted to hit Luke. Their anger with his choice had kept him away, although he was in touch with his younger sister and a handful of local friends on Facebook, who kept him up to date with what was going on.

But his mother had sounded so happy to hear from him, he wondered why he hadn't made the effort to get in touch sooner. He'd had Anna though and they were a tight little unit. To be honest, he hadn't needed anyone else, content as he was within his world.

'How are you, son?' The concern in her voice had made his heart ache.

'Oh, you know.' He told himself not to sound so miserable, but they were the only words that would come out before his emotions choked him.

'Sweetheart, we heard about Anna. Oh God, it must be so hard for you with the little ones. How are you coping now that...?' She'd stopped herself and Luke swallowed, pinched the bridge of his nose.

I will not cry. I will not cry.

'Yeah,' he said, more of a sigh than a word.

'Come home, love. Why don't you come back? Just for a bit. Get yourself sorted.' Her words rushed down the phone as though she'd been saving them up, ready. 'There's plenty of space here, you know that. Now that Granny and Grandad are gone, we're in the bungalow, me and your dad. So, our room is going spare. And then there's... well, we can jig things around, fit you all in. Ceri and Ted are still here, but there's room for all of you. This is your home, Luke. It'll always be your home and there will always be room for you. Always.'

Tears had spilt down his cheeks, his throat so tight he couldn't speak. Silence filled his ears for a long moment, and when his mum finally spoke, her voice was as gentle as the hug he so desperately needed.

'Whatever we all fell out about, Luke, well it's water under the bridge now, love. Water under the bridge. Just come home, son.'

He ended the call without saying goodbye, and sat with his head in his hands, sobbing. He hadn't even invited his family to the funeral and it suddenly seemed important, wrong. But at the time he'd just wanted the people who loved Anna to be there, not people who were there out of obligation. She didn't deserve that and he hadn't been in the right frame of mind to deal with any sort of conflict, his focus being to get through the day and be strong for the children. Nothing else had mattered. Now he wondered if it should have.

Anna had been a jewel, a shining bit of magic, able to light up every corner of his soul with just one smile, one gentle touch. Soulmates. That's what they'd been. Bloody soulmates. And without her, he felt so vulnerable, like all his skin had been peeled off, exposing organs and muscles that ached and pinched with every breath. There were still times, eight months after her death, when he wondered what it would be like to just swallow all the paracetamol and go to sleep.

He swiped the back of his hand over his eyes. *Stop it! You can't think like that.* He glanced in the rear-view mirror, glad to see that both the kids were fast asleep. A friend at school had committed suicide and he knew what it felt like to be abandoned in that way. He'd like to believe that he'd never do that to his children, but there were times when he'd frightened himself. Times when it had been close.

Coming back home was the only way he was going to make things work. He had to accept that he needed support, a little bit of nurturing to get him through this and help them all to move on. His jaw tightened as he thought about the family he'd left behind in Wales. It would be good to see his sister, Ceri. She was only fourteen months younger than him and they'd been close as children, although they'd drifted apart a bit as teenagers. His cousin, Ted, well, that was a different matter, the mere thought of his name bunching the muscles in Luke's shoulders.

It's only for a little while, he told himself. *Not forever. And fifteen years is a long time. People change. Mature.*

CHAPTER THIRTEEN

Luke drove with a mind full of memories, the good times he'd had as a child, the freedom to roam. In many ways it had been the perfect childhood. He would be apologetic, he told himself. He would grovel to his father, be nice to Ted. He would do whatever it took to get the support of his family and give his kids the sort of childhood he'd enjoyed. If he could just get a good night's sleep he might have a bit more patience and make time to play with them, rather than let them spend all their time in front of their tablets, which had become a handy babysitter while he nursed a glass of whiskey and stared into space, numb all the way through.

It's not good enough.

He heard her voice sometimes, telling him off. Anna was good at that. Her a mere slip of a thing and him at least a foot taller. She was doing it now, urging him on when he wanted to turn back, not sure if he had the mental energy for the reunion, however it might go down.

An image of his mother came into his mind, tall and blonde with inquisitive blue eyes, and he wondered how she was doing, if her MS had progressed any further. Before he'd left, she'd been having a hard time with mood swings and fatigue and some days she just took to her bed. At the time, the doctors had given her medication which had seemed to smooth things out for her, and he hoped it was still working. His overriding memories of his mother were of an active woman, always out in the fields or the polytunnel with her horticultural ventures. Experimenting with new crops to grow. She was the backbone of the farm, the organiser, the business mind. She was the cog that made the wheel turn and if she wasn't well, he wasn't sure how it would all function.

I can help now, he thought. *Time to give something back.*

He turned off the main road and onto the single-track lane that led up the valley to their farm, which stood right at the end, like a full stop at the end of a sentence. His pulse rate started to quicken, his palms slick on the steering wheel. How would they take to him just turning up like this? Whatever his mother had said, it was his father's words that took prominence in his mind.

'If you leave here, then you don't come back!' His dad had banged the table with his fist to emphasis the finality of his words and the anger in his eyes told Luke that he'd meant it. A lot more was said, his father becoming ever more clear that Luke's decision was final. It was either the forces or the family. He couldn't have both.

At the time, the argument had spurred Luke on rather than made him reconsider, because, by the time he'd told his parents about his plans, he'd secretly been through the selection process and had been offered a place. Two weeks after the argument, he'd left home and he hadn't been in touch with them since. Although he'd thought about them often, and he messaged Ceri every now and again, he'd never pushed himself to make the phone call and get back in touch and the longer he left it, the harder it became to make that first move. He thought he didn't need his family once he had his own. He shook his head as he pondered on this now, marvelled at his arrogance, his naivety.

Stupid, pig-headed bastard, that's what you are.

He hoped the presence of the children would keep things calm, civil at the very least, because his father was a big man with a big temper and was pretty scary when he was in full flow.

The road wound steadily upwards, round tight bends, past familiar driveways leading to familiar farms and houses. Mountains rose steeply on either side, the lower wooded slopes of the Nantlle Ridge on his left, the tops of the mountains forming a jagged edge on the skyline. To the right was the huge, bare hump of Hebog, the highest mountain in the valley. The air smelt different here, earthy and fresh, as it wafted through his open window, touching a place in his heart that had been tender ever since he'd left.

He turned the last corner and could see the house, a large, stone-built monolith standing tall in the face of the elements, extended over the years, so now it looked like two houses joined together, mirror images of each other, with two roofs and four chimneys. A broad expanse of flat fields surrounded the property, edged by a stream to the left, before the mountains rose steeply on three sides. To the right of the house was a long line of stone outbuildings; some used for stables, others for storage. In front of these was a yard, where a car, a pickup truck, a tractor and a range of agricultural machinery were parked. Behind the house, the edge of the large, corrugated-metal barn could be seen poking out.

He felt like he'd travelled back in time and remembered how, as a child, he'd loved to hear the story of how his world came into being.

'Once upon a time,' his father would say, grinning at his mother, 'a lonely farmer was out tending his sheep when he met a beautiful young scientist who'd gone and got herself lost. She'd been walking on the Nantlle Ridge and had taken a wrong turning in the mist.' He'd always shake his head at this point and widen his eyes, as though getting lost was the most stupid thing anyone could do. 'She was soaked through, tired and hungry, so the farmer took her to his home, which he shared with his grandparents. She borrowed some warm clothes and stayed for something to eat, enchanting him with tales of Cornwall, where she grew up.'

'You fell in love,' Luke would pipe up at this point, nodding sagely as if he knew what it meant.

'We did indeed.'

'And then Grandad had an accident.'

His father would nod. 'A runaway tractor broke poor Grandad's legs and he and Granny decided that it was time to retire.'

'So you built them a bungalow.'

'Who built the bungalow?'

'You and mummy and Uncle Robin and Auntie Bea.'

'That's right. The four musketeers we were in those days. All for one and one for all. Do you know what that means?'

'You all help each other. Like you do now.'

'That's right. Well, I couldn't run the farm on my own and Mum was still a student, so she had no money. We were poor as poor could be.'

'So you all lived together.'

'We did.'

'Because it's good to share.'

'Yes it is.' His father would chuck him under the chin. 'That's right, son. We all need to share and to help each other.'

Luke gave a wry smile and hoped that his father remembered those words now.

Looking back, he could honestly say that Phil had been a great dad. Not just Phil, but all of them. You couldn't wish for a better set of parents and with four adults sharing the job, there was always one of them with the energy to be patient.

The family dynamics had changed when his aunt and uncle went away for a weekend to celebrate their tenth wedding anniversary and never came back, killed in a pile-up on the M6, leaving six-year-old Ted orphaned. But he was absorbed into the family, Luke's parents smothering him with love and attention to make up for his loss, and he became more like an annoying younger brother than a cousin.

Everything altered again when Luke hit fourteen, though. Or maybe it was him that changed? With the onset of puberty it just didn't work anymore. Angry and intolerant, he'd felt like a prisoner stuck out there in the middle of nowhere, and he always seemed to be in a fight with some member of his family. Especially Ted, who was two years younger than him but taller and stronger and liked to make him look a fool at every opportunity. Anyway, Luke had never wanted to be a farmer; he'd wanted to travel. There was a big world out there and he'd wanted to see some of it before he even thought about settling down.

He parked in the yard now and sat for a moment, pulling his thoughts together.

'Okay, kids, we're here,' he said, turning and shaking their legs. Tired eyes blinked open and they looked around, cautious, as if they'd just landed on the moon. Bernie uncurled himself from the floor, where he preferred to sit when they travelled, and gazed through the window, his tail giving a cautious wag.

'Where are we?' Tessa asked, lifting herself up in her chair, her face pale and drawn as she glanced around. 'What is this place?'

'I told you. This is Nana and Pops' house. You've never met them, but now we're going to stay here for a little while.'

'But it's huge,' Tessa said, eyes wide. Then they widened even further. 'And they've got ponies! Dad, they've got ponies.' She jigged up and down in her seat. 'Look, over there, Dad. Ponies!'

Luke laughed. A couple of rescue ponies had arrived when he was still at home, and his mother had obviously added to the herd while he'd been away. Tessa was mad about ponies and now she could learn to ride, which would be the perfect distraction.

'Look at that cool tractor, Dad.' Callum was staring at the huge blue tractor parked next to the barn. 'Its wheels are bigger than you!'

'They are, aren't they?'

'Can I help you?'

Luke swivelled round to face the voice. A man, wearing muddy green overalls tucked into knee-high wellingtons, was leaning towards the car window, frowning. His hands were tucked into his pockets, the cap on his head, shading his face.

'Ted?' Luke's heart lurched in his chest, catching him by surprise. 'Christ, look at you with all that fuzz on your face.'

'Luke! Fuck me...' Ted covered his mouth when he spotted the children in the back seat. 'Oops. Flipping heck, Luke. We thought you were trouble for a minute there. Unmarked police car or something. Gave us a bit of a fright.' His hand dropped to the roof of the car and his mouth twitched as his dark eyes gazed at Luke, holding an expression that was hard to read. Then his face broke into a grin. 'You getting out of the car or what?'

Luke climbed out, watching as Tessa raced off to look at the ponies and Callum ran over to the tractor. He hugged his cousin, unable to speak for the weight in his chest and, after a few moments, the warmth of Ted's body, the solid feel of him, broke all his resolve and he started to cry. Big, ugly, heaving sobs shuddered through him and his cousin held him tight, muttering in his ear, 'Hey, hey, it's alright mate. You're home now. You're home.'

CHAPTER FOURTEEN

After a few moments, Luke released Ted from his grip and wiped his face on his sleeve. He watched Callum inspecting the tractor. Ted started walking over to him and shouted:

'You want to sit in the cab?'

'Can I?' Callum looked at his uncle as if he'd just announced it was Christmas, his eyes shining with excitement.

Ted grinned, lifted him onto the steps and followed him up, letting Callum sit in the driver's seat while he stood behind. Luke could see Callum jigging up and down on the seat, his hands flicking switches and pretending to steer the wheel.

Luke's heart swelled when he saw his son looking so excited, and Tessa too, standing on the gate, stroking a Shetland pony that had coming dashing over, obviously thinking there might be some treats going. He heaved a sigh of relief at Ted's welcome. It could have been so different, given the animosity that had grown between them as they'd gone through their teenage years. He put it down to male hormones, thinking they'd been like stags banging their heads together, each wanting to be the boss. But none of that mattered to Luke now, and it seemed that Ted felt the same.

Luke opened the car boot and started to unload their luggage, Bernie snuffling round his feet. A flutter of something to his right caught Luke's eye, making him turn, and there was Fay, his mother, running across the yard, or trying to run, a rapid hobble being the best she could manage. Luke gasped as she flung herself at him, holding him tight, her breath hiccupping out of her while she worked out whether to laugh or cry. He squeezed her in a hug, shocked by the thinness of her, by the way time had ravaged her body. Over her shoulder, he spotted his sister, Ceri, sauntering towards him, a huge smile lighting up her face, which was now a carbon copy of their mother's. And in the doorway of the house stood his father. Luke watched him for a moment, unsure what his reaction was going to be. His heart started to race as he remembered the full force of his father's anger. Did he still feel the same? Was his welcome about to be cut short?

His mother let him go and wiped the tears from her face, laughing now. She turned to see what Luke was looking at and gave his arm a squeeze. 'Don't you worry, love. He's missed you as much as I have. As much as we all have.'

His father walked towards him and Luke held his breath, until the older man stopped and held out his hand. 'Welcome home, son.'

Luke pulled his father towards him. 'Sorry, Dad,' he murmured as they held each other close. 'I'm so sorry.'

His dad patted his back. 'I'm sorry too, son.' His voice was gruff. 'Takes two to tango, doesn't it? Anyway, you're here now. And I'm so glad you've come home, son. I really am.' They held each other for a long time, unspoken words transmitting themselves through the tight clasp of their arms, and Luke felt a weight lift from his mind.

It's going to be okay.

There was so much to do; unloading the car and sorting out sleeping arrangements, getting the kids' rooms sorted, giving the children time to meet their two cousins, and finally eating supper. It had been a constant blur of chatter and activity, with no time for proper conversation, just the froth of words that happens when you should know each other but you don't, because fifteen years' worth of life had been and gone since the last time you met.

The children were late to settle with all the excitement of new people and surroundings, but Ceri had taken them all upstairs and was reading to them in the hope that it might calm them down. Luke slumped in a chair at the kitchen table, a cup of tea in front of him, his head resting in his hands and Bernie curled up at his feet. Exhausted after the long drive and all the emotion of his homecoming, his mind was so full of new information, he wasn't sure what he felt.

He knew Ceri had kids, as she'd posted the news on her Facebook page, back when she was a regular social media user. Now she tended to just use messenger and even that was pretty intermittent. He was surprised that his niece was already four and his nephew was now five. It was a pleasant surprise though, because Callum and Tessa immediately had kids to play with, and that could only help with the stress of the move away from their friends.

What had shocked him was how much older his parents both looked. His father was bald on top, just curly grey tufts bushing out at the side of his creased and careworn face, and although he smiled, there was a sadness in his eyes and a faraway look that Luke had glimpsed, when the conversation had buzzed around him but he was not involved. Lost in his thoughts, his father's face had sagged, the corners of his mouth drooping, making him look all of his sixty-four years. Luke's mother seemed to have shrunk, and deep grooves had appeared around her mouth and eyes after working outside for years, her coarse hair tied back in a long grey plait. Her eyes were bright, though, her mind as sharp as ever, but she looked closer to her husband in age, even though there was a ten-year gap between them. He wasn't sure what he'd been expecting after fifteen years, but their appearance had been a reminder that they wouldn't be here for ever and he was thankful that he'd made the decision to return.

His thoughts were interrupted by the sound of footsteps coming into the kitchen.

'Luke, we need to have a chat.' He looked up to see his dad standing in the doorway, a stern expression on his face, and a groan rumbled round Luke's mind. This was what he'd been dreading; being alone with his father. Before he could mentally steady himself, his mother walked in, followed by Ted. They all took seats at the table and Luke felt like he was in an interview, nerves tugging at his mouth, making it twitch.

A family meeting. This could go either way, Luke thought, his palms sweating. *Have they changed their minds? Are they going to tell me to leave?* He could hear his blood pulsing in his ears.

'I'm sorry,' he said again, pre-empting anything his father was going to say. 'I want to say I'm really sorry I haven't been in touch.' His hands found each other on the table, as if for reassurance. 'And for turning up like this. I won't stay long. I just…'

His father reached over the table, putting a hand over Luke's, looking him in the eye. 'Son, I'm sorry too. It's not for me to tell you how to live your life. Impose my morals on you. Serving your country is a brave and noble thing.'

Luke saw Ted wince and he felt his cheeks start to burn.

'I was in Cyprus, Dad. Fixing helicopters. I didn't go anywhere near danger. And I definitely wasn't a hero.'

His dad nodded and took his hand away. 'Yes, but they could have sent you somewhere dangerous, couldn't they? It's the principle of the thing. You were willing to put yourself in danger for the benefit of others. That's what matters.'

'Yeah, I suppose.' Luke looked at his hands, twiddled his wedding ring round his finger.

Silence crept between them all, separating them into their own worlds, and when Luke finally looked up, he saw his mum nudge his dad. They had a conversation with their eyes, his father giving a barely perceptible nod.

'So, Luke,' his father said. 'There's a… a few things we need to go through with you, before you make any decisions about your future.'

'You mean like house rules? I haven't forgotten, you know.' Luke was willing to do anything to fit in at this point, exhausted as he was by trying to cope with his young family on his own. It would be so much easier here, so much better for all of them.

'No, Luke, not house rules. No, it's…' He turned to his wife and she put her hand on his shoulder, urging him on. 'First things first. I couldn't… we couldn't be happier that you've come home.' He sighed and shook his head. 'I said some daft things… well, we both did, didn't we? Both too stupid and pig-headed to make up. I've regretted it every day since you left, son. Fifteen years is a long time and only snippets from Ceri. No address or phone number and…' His mum squeezed his dad's arm, to stop him heading down a road Luke really hoped he wasn't going to go down.

Luke sighed. He hadn't thought about how his silence would affect his parents, he'd just taken his father's words at face value. And there were so many times he'd wanted his parents to be there. At his wedding. When he held his first child. And his second one. *Pig-headed and stupid*, he thought, *that just about sums me up.* And the longer he'd left it, the harder it had become to make the call.

'I've missed you,' Luke said. 'Missed all of you so much.' He closed his eyes, biting his lip to stop his emotions getting the better of him. It happened so often since Anna's death; tears so close to the surface that the merest act of kindness would set him off. Emotional incontinence, that's what it was. Embarrassing. And everyone had been so kind, it had just made it worse. It would do him good to have a few weeks off before he started looking for work, he thought, get himself stabilised.

'Oh Luke, we've missed you too,' his mum said. 'But we can't look back, we can only go forwards and that's what we need to talk to you about. You can stay here as long as you want and if you help out, then you don't need to get paid work. We've got plenty you can do here.'

Luke turned to look at his cousin and wondered if anything had changed, whether the bad feeling still simmered under the surface. Ted's face told him it did and his gut clenched. His cousin's expression was so different now to when Luke first arrived, he felt something stir in him, dark and tense. Something that he'd hoped had died, but was clearly very much alive. He glanced away, turned to his parents instead, telling himself that it was early days. *I've got to make this work, for the sake of the kids.* Childhood arguments were surely dead and buried by now.

His mother's glance flickered between the two men and she gave a rueful smile. 'It was so great for you kids, growing up together, wasn't it?'

Luke swirled the remainder of his tea in his mug. 'Yeah, it was great. Till I was a teenager. Then it got a bit… I don't know.' He sighed, remembering all the friction he'd caused, all the arguments. 'I just needed to see what else was out there.'

'I don't blame you for that.' His dad patted Luke's hand. 'How do you know how great things are at home until you've been and had a look around elsewhere?'

Luke nodded. 'True enough. You know, as soon as I saw the farm when we came up the road, I felt it in here.' He tapped his chest with his fist. 'Like something was set free.' He looked from his mum to his dad and back again. 'I'd love my kids to have the same childhood I did. If you don't mind me being here.'

His mum beamed at him, her eyes sparkling. 'Oh sweetheart, that's wonderful news. I can't wait to get to know my other grandchildren.'

Ted scowled and spun a teaspoon round and round on the table until Fay leant over and took it off him.

Phil held up a hand. 'Let's not jump the gun. You might not want to stay. Let's just lay things out for you and let you think about it tonight, then we can talk again tomorrow.'

A shiver of unease ran down Luke's back.

'The thing is, we're a bit short of help around here. There's Ted and Ceri and that's it. I'm not getting any younger and your mum, well, she hasn't the stamina any more. Ceri's got the kids to look after, so she helps in the house, but the outside work… the production side of things. Looking after all the animals.' His father shrugged. 'It's a bit of a struggle keeping up with it, to be honest.'

'I can help on the farm,' Luke said quickly, eager to do his bit. 'No problem. I know the score. Sheep and cattle. I can do that.'

'Ah well. It's a bit more complicated than that.' His dad sat back in his chair. 'We do a bit of different work now. Just to balance the books, you know. I'm sure you're aware that all the European grants have changed and the subsidies are nowhere near what they used to be. It's never been easy to make a hill farm work, but now it's nigh on impossible.'

Luke frowned. 'What sort of different work?'

His dad cleared his throat. 'Well, it's a bit of a long story but, in short, your mum didn't react well to all the medicines they were giving her. Especially those corticosteroids. She hated what they did to her and so we looked for herbal remedies. And… well, we found that cannabis worked to manage the pain, and it kept her… kept her balanced, shall we say.' Fay pursed her lips, but nodded. 'And so, we… we started to grow it.'

'Cannabis? You're joking?' The blood drained from Luke's face. *Cannabis!*

'It's medicinal. Legal in all sorts of countries and lots of American states. Because there's so much science supporting it as a herbal remedy for pain management but also for anxiety and depression. And all of that helps your mum.' His dad sounded defensive and looked at Ted, who was nodding his encouragement.

'That's right, Da. Spot on. The Welsh Assembly are even talking about making it legal in the future. And parliament are allowing it for some medical cases.'

Luke's mind was having a hard time taking it in. *Growing cannabis?*

'Well, I suppose the odd plant isn't going to hurt anyone,' Luke said, trying to be reasonable. 'As long as the kids don't know anything about it.'

His dad shook his head. 'No, Luke, you've missed the point. It's not just one plant. We grow it as a crop, a sideline. Not just for us. Then we dry it and produce capsules, which we sell.'

Luke's eyes widened.

'We've been doing it for a few years, taking our time to get the growing systems right, but now it's developing pretty quickly. We need another growing area, but we also need new outlets.'

'Farming hardly makes any money,' Ted said, leaning forwards, elbows on the table, an intense look in his eyes. 'You have to diversify. Farm shops. Homestays. Campsites. Because farming's broke. If it wasn't for the cannabis, we'd have lost the farm years ago. It's our future.'

Luke leant back in his chair, away from Ted, arms folded across his chest. 'It's also illegal and probably will be for quite a while yet. Even then you'd have to be a licensed grower to be able to sell it. All regulated and stuff. What you're doing would still be illegal. What if you get caught? That could be all of us in prison.'

His dad laughed. 'Not when the local policeman is one of our customers. Anyway, who comes up here? Nobody. That's who. Nobody really cares what we're doing. It's not hurting anyone, but it is providing an awful lot of people with pain relief. And, more important, it's giving people hope. Saving lives.' He looked at his wife and back to Luke. 'Including your mother's.' Fay reached for her husband's hand, a show of solidarity that was the hallmark of their marriage.

Luke gazed around the table at the faces of his family. Drug producers. He was lost for words, unable, for the moment, to process what he'd been told.

'It's alright, son,' his dad said, sensing Luke's unease. 'You don't have to give us an answer now. We can talk again in the morning when you've had time to think it over. But the truth is, you couldn't have come back at a better time. We need your help if we're going to be able to keep the farm going. Not just with the animals. We need you to help sell the cannabis capsules too.'

Luke's mum looked at him, uncertainty in her eyes, scanning his face to see if there was an answer. 'It's a lot to ask. We know that. But we wouldn't get you involved unless we had to.' She put a hand on his arm and he covered it with his, while he searched his moral code for an answer.

The conversation changed tack, as his father started telling him about the organic certification they had just received and how both the sheep and cows would now earn a premium for their meat, which would help to counter some of the reduction in subsidies. Luke listened and realised that the family had done everything they could to make the traditional side of the farm work. He understood that there were few options to fill the income gap, but still he wasn't comfortable, wasn't convinced.

Later, as he lay in bed, staring at the ceiling when sleep refused to come, he thought of all his ex-colleagues, the ones who went into the danger zones, who saw things that no person should ever see and would never forget. He knew so many with Post-Traumatic Stress Disorder. Plenty who had lost limbs, taken shrapnel wounds and lived with permanent pain. Maybe this was a way of helping them. Wouldn't that be a worthwhile thing to do? And anyway, if he didn't agree, he had nowhere else to go. This was his family, the only one he had, and now he was home, he was sure in his mind that he didn't want to leave them ever again. *If I want this to be home for the kids I've got no choice.*

With the decision made and his conscience salved by the idea that he would be doing good, rather than committing a crime, he finally fell asleep, sure that he'd do whatever his family needed to keep their farm going.

He thought he'd come home to solve his problems.

If only he'd known it would be the start of them.

CHAPTER FIFTEEN

Luke gritted his teeth, fists clenched as he walked away from Ted's rant on how to load the pickup properly. 'For God's sake,' he muttered under his breath. 'Does it really matter?' They were going to sort out some broken fencing round the bottom pastures, a job that needed doing before they could let the lambs out, and it was a fag to come back if they'd forgotten anything. He understood that, but Ted liked everything to be in its particular place so he could double check before they set off, and Luke had apparently got it all wrong. Again. *Talk about OCD!* Ted had made it into a fine art, and he got so worked up and aggressive if things weren't exactly right he was a pain to be around.

After a month back at the farm, Luke was wondering if he'd done the right thing. *Can you ever move back home once you've been away for so long?* Every day, the reasons why he'd left all those years ago came into sharper focus; the claustrophobic nature of living and working with family, the remoteness of the farm, the lack of social interaction. It all simmered within him, making him edgy and irritable. He hooked his hands in his pockets to stop himself from hitting something, or someone, and went back into the house, needing to calm himself down before he could trust himself to go and work with Ted for hours on end.

His mum and dad were making the cannabis capsules in one of the outbuildings and only Ceri was in the house. Which was an opportunity he'd been waiting for. There were several things that had puzzled him since he'd come home, especially with regards to

Ceri, who had turned from a bubbly extrovert into a little mouse, who scurried around looking after everyone's needs and very rarely spoke, except to the children or the animals. He wanted to ask what had happened but he was never alone with her for any length of time and the right moment hadn't presented itself. But now here she was, in the kitchen, on her own, sorting out the crates of shopping that had just been delivered from the supermarket. He could hear a voice chattering in the next room and knew that's where his nephew and niece would be, watching some home-schooling video that Ceri had put on for them. Tessa and Callum were at school. This was the best chance he was going to get.

She looked up and frowned as he walked in.

'I thought you were fencing with Ted this morning.'

Luke gave her a quick smile. 'Yes, well, I will be once he gets his head out of his arse. He's just thrown a fit because I wasn't loading the pickup properly.' He sank into a chair by the kitchen table. 'Tosser.'

Ceri giggled and he realised that it was a sound he'd rarely heard since he'd arrived. *What's going on with her?* He decided to find out. 'So how are things with you, Ceri?'

She looked at him, flummoxed, as though she had no idea how to answer his question.

'Look, tell me I'm being nosy if you like, but how come you're here on your own? What happened to the father of your kids?' She'd never really mentioned him in her messages, but Luke had seen pictures of him when the babies were born, recognised him as a guy he used to go to school with, but couldn't quite remember his name. He'd assumed he would still be around, given that she'd never said anything to the contrary.

Ceri put the tin of tomatoes she was holding on the table. Then unloaded another and another, keeping her eyes away from Luke's keen gaze. A blush coloured her cheeks and he could see that he'd made her feel awkward.

'It's okay, you don't have to tell me.' His voice was gentle. 'I don't want to upset you. I was just curious.' Luke stood and started loading the tins into the cupboards while Ceri carried on emptying the crates, an uneasy silence surrounding them as they worked.

'I suppose I better get back to Lord Muck before he starts making a fuss,' Luke said when they were finished. He watched Ted through the kitchen window as he checked over the contents of the pickup, adjusting the position of things.

'Wait, Luke.' Ceri grabbed his arm. 'We probably need to have a quick chat before you go.'

'Okay, but I don't suppose I've got long before Ted comes looking for me.'

She swallowed. 'The children's father… Dylan. You remember his dad had the music shop in town?'

Luke nodded. 'Oh yeah, I know who you mean, just couldn't quite get to his name.'

Ceri sighed, a wistful expression on her face. 'It worked for a little while. Us living here was only supposed to be temporary, while we got some money together to travel. Then the babies came along, which added a different dimension to everything and…' She looked down at her hands. 'Well, he wanted to be a DJ. Not a lot of work round here, so he had to travel away and was doing well. He started to earn some good money, but the more he was away, the harder Ted made it for him to come back.' She looked up at Luke. 'Basically, he and Ted didn't get on and it all got a bit nasty. That's why he's not here.'

'What? Ted scared him away?' Luke sounded incredulous and he wondered how extreme Ted's behaviour must have been to make a father want to leave his children.

'It was a bit more complicated than that. There were other reasons why it wasn't going to work.' She shook her head, sadly. 'He wasn't ready to settle down and be a dad. That was the main problem. And Ted's always been so protective of the kids, Dylan couldn't live up to his standards.' She let out a big sigh, laced with regret. 'Anyway… what I wanted to say was… there's no point winding Ted up. It just makes him lash out. Just… try and get along, will you? For your own sake. If you want to stay here, you're going to have to let him be in charge. Then everything will be fine.'

Luke huffed. 'What? I've got to let him treat me like shit, is that what you're saying?'

Ceri frowned, her voice snappy. 'No. No, I'm not saying that, but he'd be a lot nicer to you and life would be better for all of us if you two could stop sniping at each other all the time.' She put a hand to her forehead. 'I can't cope with it. And it might set Mum off and we really can't have that happening. Stress is the one thing that makes her struggle, you know? Emotionally as well as physically.' She gazed at him and he saw the weariness in her eyes. 'You haven't been here to see it, but she's been getting worse, and now the cannabis isn't working as well as it used to and Dad won't let her take the tablets the doctor has given her, not after what the last lot did to her.' She took a big breath. 'So, do it for Mum, Luke.' She took his hand, her voice quivering, on the edge of tears. 'Please?'

He felt bad then that he hadn't been thinking about anyone else and how the niggling between him and Ted would affect them, hadn't considered the repercussions, just slipped back into their old patterns of behaviour. But he could see it now and squirmed inside.

He nodded and squeezed her hand. 'God, I'm sorry, Ceri. I didn't mean to make things difficult for you. Or Mum. It's…' He stopped himself from justifying his behaviour and sighed. 'I'll try harder. I will, I promise.'

And that's what he did.

He tried not to rise to the bait when Ted goaded and belittled him, told everyone how useless he was. He tried. But he was only human and it didn't always work. Even though he could hear the annoyance in his mum's voice when she had to act as referee, there was something in him that couldn't let Ted get away with being a bully, trying to control everyone's lives. To his shame, there were times when he did lash out, and he was back to being a teenager again, scrapping with Ted, spurred on by a rage in his heart that he couldn't control.

Over the weeks, the tension built like thunder clouds gathering in the sky, threatening one humdinger of a storm, the air crackling with things unsaid and pent-up emotion. On several occasions, he saw his mother talking to Ted – animated conversations that he couldn't hear – and Luke knew they were talking about him, that some form of negotiation was in process. Luke was coming to realise that he resented Ted's dominance and he hated the flurry of anger that swirled within him. Instead of settling in to farm life, it seemed to itch at him like a rough shirt, making him twitchy and unsettled.

The kids loved life on the farm, though, and it was so different from the suburbs where they'd lived in Aberdeen, it made a proper new start for them, with plenty of distractions. Not least their two cousins, Ella and Finn. Callum loved five-year-old Finn, and was delighted to have a playmate younger than him, who he could boss about. Tessa, on the other hand, was all about the animals. She'd adopted one of the ponies as her own and Ceri was showing her how to look after it. They had a bit of girl time together every morning – no boys allowed, she'd earnestly told her father, when he'd asked if he could come along. Yes, the kids were happy enough. School was a bit tough though, given that they were taught in Welsh, but on the whole they'd settled in well. Even Bernie had made himself at home, and clearly enjoyed having the farm dogs to play with when they weren't working. It was Luke who was struggling, each day making him feel more and more like a trapped animal, pacing around his cage, unable to escape.

I can't stay, he realised after four months at the farm. *With the best will in the world, I can't stand it much longer.* And that was a problem, because he had nowhere else to go.

CHAPTER SIXTEEN

Luke felt nervous as he walked into the school building in Bangor, his stomach griping and growling. It was a long time since he'd done anything like this. *What if I can't sing anymore?* It was a distinct possibility and he turned to go back out of the door, bumping into a woman coming the other way, who'd been rummaging in her handbag and hadn't noticed him.

'Christ, I'm so sorry,' she said and smiled. She had perfect teeth, he noticed, olive-coloured skin and very shiny dark hair, which swung round her face in a shoulder-length cut, a fringe shading brown eyes. She was tiny, with a delicate frame; even in heels she only came up to his shoulder. Just like Anna, he thought, his heart pumping so hard it hurt for a moment.

'No, no, my fault.' Luke looked over her shoulder at the door and his escape route.

'Are you here for the choir?'

Luke hesitated, told himself to stop being such a wuss and smiled at her. 'That's right. I thought I might be in the wrong place.'

'No, right place. We're down here.' She pointed down the corridor and now he was trapped, obliged to go, which was good, because his mum would have been disappointed if he'd gone home early.

It was just over a year since Anna had died and now the anniversary had passed, his mum had been trying to encourage him to move on with his life.

'You need a hobby, Luke. Something to take your mind off things. Something that's just for you. Nothing to do with the kids. And –' she'd checked behind her to make sure they weren't overheard – 'something to give you a bit of space from Ted.'

He'd jumped at the idea and decided to start with singing. He'd loved singing when he was younger and he thought it might be a good way to get rid of some of the emotions that filled him to bursting, threatening to overflow whenever he was around his cousin. His mum was right, he decided, and maybe if he had a bit of time doing something just for him, the farm might not feel quite so claustrophobic.

Luke smiled to himself now, excitement thrumming in his belly as he followed the woman, noticing the confidence in her walk, sensing a lively presence about her that seemed to fill the corridor. They entered what must be the assembly hall, with a stage at one end and a piano in the corner.

She turned and gave him a beaming smile. 'Silly me, I didn't introduce myself, did I? Just left you following along like a lost puppy! I'm so sorry. I'm Mel.' She held out her hand.

'Luke.' Her handshake was firm and warm, no nonsense, which he liked. He could smell her perfume, not overpowering, just a floral scent in the background. Clean and wholesome. *Nice.*

'So, we're a bit sexist here. Men are over there.' She pointed to the opposite side of the hall, where half a dozen men stood chatting. 'Women over here. Come on, I'll introduce you to Geraint, our choir master. He'll sort you out with the song sheets.' She gave him that wonderful smile again. 'What do you sing, by the way?'

'To be honest, I haven't really sung since I was at school and my voice hadn't broken then.' He shrugged, gave a nervous laugh. 'It's going to be a bit of a surprise to everyone, including me.'

Mel laughed. 'Well, you can guarantee it won't be as high as me. I'm soprano all the way.'

The choir master welcomed him with enthusiasm, the men being outnumbered by the women by at least two to one. 'We're all out of balance,' Geraint said with a shake of his head. 'Let's hope you're a strong tenor. Ours aren't the youngest and their voices have seen better days.'

Luke looked at the huddle of men gathered at the right-hand side of the stage. Ten of them now and apart from a young man in his twenties, the age range did seem to fit in the pensioner bracket, whereas the women were a complete mix of ages. Mel had settled herself in the front row of the ladies' group and when he caught her eye, she smiled and gave him the thumbs up. He smiled back, a burst of heat making his cheeks glow.

Over the course of the evening, it was surprising how quickly he found his voice again and it was, indeed, a tenor. The music swelled through him, smoothing the rough edges of his ragged emotions, and after a couple of songs, he started to relax. They were singing a mixture of gospel and pop anthems, many of which he knew. But he could read music, so even the songs he didn't know weren't too much of a problem.

'Final song,' Geraint said after what seemed like ten minutes, but was really an hour and a half. 'Luke, I wonder if you'd do the solo on this one? "You Raise Me Up". You must know it?' He peered at Luke over the top of his glasses. 'If you'd come down to the front here. And Mel, if you do the other solo? You know how it goes, don't you?'

Mel nodded and walked over, so they were standing facing each other. She winked at him, eyes shining. *She really is a gorgeous woman*, he thought, and before he knew what he was doing it, he winked back. His heart was pounding. It must be twenty years since he'd sung solo, but he'd done a lot of it at school and had competed at the local music festivals, the *Eisteddfodau*. This was no different, he told himself, and took a few deep breaths as Geraint played the introduction, then he gave the song everything he'd got, his voice blending with Mel's harmonies like sugar and spice.

When they finished there was silence for a moment and then an enthusiastic round of applause. He was tingling from head to toe and felt like he'd grown six inches taller. *That was brilliant*, he thought. *Absolutely bloody brilliant.* Mel took his hand and started bowing, like they'd done a proper performance, hamming it up, and he joined in, his cheeks flushed, and for the first time since Anna had died, he felt a flutter of happiness rise up in his chest, like a bird taking flight.

'Do you fancy a drink?' Mel said when they were all packing up. 'A few of us go to the pub after practice. You'd be very welcome. Get to know some of the others.'

'Oh, um, I should probably get back,' he said, quickly. Then he wondered what the rush was. The rest of his family were at home and given that it was half eight, the kids were probably already tucked up in bed. Mel gazed at him, her large brown eyes clear and bright and he found he couldn't look away. He smiled. 'Okay then, why not?'

CHAPTER SEVENTEEN

Around two months later, Luke put down the hay bale he was loading into the back of the pickup truck and answered his phone, a shiver of excitement working down his spine when he saw the name of the caller.

'Hey, Nick. How's things?'

'Pretty good, mate. Pretty damned good.'

'Any news?'

There was silence for a moment and Luke smiled, knew that his friend was keeping him waiting for a good reason, rather than bad. Nick was a bit of a joker, but honestly, he was so easy to read it was ridiculous.

'The answer is yes.'

Luke smacked the side of the pickup. 'Yes!' he shouted, making Ted turn and glare at him. He walked away a few steps and turned his back, lowered his voice. 'So, there's an opening?'

'That's right. They're looking for a couple more engineers with your background. Lucky you've had experience with the new helicopter they're using for mountain rescue. Anyway, I mentioned you to my boss. Told him we'd served in Cyprus together and he's going to get in touch.'

'Bloody brilliant!'

'The wonders of Facebook, eh? If you hadn't popped up on there, I wouldn't have known you were back in Wales.'

Luke grinned. He'd given up on social media after Anna died; everything seeming trivial and other people's lives so happy compared to his. But he'd realised that he needed to broaden his

circle of friends now, if he was to keep himself sane stuck away
up the valley, and even if they were only virtual friends, at least
they were people to chat to.

After a few months at home, Luke felt a lot steadier in himself,
had more energy and experienced fewer days when his emotions
threatened to overflow. But the stronger he felt, the more restless
he became, remembering the real reason why he'd wanted to leave
this place all those years ago.

Ted.

It was very clear that even if the rest of his family wanted him
to stay at the farm, Ted definitely did not.

Now that Mel was in his life, Luke wanted to spend more time
with her, but that involved so much driving it had really started to
piss him off. A couple of days ago, he'd finally decided it was time
to make some changes and it was Mel who'd got him thinking
about work opportunities away from the farm.

They were curled up on Mel's sofa, an empty bottle of wine on
the coffee table, the remnants of a delicious meal she had cooked
for him stacked up in the kitchen. Her perfume filled the air, the
skin of her thigh soft beneath his hands, her bare breasts snuggled
against his chest, their legs entwined.

'Well, that's the best choir practice I've ever had,' he said.

She laughed. 'Does nobody at the farm think you're doing a
lot of singing these days?'

'Hmm. Mum did say she was glad I'd found a new hobby.'

They both laughed and Luke held her tighter.

'I don't mind being your hobby,' Mel murmured, dropping
gentle kisses up his neck, giving his earlobe a nip. 'But it would
be nice if we could do this more often.'

A groan escaped him as his body came to life again and he
swung himself on top of her. Even Anna hadn't got him stirred up

like this. But then Mel was older, more experienced, with plenty of little tricks to excite him. And she loved sex. But that wasn't the only thing that excited him about her. She was funny and smart and nothing was a problem, so easy to be with he forgot all his worries when they were together, her personality like a balm to the bruises Ted inflicted on his ego every day.

'You want more?' he murmured as he kissed her breasts.

She arched her back. 'Every damned night.'

He stopped for a moment, her words linking with a decision that he'd already half made, one he'd toyed with in the early hours of the morning, when he couldn't get back to sleep.

'I'm thinking about moving out.'

She stilled then, and opened her eyes. 'You are?' She grinned at him, excitement flashing in her eyes.

He nodded. 'Yep, I am. The sale of the house in Scotland has just completed. And I've got some money from Anna's life insurance. Plenty to buy a nice house.'

'Right.' She shifted position so she could see him better, her breathing shallow, excited.

'I've had a quick look and there's a new estate being built up by the hospital. A spanking new three-bed house wouldn't even take all my money.'

'You want me to move in with you? Is that what you're saying?' Her voice was thick with emotion, her eyes full of anticipation as she waited for his reply.

Luke gazed at her for a moment, suddenly unsure. *Is that what I'm saying?* In his mind, he'd been moving closer so they could see each other more often. Panic flickered in his chest and he started to backtrack a little.

'We'd have to take it slow. You know, for the kids. So they can get used to you in their lives. It's been such a big change for them coming down here. New place, new people, new school, and a new language. It's been a hell of a lot.'

'But if you're in Bangor they could go to an English-language school, couldn't they? A private one?'

Luke sighed. 'Sounds expensive.'

'I could help. Financially, I mean.'

Luke shook his head. 'Don't be daft. I couldn't expect you to do that.'

She stroked his face. 'You know, you could always see if you could get a job using your engineering skills. If you're moving to Bangor, then RAF Valley isn't too far away for a daily commute, is it? Then you'd get a proper salary.'

He'd smiled at her. 'See, I knew you were smart. That's not a bad idea, is it?'

'No,' she said, her hands running down the length of his back, making him shudder with anticipation. 'If it gets you out of the sticks and into town, then I reckon it's the best idea I've had in a long time.'

It had been late when he'd left her apartment, satiated and pleasantly tired, but the drive back had seemed to take an eternity. *Imagine if I only lived five minutes away from her. Imagine…* But he didn't let himself go any further than that. He had the children to think about and he wanted them to be settled in a house of their own first, before he could consider her suggestion that she move in with them.

He thought it all through as he drove. A job working on helicopters again, with people like him. Now that was something he could look forward to. The farm was alright, but now that the old animosity with Ted had reasserted itself, he couldn't stay for much longer, especially now that Ted had started calling him PS, short for prodigal son, reminding his parents at every opportunity that he, Ted, was the one who had stayed behind and put the work in to keep the place going. He, Ted, was Mr Reliable, implying that Luke wasn't.

By the next morning, the idea of moving away from the farm had set like concrete in his mind. It felt right. It would be better for him, better for the kids and he'd have money to put back into the farm if they needed it. Of course he'd carry on helping with the cannabis side of things, doing his bit with deliveries. There was no problem with that; it wasn't as though it took too much time. And anyway, if he was at RAF Valley, he'd be building up a whole network of new contacts for them.

As soon as he got up, he went straight onto the contractor's web page, looking at their staff to see if he knew anyone. And that's where he found Nick.

Luke grinned to himself now as he put his phone away. He was taking control of his life again and it felt good. A shout made him glance round, but he was too late to see Ted launch a haybale at him, too late to stop it smacking into his chest and toppling him backwards on to the packed earth of the barn. He landed on his back with a *whoomph*, all the air driven out of him, leaving him rolling around, gasping for breath.

Ted stood over him, sneering. 'You should have been ready,' he snapped. 'Oh, unless your social life is more important than helping us keep this place going. Can't you think about Ma and Da for a change?'

Ma and Da, that's what Ted called Luke's parents, and they did nothing to stop him, even though he was their nephew. To Luke, it sounded weird, possessive, and had started to rankle every time he heard him say it.

Ted had always been jealous of Luke about something or other and the only real solution was to put a bit of distance between them; try and get their relationship on an even keel again, because stunts like this were wearing so thin that Luke was a whisker away from beating the shit out of his cousin. And then he'd be in all sorts of trouble.

Luke rolled himself onto his knees and got himself up on his feet, dusting himself down without looking at Ted. In that moment, his hatred for his cousin was like a festering sore. What he wanted to do was go on the attack, use his fists, which curled by his sides whenever he was within touching distance of the guy, but he remembered the look on his mum's face the last time they'd fought and he made himself turn and walk away.

He went in search of his mum. The decision had been made. He was getting a job and moving out, but he understood that it would affect his whole family, not just him, and it was only right that he discussed it with her first, settled any worries before they rooted in her mind. He'd been startled enough by her condition as it was and after Ceri's warning, he really didn't want to be the one to make it worse.

'Hi Luke, what's up?' His mum was sitting at the kitchen table, laptop open, a pile of receipts by her side.

'Oh, I just…' Luke looked around to check they were alone. 'I just wanted a chat.'

His mum's eyes narrowed, her brow creased into a frown, and she sighed. 'You're going to tell me something I don't want to hear, aren't you? You've not been fighting with Ted again, have you?'

Luke went over and flicked the kettle on, making them both a mug of tea while he marvelled at his mother's ability to read his face, unsure how to start a conversation that he was certain would upset her. He put the mugs on the table and sat down, the right words elusive, slipping from his grasp as he tried to string a sentence together.

He took a deep breath. 'Mum, I just want to thank you and Dad for welcoming me back after… you know.' She gazed at him, and Luke looked down at the table, picking at a knot in the wood. 'But I feel much stronger now. And I think… I want…' Luke felt a burning in his chest, his lungs constricting as he tried to make his words palatable. In the end, his news came bursting out. 'Thing is, I've got a chance of a job at RAF Valley. On the rescue helicopters.'

His mum reached out and put her hand over his, mustered a shaky smile. 'That's wonderful news, love. Wonderful. Farming never was your thing, was it? I understand that.' Her smile broadened. 'A local job! Well, that's… wonderful.'

She gave a strangled laugh and put her mug down, her hand shaking so much the tea was spilling over the rim. 'I thought you were going to tell me you were going back to Scotland or something.' She clasped her hand to her chest, eyes wide. 'Overseas, even. Honestly, you scared the life out of me. I just got you back – I couldn't face losing you again.'

'So… um, there is something else.' Luke's heart raced.

'Whatever you tell me now, love, it's fine. We can get one of Ted's friends to come over and help.' Her relief was making her gabble, as she worked through the logistics of how they'd fill the gap when Luke no longer had time to do the farm work. 'Nathan's a good lad. Got to help on his dad's farm as well, but if we're stuck he's pretty reliable. And Ceri can do a bit more outside. She won't mind. Sod the housework, eh? And maybe on a weekend you could still pitch in at times. Then—'

'Mum, I just need you to listen.'

She gazed at him, uncertain.

'I'm moving to Bangor. Otherwise the travel's going to be too much. And the kids have struggled with being taught in Welsh, so I thought… there's an English school in Bangor they can go to. I think they'd be happier—'

'Bangor?' She sounded horrified, like he'd told her they were moving to the slums of Delhi. 'Why would you want to live in Bangor?'

Twenty-seven miles didn't seem that far to Luke, but to his mum it was obviously another world.

'Because it's easier to get to places, Mum. If I don't get this job, then the A55 is on the doorstep if I'm in Bangor. I can look for something up the coast. There's no jobs here for me, are there?'

'But what about…'

She stopped herself and he knew what she was thinking.

'I can still help with sales and deliveries of the cannabis capsules. Don't worry about that. We'll just have to be a bit better organised.'

She let out a long sigh and looked at her hands, fiddled with her wedding ring, twiddling it round her finger. He noticed then how thin her hands were, how much weight she'd lost, and wondered if he was doing the right thing.

'It's a lot to take in, love.'

'I know. But I've got to put the kids first and I want school to be something they enjoy. Especially at this age. You know they're finding it a bit of a culture shock at the moment.'

'But they love it here on the farm.'

Luke nodded. That was the thing, the sticking point. Was he going to rip them away from the people they had grown to love and a lifestyle they had taken to like ducks to water?

Ted walked in and stopped in the doorway, a frown on his face.

'This is very cosy,' he said. 'What happened to drinks for the rest of us?'

'I was on my way,' Luke said, standing up. 'Just needed to have a chat with Mum.'

His mum looked up at him and grabbed his hand. 'It'll be fine, Luke. You just do what you have to for your family.' She gave him a sad smile. 'And what's best for you.'

'That's right,' Ted sneered. 'Make sure you put yourself first, as usual.'

'Ted, will you give it a rest!' Fay snapped, her face contorted in anger, her words making her nephew flinch. Ted gave Luke a look that made him shiver inside. Because that look was full of rage. That look said he'd like to see him dead.

CHAPTER EIGHTEEN

A month later, the children's faces shone with delight as they unwrapped the presents that Mel had bought them. A book on how to look after ponies for Tessa and a model tractor for Callum, identical to the one they had at the farm, both sure-fire winners. Luke's grin widened when he saw what she'd bought. She'd listened to him when he'd talked to her about the children. Really listened. She'd made these choices herself and they were absolutely perfect. Exactly what he would have chosen if she'd asked him what they would like.

'Cool,' the children said in unison, making Mel and Luke laugh. Callum started opening the plastic packaging, to free his bright-blue tractor, while Tessa flicked through her book, studying the pages and calling out at the pictures. 'Look at this one, Dad,' she said, excited. 'This is my favourite colour. Dappled grey, isn't it lovely?'

Luke threw Mel a glance and mouthed 'thank you'. She gave him the thumbs up and his heart swelled with love. *She really cares*, he thought, and that alone lifted his spirits. If she was willing to try, then they could make this work. This was the best possible start to the day.

'Say thank you,' Luke prompted as his children studied their presents. 'That was so thoughtful of you, Mel,' he said. 'Wasn't it, kids?'

'Thank you! Thank you!' they both shouted, their gifts clasped tightly in their hands.

They were standing in the small lounge in Mel's apartment, nobody sure what happened next until Luke took charge. *That's my role, isn't it? Head of the family.* A role he wasn't allowed to have at the farm, because Ted had to be in control, everybody tiptoeing round him as if he was an unexploded bomb. Luke felt his resolve harden and he knew that his decision to move out was for the best.

'So… Greenwood Centre, kids?'

His question was received with whoops of delight. They'd only been once before, but it had been a big hit with the kids and they had chattered on about it for weeks after the event. Luke grinned at Mel. He'd warned her to wear casual clothes that she didn't mind getting a bit grubby and was pleased to see the jeans and fleece, which weren't her usual style of dress and looked brand new. As did her white trainers. He'd winced when he'd first seen them, knowing that they'd be a few shades grubbier by the end of the day. Still, they'd wash, he reassured himself. And they were only a pair of trainers. They bundled into Luke's car and set off while Luke explained to Mel where they were going.

'It's not far. Between Bangor and Caernarfon. Brilliant place for kids.'

'So, what is it exactly? You didn't really explain. Did I get the dress code right?' She sounded a little anxious.

'You'll be fine. It's all outdoors, but it's quite physical, so even though it's a little chilly today, you'll soon get warmed up.' She still looked unsure. 'Honestly, I think you'll love it. It's an eco theme park. Loads of rides and activities for the kids. Beautiful views all around and the kids just run themselves ragged.'

Mel smiled at him. 'So, we do that as well, do we? Run around?'

Luke put his hand over hers. 'You do as much or as little as you want. If you want to go on the go-karts, you can. There's a brilliant roller coaster. Mega slides, where you sit on these trays. Then there's this climbing frame thing up the hillside with nets and ladders and tunnels. Unfortunately, I'm too big for that. Got a bit stuck last time, and felt like a right idiot, so I won't be doing that again. Kids love it, though, so we can sit that one out, have a breather. And it's right next to the ice cream shop.'

Mel laughed, eyes sparkling with excitement. 'I can't wait. Sounds like great fun.'

He let out a quiet sigh. He'd been hoping she'd say that. He supposed this was quite a big test today; the first time she'd met the kids and the first time they'd all been out together. He couldn't pretend he wasn't nervous. He'd been awake half the night, wondering if he was being too ambitious, if it was too soon, hoping that the weather would be fine. So many variables that needed to come together to make this a happy day out.

It wasn't that he didn't miss Anna. He'd always miss her, and his memories of her and the time they had together were ingrained in him. But this connection he had with Mel was completely different. There was a level of passion he'd never experienced before, not even with Anna, a sexual attraction that he couldn't seem to resist. After a year of grieving, she'd awoken him. Given him back his life, almost. Yes, it was as big as that. And she was so kind and interested in him and his family, which showed in her choice of presents for the children.

He glanced at her now, her beautiful profile, the healthy glow of her skin, hair as dark as a raven. However you looked at it, she was one hell of a woman, in control of her own destiny, running a successful consultancy business. And he wanted her. Right here, right now, he wanted her in his life more than anything because she made things better, she made him laugh, made him forget his sorrow and helped him to look forwards rather than back. She was full of ambition and plans; places she wanted to go, things she wanted to achieve and there was no doubt she was wringing every ounce of pleasure out of her life. He wanted to be like her and when he was with her, the *joie de vivre* rubbed off on him.

The weather had decided to be kind, only a few fluffy clouds dotting the brilliant blue sky and a gentle breeze shivering through the leaves. The park was set in a large patch of woodland and although there were lots of families there, the way the paths meandered through the trees meant it didn't feel too crowded, the rides hidden round corners, in little clearings, picnic tables dotted everywhere.

'Go-karts next!' Callum shouted after they emerged from the boat ride round a swampy track.

'Race you,' Tessa yelled and sprinted off, Callum at her heels. Luke caught hold of Mel's hand.

'Thanks for the presents,' he said.

Mel grinned. 'Thank God I got it right. I can't tell you how long it took me to choose those. I've not had much experience with kids and I was so worried I'd get it horribly wrong.'

'You're a star, Mel.' He pulled her to him and kissed her, smoothed her hair back from her face. 'It's going to take a little time, though. Let them get used to the idea of a new woman in our lives. Like I said, we've just got to take it slow.'

Mel pulled a face and laughed. 'Patience is not one of my virtues, Luke. You must have worked that one out.'

He kissed her again. 'Sometimes you have no choice,' he said, teasing.

She pushed him away. 'You know, this is killing me. Seeing you twice a week isn't enough. I can't wait till you move to Bangor.'

'Another month, and it should all be sorted. You were right about the bigger house. The four bedrooms gives us a spare room for guests and it's not that much more expensive. As the agent said, in terms of an investment, it's much better value.'

She looked at him from under her lashes. 'And room to expand the family.'

He gazed at her then, lost for words. This relationship was hurtling along at a hundred miles an hour and the more he told himself he needed to slow down, the more things seemed to speed up.

What's she saying? She wants a long-term relationship with me… and a baby?

He hadn't given the possibility of a baby any thought, which had been stupid. Why wouldn't Mel want kids? Just because the opportunity hadn't arisen for her yet, didn't mean it wasn't something she wanted.

Another baby. Well, well, well.

He pulled her to him, his hand resting on her waist as they walked towards the go-karts, feeling excited and unsettled at the same time. What about Tessa and Callum? They'd had so many changes in their lives over the last year, would it be fair to expand the family? Or would it give a new focus, something to bind them all together? *Christ, this needs a bit of careful thought.* But a seed of excitement had been planted in his chest, spreading a warmth around his heart.

Another child.

It didn't feel like a bad idea. More like a new beginning.

CHAPTER NINETEEN

One year ago

Luke sat in the dining room of the hotel, feeling more relaxed than he had for quite some time. Just him and Mel on a romantic getaway in Scotland. It had been exactly what they needed. Things had started to get a bit fraught for a while at home, but she'd been a different person while they'd been away. Or maybe it was him who'd been different.

He would have to admit that he'd seriously underestimated how hard it would be to integrate their little unit into a harmonious family. Mel was different to Anna in so many ways and although he knew he shouldn't compare them, it was hard not to, especially when the kids kept making comments.

'She's trying to be Mum and she's so not,' Tessa had said, arms folded across her chest. Callum had nodded his agreement, the two of them standing there, swaying slightly from side to side, all indignant. It had been a few weeks ago now, the weekend that Mel had stayed over for the first time, a gentle move to a more permanent living arrangement, the four of them together. Luke sighed. He'd known it was too soon, but he'd let Mel persuade him.

'It'll be so much easier with two of us to look after the children. I work from home a lot, so I can organise things around the kids. I want to help, Luke. I want to look after them.'

She'd been dead right when she'd said patience wasn't a virtue of hers, but that woman had a way of winning him over with logical arguments that he'd found impossible to counter. Without his parents and Ceri to help, he had to admit that it had been hard to start a new job and get the kids to school and organise after-school childcare and keep up with the housework and the washing, making meals and getting the shopping in. Another pair of hands to help was a welcome thought and Mel was so very keen to get involved. Only a fool would have said no. And anyway, it had to happen sometime, if their relationship was to move in the direction he wanted it to go.

Luke had sat on the bed, gathered his children to him, and held them tight, breathing in their scent. A smell that reminded him of Anna. *What would she think?* Well, he knew exactly what she thought because they'd had long conversations about death when they were in Cyprus and had no idea if he'd be posted to a war zone. They'd both agreed that if either of them died, they would never want their partner to be lonely. All she wanted was for him to be happy, whatever that took. 'And anyway, what would I care if I'm dead? Crack on,' she'd said. He sighed at the memory, knowing now that cracking on was so much harder than it might sound.

'Look, guys, I know this might take a little bit of getting used to, but Mel is part of our lives now and I want you to be nice to her.'

'But she's not nice to me.' Callum had poked at his chest with a finger.

'She tells us off all the time,' Tessa had whined. 'And she took my phone off me. And she shouts at Bernie.'

Luke had taken a deep breath. He'd have to have a conversation with Mel about phones. And dogs. House rules in general, really. They needed to be consistent and at that moment they were pulling in opposite directions.

'I know. But maybe we've got a bit sloppy. Perhaps it is best if you make your beds in the morning. And put the top back on the toothpaste.' He'd thought through the sources of arguments over the previous couple of days. 'And take your shoes off by the door. Hang your coats up.'

Callum had shaken his head. 'That's a lot of work, Dad.'

Luke had had to hide a smile. 'Well, if you don't do it, then it's a lot of work for somebody else, isn't it?' Callum and Tessa had stared at him with serious eyes, clearly not convinced.

'Well, I'd like it if you could at least give it a try. And if Mel asks you to do something, then I'd really like it if you did whatever she asks you to do.'

'Just when she's here?'

Luke had nodded. If it was only one night a week, or the odd weekend, it was a start.

But now, just a few weeks later, Mel more or less lived with them. Luke wasn't quite sure how that had happened, but one night had quickly become two and then three. He'd put his foot down then, told her that they needed to slow down a bit, give the children time to adapt, because he felt they were a bit unsettled. In reality, mutinous was a more accurate word.

Still, he didn't think a bit of discipline did them any harm and he liked having her around. It was so much easier with the two of them sharing all the household tasks, fun even, to make meals together and plan outings. For the last couple of weekends, the children had stayed at the farm; Tessa keen to help with the ponies and Callum desperate to ride on the tractor and see his cousins. It suited everyone, providing Luke with a bit of breathing space and Mel, he realised, liked his undivided attention.

On holiday, they'd done a lot of talking, as he gently tried to educate her on some of his basics philosophies of parenting, while she'd said all the right things. She'd apologised for being picky and admitted that should could be a bit OCD about tidiness and agreed that maybe she'd have to relax her standards a little for the kids. She'd really listened to him and responded to his concerns with an eagerness to please that swept away all his reservations.

They'd become closer, he felt, understood each other better, and he was sure that their new togetherness would make everything run more smoothly when they got home.

Today was Valentine's Day and he'd had to hastily arrange for the hotel staff to get Mel a present, because her face at breakfast, when she realised that he might have forgotten, was a picture of hurt, however much she tried to hide it. He gave the present to her now, as they sat in the bar after their evening meal.

'I know it's late, but I've got a little something for you.' He took a flat box out of his pocket and saw her smile flicker for a moment. 'Happy Valentine's Day.' He hoped he'd got it right. Buying presents for a woman was always tricky, he'd found, and Anna had often told him he was hopeless when it came to gifts, but she'd always seen the funny side and knew that the intention was right, even if the present wasn't.

Mel took the bracelet out of the box and wrapped it round her wrist. Luke leant forwards and closed the clasp for her. It looked a bit insignificant, cheap, and he cringed inside, wishing he'd had time to go and choose something himself. He waited for that stare, the one that heralded trouble, but instead he got a full wattage smile.

'Oh, it's lovely, darling,' she gushed. 'I have something for you, too.'

She opened her handbag and put a little square box on the table. Red velvet on the outside. He swallowed. The box alone was more impressive than the present he'd bought for her, but it was the thought of what might be inside that was making his stomach churn. *I'm not ready*, he thought, suddenly hot, hoping he was wrong.

He flipped the box open and there was a gold ring, set with a red stone.

She reached over and took his hand, gazing at him with love in her eyes. 'Luke, will you marry me?'

He flipped the box lid shut, a band tightening round his head. *Oh my God! What to say?* He squeezed her hand and swallowed. 'Wow. I… um… Don't you think we might be rushing things?' Mel blinked, the smile falling from her lips and the hurt in her eyes squeezed his heart. He stumbled on, his voice breathy, his chest heaving as adrenaline chased through his veins. 'We've got to give the kids time to settle down. You know that.' But his words sounded hollow; obvious delaying tactics while he could get his arguments properly laid out.

She closed her eyes and when a tear rolled down her cheek, his resolve started to crumble. He couldn't bear to see her upset and for him to be the cause of it.

'Tell you what, let's get a bottle of bubbly and take it up to our room. Talk it all through.' She gazed at him and he stroked her hand, pleading with his eyes. 'It's not that I don't love you, you know that. It's more… more to do with timing.'

But Mel didn't move, just sat there looking at the little box and her rejected proposal. The most hurtful thing a man could ever do to a woman.

Luke's heart clenched. *I can't be that cruel.* Rejecting a proposal would surely signal the end of their relationship and that was the opposite of what he wanted. *I can't lose her.* He let go of Mel's hand and picked up the box, opened it and put the ring on his finger, while she watched wide-eyed. 'A perfect fit. It's lovely, Mel.' He reached over and took her hand, raised it to his lips. 'Of course I'll marry you.'

It's just an engagement, he told himself. *One step down a path that you want to go down eventually anyway.*

Well, he got that one wrong.

As soon as they'd finished the bubbly, she sprung the wedding at Gretna Green idea because surely, if he wanted to marry her, there was no need to wait? And at her age, she didn't want a fuss, no need for crowds of guests. No, small and intimate would be way more romantic.

His heart hammered in his chest, his brain too shocked to provide him with any rational counter. *How can I refuse without her feeling that I'm not committed?* Stability for the kids, she said, two parents to share the load instead of one, she said, more money if they ran one household instead of two. Lots of time together, wouldn't that be wonderful? A proper family. There was no logic that he could come up with to deny her.

A niggle of doubt tapped away at the back of his brain, a doubt that said this shouldn't be about logic, this should be an irresistible yes. A yes that sprang out of him the moment she'd asked. But maybe, he told himself, life had to be different the second time around. When you had children to protect and nurture, perhaps your heart wasn't allowed to rule your head. It had to be about logic and finding practical solutions to life's difficulties. Marrying Mel was the sensible thing to do, a show of commitment that would demonstrate to everyone that they were now a proper family unit.

It was only after they were married that he understood that his doubt was right and he really should have listened to it.

On their wedding night, she hit him for the first time.

CHAPTER TWENTY

Their wedding was a joyful adventure, full of laughter and disbelief at the speed at which everything was happening. The arrangements fell into place so easily, Luke told himself it was meant to be, the stars were aligned and it was clearly the right thing for him to do. He had no time to think, no time to back out, or turn his doubts into action as Mel hustled him round the shops, getting everything ready. She got him fitted for a suit, ordered the flowers, and sent him out to buy some smart shoes, while she found herself a dress and conjured up a couple of witnesses.

She had booked Gretna Green's famous Blacksmith Shop for their wedding, a venue that had been used by eloping couples since 1754, and it was more like a barn than a chapel, with stone slabs on the floors, wooden rafters and whitewashed walls. Romantic in the extreme, with just the two of them, the official and two witnesses. Mel looked beautiful in a simple floor-length ivory dress, with long sleeves and fake fur round the scooped neckline and cuffs. A beaded bodice hugged her figure, and she carried a small posy of red roses to match the flowers in her hair. And when he saw her, any doubts Luke might have had were crushed by his desire for her, to have her to hold and be by his side for ever.

With a heart full of love and a mind full of happy memories from their special day, they finally made their way back to their hotel and ordered champagne to take up to their room. By this point, Luke was mentally exhausted by the blur of events and completely stuffed with the wedding meal they had enjoyed after the late-afternoon ceremony. They had already drunk a bottle of champagne, or was that two? He was feeling distinctly queasy and in need of a lie down.

Mel stopped outside their bedroom door and he looked at her for a long moment, wondering why she hadn't opened it, given that she had the cardkey in her hand. She frowned at him.

'Oh Luke, I swear there isn't a romantic bone in your body, is there?' She smacked his arm to get his attention. 'Do I have to do everything?'

He was startled by her tone of voice and the force of the smack, which left his arm stinging beneath his suit. He wondered what he might have done wrong, afraid to ask because he obviously should know what was expected. Except he didn't. He stared at her, a growing sense of panic stirring up the contents of his stomach.

'The threshold, Luke. This is the threshold to our new life.' She pointed at the door and he realised, with a flash of relief, that he knew what she wanted.

He smiled at her and whisked her off her feet, planting a lingering kiss on her lips as he fumbled to get the door open, which was tricky with his arms full, but after a couple of attempts, he finally managed it. He staggered into the room, almost stumbling over a pair of shoes he'd left on the floor, and deposited her on the bed, flopping down beside her, glad that he'd avoided a catastrophe by not dropping her on the floor.

His mind was spinning with all the alcohol, the rich food swirling in his stomach, and it was a moment before he realised that she hadn't moved, hadn't said anything. When he turned towards her, squinting to get her face in focus, she was still looking a bit cross.

'I love you, Mrs Roberts,' he whispered, before his lids fluttered closed and he started to succumb to the irresistible pull of sleep.

A stinging slap to his face stopped that from happening.

'Don't you dare fall asleep on me.' He opened his eyes to see that her face had transformed into a mask of fury. 'It's our bloody wedding night. You can't just fall asleep!' She slapped his face again, harder this time, and the force of it made his head whip to the side. His mind was blurry with drink, his heart racing as he tried to work out what was going on.

She raised her hand again.

'Mel, no, stop it. I'm awake. I'm awake.' But he was too late and his other cheek felt the sting of her wrath.

'You've spoilt it all. Ruined my special day.' She was sobbing with rage. 'If you really loved me you wouldn't fall asleep on our wedding night. You'd want to make love to me, make me yours.'

'But it's not the same when you live together, is it?' A slap told him he'd made another mistake and his befuddled brain started to understand. Romance. She wanted romance and he'd let her down. He managed to roll out of her way before she hit him again and got himself upright on the other side of the bed, glad of the distance between them.

'I'm sorry. I'm really sorry,' he gasped, his insides swirling with the sudden movement. 'You're right. Look, I'm wide awake now. Let's open the bubbly, shall we?'

The last thing he wanted was more champagne, but he really wanted to make Mel happy and he knew he'd got it badly wrong. Whatever it took, he'd do it to make things right between them. This was no way to start a marriage and it was all his fault. He rubbed at his face, his cheeks still stinging. It was a heck of a whack she'd given him, but then they were both a bit drunk, he told himself, and he knew how easy it was to misjudge things. Still, he didn't want it happening again and he started to undo the foil on the bottle, fumbling with the cork.

Mel knelt on the bed, still seething, her chest rising and falling as she took in big gulps of air, obviously struggling to keep her anger on her side of the bed.

'You look so beautiful today, so gorgeous.' Luke grasped at the words, any words he could find that might reassure her that he found her attractive and take away the hurt. 'Please? Can we rewind?'

After a moment she gave a heavy sigh and shuffled up to rest her back against the headboard, quiet now, dabbing at her face with a tissue while he poured them glasses of champagne. Just the smell of it was making him nauseous, but he passed her a glass and raised his in a toast. 'To us, my love. To our marriage.' He forced himself to take a sip and put his glass on the bedside table, not intending to drink any more.

He got on the bed beside her and took her hand, twined his fingers with hers. 'I'm so sorry, Mel. Really. Tell me what I have to do to make it up to you? Anything, just say.'

She smiled at him then, and downed her champagne. 'Well, Mr Roberts, I have a surprise for you and one I think you might like. But you're going to have to get me out of this dress to find out what it is.' She gave him a cheeky grin and he was relieved to see that the rage had passed and she was back to the woman he loved.

He blamed himself.

Of course it was his fault, inconsiderate idiot that he was. It was his job to make his wife feel special and falling asleep on his wedding night was definitely out of order. It wasn't surprising that she'd hit him. What surprised him was that she'd hit him so hard and, in the morning, his cheeks were still a bit red. But there was no apology on her part, no mention of it at all, which made him wonder exactly what had happened and if he'd remembered it right. Alcohol could do funny things to your memory.

So, he put the whole incident to the back of his mind, vowing that he'd learnt a valuable lesson and he would strive to make Mel feel special, do whatever it took to make up for his selfish behaviour.

CHAPTER TWENTY-ONE

Seven months ago

'Dad, where's my picture gone?' Tessa stood, hands on her hips, frowning. 'The one of Mum that's always by my bed.' Her voice wobbled. 'Where I can see her.'

Luke looked up from the sink, where he had a bike tyre immersed in water, looking for a puncture. He had to be quick, because Mel hated him doing this sort of thing in her kitchen. It had caused one hell of a row last time and he had no intention of instigating a repeat performance.

'Just let me finish this, sweetie, then I'll come and have a look with you.' He glanced at his daughter, and knew that something had changed. Something was bothering her. *Is it the new school?* he wondered, very aware that two school changes in the space of a year was a lot for any child to cope with. He sighed. *Who am I kidding?* It was more likely to be the new living arrangements. *We're all taking a bit of time to adjust*, he told himself. *That's all.*

'Shall we go and see Nana and Pops later?' He was rewarded with a grin and he wondered again whether moving to Bangor had been the right choice. In fact, had anything he'd done over the last year been the right choice? He really was beginning to doubt his decision-making ability these days.

'Gotcha,' he said as bubbles flowed from the site of the puncture. It was unreal how many punctures he'd had recently. Every time he planned to go out with kids on their bikes at least one tyre had a puncture and then, by the time it was all fixed, it was getting dark and too late to go. He marked the spot with his finger, pulled the tyre out of the water, dried it off and patched it, while Tessa watched him, a shadowy, silent presence in place of the chatterbox she'd always been. He'd have to see if he could winkle the problem out of her when they were on the way to the farm. He hoped it was something simple, something he could fix.

'My picture, Dad. You said you'd help me find it.' Tessa was standing behind him as he wiped down the sink and the worktops. He'd almost forgotten, his mind on work and the delivery of cannabis capsules he'd promised his mum he'd make at the weekend, wondering how he could fit it all in with Mel's plans. She'd booked lunch at a place up the coast, somewhere fancy that was going for a Michelin star. Not his cup of tea, but she loved that stuff and, more than anything, he wanted to make her happy. She hadn't let him forget the way he'd let her down on their wedding night and he knew he still had a way to go to make up for his bad behaviour.

'I know, poppet. Just got to finish this, then I'm all yours.'

He looked around, satisfied that everything was up to standard, then took his daughter's hand and let her lead him upstairs.

'Look how tidy it is in here, Tess. You've done a great job. Must be nice to come back to such a clean room.' It actually looked a bit bare, he thought, and nothing like the colourful tumble of toys and possessions she used to exist in.

'I like all my cuddly animals out, actually,' she said, hands on hips. 'They don't like being stuffed in a cupboard. They'd much rather be on my bed, so they can see what I'm doing.'

'Well, why don't you get them out again?'

'Smelly Melly won't let me.'

'Tessa! You mustn't call her that.' Luke tried to hide his panic, but his face gave him away.

'See, Dad, you think she's smelly too.'

'Only in a good way.' He sat on the bed and Tessa sat next to him. 'Don't you think it's a bit rude to call her that? You wouldn't like it if people called you smelly, would you?'

'She calls me horrible things.'

'She does not!'

Tessa stared at him, the look in her eyes making Luke's heart clench. 'Yes, Dad, she does. She called me…' Tessa stopped and chewed at her lip as if she'd remembered something.

'Called you what?' Luke frowned.

Tessa looked at him, a glimmer of fear in her eyes. 'Promise you won't tell? 'Cos she said if I told you then she'd take all my toys to the tip.'

Luke felt a weight thud to the pit of his stomach. He knew how much those toys meant to his daughter. How they were her little friends.

'Promise.' Luke nodded and when he put an arm round her, and pulled her close, he could feel her body shaking. Something was seriously wrong here and he wondered how he was going to put it right.

'She called me a spoilt little bitch.'

Luke gasped. 'When, sweetie? When did she call you that?'

'When you weren't here.'

'Once when I wasn't here?' *Maybe she'd caught her at a bad time?*

'No, Dad. It's happened a few times now.'

Luke's scalp seemed to tighten, as the news swelled inside his head and the implications made themselves real. His work hours were prone to change, his workload unpredictable, and he relied on Mel to organise the school run, as her work was more flexible. Anyway, she'd offered to do it. Had insisted, in fact, as soon as they'd got back from Gretna and she'd moved in with them.

'It's my job,' she'd said to him, smiling. 'My priority is the children now and they come before work. Anyway, I'm self-employed, so it's up to me when I organise meetings. And I work from home a lot anyway, so it's not a problem.' She'd put a reassuring hand on his arm. 'I want to do it. Honestly, I do. And it means I'll get to meet the other mums, get involved in all the school stuff.' She'd actually been excited about it and he would have to say it was a relief. Juggling the kids and work had been a bit of a nightmare previously and he'd used up an awful lot of favours in the last few months.

Tessa snuggled up to him. 'I liked it at the farm, Dad. I want things to go back to how they were. I'll learn Welsh. Honestly, I'll try harder.'

Luke stroked his daughter's hair and he wished that he could turn back time. Undo decisions. Make them again with hindsight. Why on earth had he been in such a hurry to move out?

Ted.

There was no doubt that he was a big part of the answer. Mel was the other. Push and pull. That's what had done it. Ted wanting him gone, the animosity between them making it too uncomfortable to stay, and Mel pulling him towards her, bewitching him with her passion and love, sorting out all sorts of practical problems for him, showing him how his life could be so much better with her in it. He swallowed, his mouth as dry as dust.

He'd got what he'd wished for. A life with Mel.

The second time she'd hurt him, it had been in the heat of the moment, during sex. Her fist had caught his ear when he'd climaxed before she did and he'd thought it was an accident.

'Oh God, I didn't mean it.' She rubbed at his throbbing ear, apology in her eyes. 'Honestly, I just thought it, I didn't mean to do it.'

He frowned, not sure if he'd heard her properly. *Why would she even think about thumping me?* He pulled away slightly, so he could see her better. 'What do you mean?'

She looked away, her hands stroking his chest as she spoke.

'It's so hard to explain, but… it's just… I organise my life around everyone else. Put you all first, rushing about making sure that everything runs like clockwork and you don't have to worry about anything. And…' Her voice cracked. 'Sometimes my needs have to be top of the list. But you don't understand that…' He could feel her tears on his skin, warm and wet as they trickled down his chest. He realised what he'd done then, felt awful, and cursed himself for not being a better husband. But he knew where he was going wrong and he resolved to do better.

The next time it'd happened, they'd been having a row about the dog, who had stolen Mel's toast off the table while she wasn't looking. It wasn't the first time Bernie had snaffled food, but Mel was in a rush to get to a meeting and was already a bit wound up. When Luke had laughed about it, she flew at him in a flurry of slapping hands, stinging his arms and chest while he backed away into a corner, waiting for her anger to subside.

And then it was because he'd taken the kids out on a night hike and had forgotten to tell her they'd be staying over at the farm for the night. That time it wasn't just slaps and scratches; that time, she'd punched him in the face while she yelled at him, telling him how inconsiderate he was, leaving her all on her own. The bruises took a bit of explaining. A tumble off his mountain bike, he told everyone, more ashamed of the visible evidence of a fight with every incident.

He knew it was his fault she got so cross and although she might snap at the children at times, he'd never seen her be physical with them in any way and was sure she would never hurt them. No, it was his selfish and inconsiderate behaviour that got her livid, and it was up to him to learn from his mistakes and try harder.

His upbringing had made him very aware that a man should never hit a woman, that words should be used to resolve arguments, not force, given that a man would always be stronger and more able to cause harm. Actions that he would live to regret.

He'd watched, unseen, as his father towered over his mother, his body clearly thrumming with anger, his fists clenched firmly by his sides as they threw insults at each other until their anger wore itself out. That's how it had always been with Anna. Of course they'd had rows, but physical violence had never been a part of their relationship however angry they'd been. He was coming to understand that Mel lived by a different set of rules.

Now, he shook the thoughts from his mind and brought his attention back to his daughter.

'Okay, Tessa, let's see if we can find your picture?' He needed a distraction to stop his mind going down a road that he didn't want it to go down. A road that didn't bear thinking about. 'Maybe it got knocked down the back?'

Tessa sighed, exasperated. 'I've looked, Dad. I've looked everywhere.'

'Well, it can't have just disappeared, can it?'

'I think she's thrown it away.' Tessa's bottom lip quivered.

'She wouldn't throw it away.' Luke was horrified at the thought, was sure Mel must have just put them in a drawer somewhere.

'She said she was my mummy now and I didn't need Mum's picture anymore.' Tessa looked up at her father, her voice almost a whisper. 'I've already got it out of the bin twice.'

His eyes widened. 'No. Mel wouldn't do that.'

He felt Tessa's body stiffen and he winced as he realised he'd just called her a liar. And that was one thing his daughter was not. However hard it was to tell the truth, Tessa never shied away from it. Never. Tessa nodded, tears in her eyes. 'I saw her rip up the one in the lounge as well. The one on the mantelpiece. She didn't know I was watching.'

A chill ran through Luke as he got up and hurried downstairs to the kitchen. He opened the bin, but found that it had recently been emptied. He looked outside, but the wheelie bin was empty too. Today, he remembered, with a horrible sinking feeling, was bin day.

He walked round the house, looking for the pictures of Anna that had hung in almost every room. A reminder for the children, he'd told Mel when she'd complained about his dead wife watching her, judging her. He'd been so busy that he hadn't noticed they were gone. They'd been there yesterday, he was sure of it, as he had a habit of stroking Anna's face, having little chats with her.

Did Mel overhear me? Was she jealous?

His pulse was racing now, a mess of unease growing in his mind, spreading like a stain. He ran upstairs into the bedroom, looked in his bedside drawer, where he kept his favourite picture. The one when the kids were little, Anna looking so content and peaceful, the broadest smile on her face as she held her babies on her lap.

But it wasn't there.

He sat on the edge of the bed, head in his hands, finding it hard to believe that Mel would be so cruel.

He was thankful that he still had some of his possessions up at the farm, including a couple of photo albums. But that wasn't the point. The point was Mel didn't know that, so as far as she knew, she'd destroyed all his pictures of Anna. And it was the best ones that had disappeared.

Luke could feel muscles tensing in his body that he hadn't wanted to use since he'd left the farm; his fingers flexing, fists clenching and unclenching. Mel was at a meeting in Manchester, networking she'd said, to see if she could draw in some larger clients. She would be late home tonight, which was definitely a good thing, given the way he was feeling.

Verbally abusing his daughter and throwing away all the pictures of Anna; that was seriously bad behaviour and he wasn't sure what to do for the best. He rounded up the kids, ready to head off to the farm, because if Mel walked through that door right now, he wasn't sure how he'd react.

CHAPTER TWENTY-TWO

Later that evening, Luke dropped the children at the farm, without explanation to his mother, except to say he would be back later. Then he'd gone home, readying himself to have a serious conversation with Mel. He'd been sitting in the kitchen when she finally arrived back, cheeks flushed and a triumphant gleam in her eye.

'I've got a meeting with the regional manager of CBL Systems!' she announced as she walked in and put her bags on the table, along with a bottle of wine. She noticed his lack of response and frowned at him. 'You know, the company I've been trying to get a contract with.'

He gazed at her, anger sizzling through his veins.

Her hands went to her hips, confusion on her face. 'I thought you'd be pleased.'

'Yes, well done,' he said, in a monotone voice.

'What the bloody hell is wrong with you?' She had that glint in her eye, the one that signalled trouble. He should have taken notice, should have moved, but he was so angry with her that he stayed in his chair, determined to get his point across.

'I've just found out that the pictures of Anna are gone. All of them. And Tessa tells me you've—' She flew at him then, fingernails clawing at his face before he knew what was happening, before he could dodge out of the way.

'That bloody dead wife of yours!' she screamed. 'Why should I have to live with her face all over my walls? Why should I? It's as if I'm not good enough. Saint bloody Anna. Like shrines all over the house, they were.' And all the time she was shrieking at him, she was scratching his skin like a wildcat, his hands and face taking the brunt of the punishment dished out by her sharp acrylic nails.

'Mel, stop it!' He held his arms over his head and pushed her away with his foot before he stumbled out of his chair, managing to put the table between them. She glowered at him, fury in her eyes.

'Not bloody good enough, am I? You just don't care about me. Even though I look after everything. Do everything for you. I run the house, I run our lives and what thanks do I get?'

He drew a breath to say something to try and calm her down, but before he could speak, she grabbed her laptop bag from the table and smacked him in the face. It smashed into his cheekbone, sending shards of pain shooting through his flesh. He staggered backwards holding his head in his hands, gasping.

'You stupid excuse for a man. You don't love me. And you sure as hell don't respect me, or you wouldn't have had those pictures of your dead wife all over the house.'

She hurtled round the side of the table, the wine bottle in her hand now, and started whacking him with it on his arms and legs and torso, the extent of her rage seeming to have no end.

'Mel! Mel! No, don't, please,' he begged, but there was no stopping her and the more he pleaded, the harder she hit him. Fearing that she was going to do him a serious injury he finally had to kick her away and run out of the house, glad that he had his car keys in his pocket. He jumped in the car, locked the doors and screeched out of the drive, his body shaking with the shock of his ordeal as he headed back to the farm.

'Oh my God, Luke! What happened to your face?' His mother clasped her hands to her cheeks, mouth open.

Luke gazed at her for a moment. He had no idea what he looked like, but his face was stinging like crazy, his left eye was slightly closed and there was blood all over his hands. His body throbbed where she'd hit him with the bottle and he wondered if she might have cracked a rib, every breath bringing a searing pain to his chest.

His mouth clamped shut while he tried to compose himself, feeling a bit light-headed with the shock of it all. He sank into a chair and closed his eyes for a moment, exhausted beyond thought, dragging his eyelids open a moment later to see his mother filling a bowl at the sink, the first aid kit out on the table.

'Right, then,' she said as she brought the bowl over. 'Let me have a look.'

Luke felt like he was five again and actually, it was just what he needed. A moment in time to give up responsibility and let himself be looked after.

'So, what started it this time?'

Luke winced as his mother dabbed at his face. 'What do you mean "this time"?' His heart was racing as his mind scrambled to find a plausible explanation for his injuries. 'It wasn't my fault. I had a… a run-in with a bunch of youths when I went to the shop to get a bottle of wine. They just jumped me.'

'Hmm.' Fay dabbed at his wounds and he looked away, unable to meet her gaze. 'You may be thirty-four now, but I still know when you're lying, Luke.'

He felt even more stupid then, for trying to hide the truth.

Mel's right, isn't she? I'm a poor excuse of a man. Tears stung his eyes. How on earth had it come to this? But he knew; she'd told him. He didn't respect her, hadn't thought about her feelings when he was thinking about the children needing a connection to their mother. He realised how insensitive he'd been and could understand why she'd been so upset. At least it was only his behaviour that she punished; he was sure she hadn't raised a hand to the children because Tessa would have told him earlier. It was up to him to sort himself out and be a better husband.

His emotions bubbled up inside, blocking his throat and making it impossible to speak.

'She's done it before, hasn't she?' Fay said. 'Maybe not this bad, but she's kicked off.' He opened his mouth to deny it but he caught the look in his mother's eye and thought better of it. 'I've seen the scratches. The bruises. You think I don't notice, but I do. Why the hell you had to marry the woman, and so soon after meeting her, is beyond me. I thought you were intelligent, but this is stupidity, it's...' Fay's jaw tightened and she shook her head, as her anger rendered her speechless.

Luke felt himself shrivel inside and wondered who else had seen through his lies. What about his work mates, his boss, the teachers at school? He'd given all of them excuses over the last few months.

He sighed and it felt as though the will to live was flowing out of him in his every breath, his body throbbing and sore, his mind swamped by regret. It was a little while before he could summon the energy to speak.

'She got rid of all of Anna's photos. Threw them away. I tried to talk to her about it and...' He flinched as Fay dabbed at his hands. In all honestly, he was horrified by how quickly things had escalated, had been properly frightened about what Mel would do next when she'd cornered him in the kitchen with the bottle. That wild look in her eyes, the feral snarl on her face; she looked completely mad, somebody he didn't recognise at all. He took a few deep breaths to try and calm himself but that only brought slicing pains to his ribs and he couldn't stop the tears from falling. He'd made such a mess of everything, had let his loneliness and loss lead him and his kids into a situation he had no idea how to resolve.

His mother was right, of course. It had happened before. But each time, he'd blamed himself, knew that he'd said the wrong thing. Knew that Mel was struggling to slip into the role of wife and mother to two children who weren't hers, children who were still grieving for their biological mother. It had all happened too quickly, that was the problem. He should have stood his ground and waited, done things more gradually, but Mel had been so persuasive. And although she struggled to know how to parent the children, and perhaps let her tongue run away from her at times, he knew she loved them. It wasn't the children she wanted to punish, it was only him. So it was up to him to work out a solution.

He sighed. 'What am I going to do, Mum?' She looked at him, concern etched on her face, but before she could speak, Ted's voice fractured the silence.

'Ditch the bitch.' Luke hadn't seen him standing in the kitchen doorway, didn't know what he'd heard, but it was obviously enough to know that Luke had been attacked by Mel. 'It's your house. Throw her out. It's the only thing you can do.' He waited a beat. 'If you're man enough, that is.'

Luke bowed his head, the feeling of failure making him want to go to sleep and never wake up. That would be the easiest answer, would save him from messing up his kids' lives.

'You know you can stay here,' Fay said, lips pursed, frowning. It was a look Luke knew from his childhood, a look that meant that you didn't argue. 'The kids can have a day off tomorrow. You can't possibly think about going back there.'

Luke squeezed his eyes shut, willing the tears to stop, and told himself to man up. But his head was throbbing, his body ached and his thinking was blurred. He was the head of his family, it should be him in charge. Not his mum, or Ted. But it was clear that the dynamics weren't like that. Not here. Not at home. Not anywhere. He swallowed hard, the heat of shame burning up his neck.

'I have to go back,' he said, dread in his heart. 'Not tonight.' He sighed. 'I'll let her calm down. But tomorrow, I've got to go back and see if I can sort this out.' He'd be a failure if he didn't and he'd be damned if he was going to give Ted another thing to crow about.

His mum nodded, weariness in her eyes. 'It's all been such a rush, hasn't it? Everything so fast. I thought maybe…'

'It's a rebound thing.' Ted finished her sentence, a habit of his that made Luke clench his jaw. Once again, Ted behaving as if he was Fay's son, not Luke. He made out that he was closer to her, Luke the outsider. 'He let his dick make the decision. We never thought it would last. Did we, Ma?'

'For Christ's sake, she's not your mother!' Luke shouted, unable to help himself. He hated it when her called her that, but his mother never stopped him.

Ted scoffed and put his arm round Fay's shoulders. ''Course she's my ma. Good as, anyway.'

Fay's fingers went to her temples, her eyes squeezed shut. 'Can you boys just give it a rest?' She wriggled away from Ted and glared at them both, her eyes flicking from one to the other, her face an angry scowl. 'I have been a mother to both of you. But neither of you own me, just remember that.' She gathered herself and held on to the back of a chair. 'I don't want to have this conversation again; do you hear me? I thought you two would have grown out of this by now.' Her words were enunciated very slowly and carefully, like a threat, as she looked from one to the other. 'Do not make me choose between you.'

They'd had fights about this very thing when they were younger. Ted wasn't a sharing type of guy and Luke wondered why he'd thought he would be any different fifteen years on. He knew in that moment that he couldn't come back to the farm. He had to make things work with Mel, stand up for himself and prove them wrong.

A little later, when he'd been cleaned up as best his mum could manage and she'd filled him with hot, sweet tea to counteract the shock of being attacked, his phone pinged; a text message from Mel.

Forgive me, darling. Please, please come home. I've got something I need to tell you.

He typed his reply, determined to get to grips with the situation.

See you tomorrow night.

He wouldn't take the children, though. Not until he was sure that Mel understood that this couldn't go on.

CHAPTER TWENTY-THREE

Luke couldn't take the next day off work, as two of his colleagues were on holiday, so he had to fend off comments about his injuries by saying it was a disagreement in the pub. All day, he thought about what he was going to say to Mel. She seemed to be able to mould his thoughts any which way she wanted and he had to be sure that his argument was clear in his head if he was going to fight off her verbal parries.

As soon as he parked in the drive, the front door of the house flew open and Mel came dashing towards him.

He wound down the window, unsure what sort of mood she was in, but at least out here his neighbours in the cul-de-sac could see what was going on. *I'm safe enough*, he told himself, his muscles tensing while he forced himself not to drive away.

Her face was red and blotchy, tear-stained. He'd never seen her looking so dishevelled and vulnerable.

'Are you coming in?' Her voice was tentative, like she honestly believed he might say no, and that was enough to make him think that she would be willing to listen to what he had to say.

He left the keys in the car, just in case he needed a quick getaway, took a deep breath and opened the door.

Once inside the house, she flung her arms round him, her face pressed against his chest.

'I'm so sorry. So, so sorry. I don't know how things got so out of hand.' She started crying. 'I love you so much, Luke. Please say you'll forgive me. Please?'

He hesitated, then, unable to help himself, he wrapped his arms around her. He wanted this to work, didn't he? With all his heart he wanted it to work. On so many levels, it would be better if this… this incident could be forgotten, and the hole that it had ripped in their relationship repaired. Maybe it could make them stronger. Maybe it would give him the upper hand now.

He pushed away from her, hands on her shoulders as he looked into her eyes, which were brimming with tears.

'It can't go on, Mel.'

She pressed her lips together and nodded, her expression one of absolute regret.

'You're a mother now and—'

Her eyes widened. 'I'd never hurt the children. Never. You've got to know that, Luke. They're as precious to me as if they were my own.'

'I know. I know that. But the kids' needs have to come first. And I know it's difficult. Maybe you don't like pictures of Anna around, but they need them. At the moment, with all the changes that have happened, they need to remember her.'

Mel blinked a few times and nodded.

'I'm so sorry. I don't know what got into me.' She looked away. 'No, that's not true.'

He waited, the silence filling the hallway.

'Honestly, I hate myself. I do. The thing is…' She took a deep breath, her eyes searching his. 'I'm pregnant.'

Luke's chest felt tight. Too tight to breathe. That was the last thing they needed. He knew that his response was taking too long to come, but he couldn't put his feelings into words.

'That's, um… that's a surprise.'

'It's hormones. That's what it is, Luke. They've made me super sensitive. That's what the doctor said. I called in to see him today, you know, about my mood swings and…' Her voice trailed off.

'Well, that explains things, I suppose.'

She knocked his hands from her shoulders, took a step back, hurt written all over her face. 'Aren't you pleased?'

There was a glint in her eye. A glint he didn't like. His pulse quickened and he forced a smile.

'Of course I'm pleased. It's just...' He couldn't work out how it had happened. He'd been so careful, always wearing a condom, even though she'd asked him not to. He wasn't ready yet. The kids weren't ready. Anger welled up inside him, threatening to burst out in words he knew he would regret and he battled to close it down. This should be happy news. *Maybe a baby is just what we need to bond us all together.* His head throbbed with this new information, removing his ability to think straight. *Is this a good thing or a really, really terrible thing?* He couldn't quite work it out, a mixture of emotions flashing through him, rendering him speechless

'I know we've been using protection, but...' She smiled at him through her tears. 'These things happen.'

Mel took his hand and led him into the kitchen, where she'd laid the table with napkins, all fancy, the smell of cooking filling the air. It all seemed so normal in there, familiar, no sign of the ugly brawl and without his physical injuries, he might have wondered if he'd imagined the whole thing.

'I've made your favourite,' she said, pointing to the lasagne cooling on the side, a fresh green salad and garlic bread already on the table.

There was no doubt that she was making an effort, no doubt that she was sorry, but Luke felt something had shifted in their relationship.

Can I trust her?

She made him sit down and served him a delicious three-course meal, all the while chattering away as if nothing was wrong. Maybe it wasn't. *Maybe it's just me finding it hard to adjust to married life and it isn't Mel's fault.* He shouldn't be comparing life with Mel to the life he shared with Anna, should he? *Different people, different needs, different dynamics. Hormones.*

She tidied away the dessert plates and went to get another bottle of wine.

Luke frowned. 'Should you be drinking?'

Mel hesitated. 'Just tonight. I'll stop after tonight. I just feel we need to… you know.'

She lifted her glass. 'To new beginnings,' she said. He chinked his glass against hers, wondering how many times they could do this. Whether they had really sorted out their differences.

Give this a chance, he told himself. *For everyone's sake.*

And he did.

Over the next couple of months, things got better, the children seemed happier, the fight faded in his memory as his body healed and their love-making resumed with the passion it had held at the start. All the better, Mel said, for not having to use condoms. There was something about her demeanour, though, something that made him wonder if she really was pregnant. He remembered Anna's morning sickness and overwhelming tiredness in the first three months. Her insatiable appetite and the thickening of her waist. All of these things were absent in Mel, who had the appetite of a sparrow. He knew every woman experienced pregnancy differently, but surely there should be some change that a new life was creating in her body. And wouldn't she have had a scan by now? Wouldn't there be appointments that he should be attending with her?

One evening, when the kids had gone to bed, he couldn't hold on to his thoughts any longer and before he could really think about it, the words that had been circling in his mind were spoken.

'I don't think you're really pregnant, are you? I think that was just a trick to get me to come back.'

She stared at him for a moment, then looked down and started twiddling with her wedding ring. It was a little while before she spoke. 'I lost it.'

'What do you mean?'

'I had a bleed.' She sighed and chewed at her bottom lip. 'I knew it was over. The baby was dead.' She looked at him with defiance in her eyes, and his frustration burst out of him in a stream of questions.

'Have you been to a doctor? Are you sure?' His voice hardened. 'And why didn't you think to tell me?'

'Well, I thought…' Her eyes slid away from his, confirming his suspicions.

She's been lying. She'd never been pregnant, just used that to reel him back in. And that seed of doubt about their relationship started to grow again, its roots anchoring themselves in his thoughts. *How can I ever trust her?*

She took his hand and linked her fingers with his. 'We can try again, though, can't we?'

He nodded, his mind racing. One day at a time, he told himself, while he worked out how to bring the situation back on track. Maybe she was telling the truth. Maybe she had lost the baby and it had been hormones making her temper fray, shrinking her tolerance to zero. It was the obvious explanation, because since the night of the fight, she'd been lovely to the children, taking them out for treats, patiently explaining how she wanted things done in the house, instead of snapping at them, helping them with their homework. And when he'd asked them if everything was okay, which he did on a regular basis now, they assured him that it was. She'd even started letting the dog in the lounge, and stopped fussing about the muddy paw prints in the kitchen.

He watched and waited, tense and alert, ready to protect his family at the first sniff of danger. But nothing happened and he felt himself start to relax, allowed himself to believe that life could be good, that they had finally settled into being a family.

Until the incident a couple of months later.

CHAPTER TWENTY-FOUR

Three months ago

It was in the early hours of the morning when Callum pattered into their bedroom, woken by a nightmare and needing a bit of company to get settled down again. Mel had said, on several occasions, that she couldn't cope with children in the bed and she started getting snappy, reminding Luke about a meeting she had to go to the following morning. Callum had been upset by Mel's disparaging remarks and had run out of the room crying, so Luke had gone after him. Mel followed them down the corridor, screaming like a banshee and scaring the poor child, who promptly wet himself.

'You pathetic little shit!' she'd yelled at Callum, who cowered against the wall, his arms protecting his head, wet pyjama bottoms clinging to his legs, a puddle on the laminate floor.

'Mel, you mustn't speak to him like that!' Luke could feel the rage building inside, hot and fierce.

She turned on him. 'How old is he? Nearly nine and he's still pissing himself?' She stood on tiptoes, her face inches away from Luke's. 'I call that pathetic.'

'No, Mel.' Luke grabbed her shoulders to keep her out of his face, blood pulsing in his ears. There was a moment's silence while they stared at each other before she leapt at him, arms like windmills, slapping and scratching, tearing strips of flesh from his hands, arms and face.

'Why do I never come first? It's all about the fucking kids with you, isn't it?' Her eyes had a manic gleam, spittle flying out with her words. 'What about me? You bastard. It's never about me!'

Luke backed away from her, glad to see Callum dash into the bathroom, where he locked himself in. After a few minutes, Mel wore herself out, spat on him, then stomped back to their bedroom, slamming the door behind her. He waited a moment, to be sure, then spent half an hour coaxing his son out of the bathroom, while Tessa stood in her doorway, a cuddly unicorn clasped to her chest, eyes wide and fearful.

He didn't go to work the following day.

The children didn't go to school.

It was time to leave.

Once they'd had breakfast and long after Mel had left for a meeting, Luke got them organised, grabbing their most treasured belongings. He was waiting for Callum to bring his backpack downstairs when Mel came through the front door. *She's back early!* Luke tensed, fear creeping up the back of his neck. She stopped, her eyes scanning the pile of suitcases in the hallway, a frown pulling at her face.

'What's going on?'

Luke took a deep breath. 'We're going back to the farm.'

'What?' She dropped her bags onto the floor and moved towards Luke, her keys still in her hands. 'Why would you do that?'

Luke saw Callum start down the stairs, then stop and hurry back up again. He could see Tessa's face peeping over the bannister. How could this be a home when the kids were scared of their stepmother's temper?

Time to man up.

He turned and walked into the kitchen, Mel behind him, heels clicking on the floor, then he closed the door to give them an element of privacy. This was not a conversation he wanted to have in front of the children, especially when he knew that Mel would react badly. He could already see it in her face. That look. His heart started to race and he told himself to be prepared. He stepped back a pace, putting more space between them.

Mel had that mean glint in her eyes that he was coming to know so well. He was going to have to be careful here. In fact, maybe this wasn't a good place for a showdown. Not with knives and other utensils on the worktop, pans hanging by the cooker. He walked towards the dining area and sat down, hoping she'd do the same. But she didn't. She paced up and down, hands to her temples.

'What the fuck are you playing at, Luke?' She stopped and glared at him. 'You're like a little child, always running to mummy when things aren't going your way.' She leant towards him over the table, her mouth an angry line. 'This is real life, Luke. People row. They make up. Rinse and repeat. I know Anna was a saint, but this is life for the rest of us.'

She stood back, threw up her hands. 'I've apologised. Many, many times. I got cross. Sorry. I'm really sorry. It's just... it's just I need my sleep. I can't function on a few hours and make sense when I'm in meetings with clients. And once I'm awake it takes me forever to get back to sleep.'

Luke swallowed, trying to dredge up some courage, but his heart was racing. 'It's not right, Mel. I can't live like this. It's not fair on the kids.' Luke sounded defensive rather than masterful, weak rather than strong.

'You're not helping them, you know. Babying them like you do, always pandering to them, letting them get away with blue murder. That's not the way to make them strong and independent. They need to learn to abide by rules.' Her hands were waving in the air to emphasise her point. 'None of this free-thinking bollocks you grew up with.' She sneered at him. 'That's not going to get them anywhere. All that hippy shit. They've got to learn how to fit in. Have proper manners. Know how to be good little worker bees.'

Luke cleared his throat, his back damp with sweat.

'That's not what I want for them, Mel.'

'They're spoilt. You know that, right?'

'They're not.'

'They so are.' She jabbed a finger at him. 'And taking them up to that farm will make them worse.'

'We're going.' Luke stood. Mel advanced towards him. A quiver of adrenaline radiated down his legs.

'You're not. You're not going anywhere. You've got to stop this, Luke. Running away at the first sign of trouble. A bit of a disagreement and there you go, running off again.' She reached for his hand and her face softened. 'For better and for worse. That's what you promised me in our marriage vows. Or didn't you mean it?'

His mouth was so dry he couldn't speak. That was such a loaded question, a palatable response too difficult to find.

She squeezed his hand, her eyes pleading. 'Please, Luke, please don't go. I love you so much. You and the children are everything to me. Everything.'

Luke snatched back his hand. 'I can't live like this.' Not eloquent, but it was the only thing his mind could come up with. He tried to move to the door, but Mel blocked his path. His hands twitched by his sides, his heart galloping so fast he was struggling to breathe. 'It's… it's not good for any of us.'

'Luke. Don't you realise that I know?'

She stared at him. He stared back, an icy chill running through him.

'Know what? I've no idea what you're talking about.'

'I mean the pills that you keep in the garage. I know what they are. I know you're selling drugs.'

Luke's heart fluttered, his breath quickened. 'No, I'm not. Don't be ridiculous.'

She nodded at him, her mouth giving a dismissive twitch. 'Okay, so what are they then? And why do you need to hide them?'

He sighed, looked at the floor then back at Mel, could feel the perspiration on his brow. 'They're... bodybuilding pills. I'm trying to beef up a bit.'

'But you sell them to people. I have pictures.'

He rubbed his sweaty palms on his jeans, shaken by the turn in the conversation and what it might mean in terms of his plans to leave. 'What? You followed me?'

'No. I have better things to do. I paid an expert in surveillance to follow you. And he watched you make several drop-offs. Looked like a delivery route he said. Up to Deeside and back.'

Heat flooded Luke's face, his voice defensive. 'It's not illegal. It's just a bit of a sideline. Some extra money.'

She gave a tight-lipped smile and shook her head. 'I've had them analysed. I have a lab report saying exactly what they are. And cannabis is definitely illegal.'

Luke's heart was racing so fast he could hardly think straight. How could she have gone behind his back like that? Had him followed. This was bad. Really bad. Even though there was talk in political circles about making medicinal cannabis legal, it would be years before that came about and, in the meantime, she was right. He was breaking the law. A criminal.

She could bust their whole business open. Put loads of people in danger of being arrested. Including him. And what would happen to the kids then?

Fight your corner. Think about the kids now, not what ifs. She's bluffing...

'I don't believe you. And anyway, it's none of your business.'

'Oh, but you should believe me. And I think it's very much my business. I think the police would be very interested. In fact, I have a sample, somewhere safe, just in case.' Mel was staring at him, eyes narrowed. 'So, if you decide to leave me, well, I might be compelled to tell the police. For the sake of the children, you understand. I would hate to think of them growing up in a drug den. And I'm pretty sure that if you're convicted of dealing, I'll have no problem getting custody.'

'You wouldn't do that. Anyway, it's medicinal. You don't get a high from it.'

Mel raised her eyebrows. 'You think that matters? Because I don't think the law is that precise. I think the law says that cannabis is illegal. Growing it, selling it and using it.'

Luke gasped, his mouth opening and closing as he tried to think of something that might put him on the front foot, give him some sort of lead in their verbal battle. But he couldn't think of anything and her threat of taking the children from him sent shockwaves of panic through his body. *Could she do that? Was it possible?*

'What do you want from me, Mel?' He sounded whiny, feeble. 'Why can't we just put this whole marriage down as a mistake. We rushed things. It's not working.' He took a step towards the door, but Mel wasn't going to move. She stood her ground, blocking his way, put a hand on his chest and pushed him back.

'You think it's that simple? Really? I've built my life around you and your children. I have a business, a reputation, not only with work colleagues, but at the school. I have a network of mummy friends. I'm important to people. Don't you understand that? If you leave, then I'm nothing again. Worse than nothing. I'm a reject. And that –' she pushed him in the chest – 'that is not going to happen. You are not going to humiliate me. You are not!'

There was a snarl on her lips, a hardness in her eyes.

Luke tried to swallow his fear and hoped that the children had locked themselves in the bathroom. He glanced around him, and knew that his only escape route was back into the hallway. He stepped to the left. She mirrored him. He stepped back, but she followed him, her eyes never moving off his face. He had to get to the door. Gradually he shuffled round until they had changed places, and he inched backwards until his hand was on the door handle. If he was quick, he could open it, turn and slam it in her face.

If he was quick.

But she was quicker.

Without warning, she lunged towards him, fists pounding him in the chest and face, her car keys still clasped in her hand. 'You don't love me, do you? Do you? You just wanted someone to look after you all, cook the meals, do the housework. I'm just a bloody slave for you all, that's what I am. I thought we were going to be a proper family.'

The keys jabbed at him like a bunch of blunt daggers, scratching and bruising his skin.

'Mel, stop it. Stop!' he shouted, a hand over his right eye, where she'd scored a direct hit, pain searing through him. But still she carried on.

'I hate you! I hate you! You just use me, you bastard!'

Luke grunted as the blows kept falling, his arms folded over his face. He tried opening his eye, but it stung too much, the pain intense. Tears streamed down his face. Then he noticed spots of blood dripping on to the floor and his brain froze on one thought.

What has she done to me?

He peered at her from under his arms. She looked shocked, her face blotchy and red, and she stared at her keys as if she'd never seen them before.

'Christ, Luke. Look what's happened now. You stupid man. You did that. You!'

Luke's eye burned, the pain escalating outwards, almost unbearable. He still couldn't open it, and could feel the tickle of blood oozing down his cheek.

'Let me have a look.' Mel tried to prise his arms away from his face, but he shrank back, holding them tighter while his heart jumped around and his breath came out in rasping gasps.

'That's going to need seeing to.' Mel looked down at her hand, where the keys were dripping blood on to the floor.

Luke felt nauseous, his stomach swirling, his pulse pounding in his damaged eye. It was closed now, his lids stuck together with blood, and he was feeling a bit faint. He put a hand on the wall behind him to steady himself, but his knees gave way and he slumped to the floor, the room starting to spin.

Mel went over to the sink, washed her keys under the tap and turned to him, all businesslike and efficient, the rage gone as quickly as it had come. She gave him a tight-lipped smile.

'Right, sweetheart, I think we need to get you to A & E, get them to have a look at that eye. It's looking a bit nasty. Clumsy you. Fancy tripping and knocking into the keys like that.'

She called one of the mums from school, who was on the fundraising committee with her and only lived a couple of streets away, and she agreed to come and sit with the kids while they went to hospital. No problem, she'd said, only too happy to help, and she'd bring Rory with her. That would keep Callum busy.

Luke was in shock, the world going on around him, but he wasn't part of it, all of his attention concentrated in the pain in his eye. He'd had a bit of an accident, Mel told everyone, and Luke couldn't speak to contradict her.

The next day, Luke had to phone in sick to work. His eye was patched and he'd been told to rest in a dark room for a few days, minimal eye movements, to give it a chance to heal. Mel fluttered about, making sure he was comfortable, bringing him hot drinks and food. She cancelled her plans for the week and put all her efforts into nursing him better. It was hard to believe, when she was like this, that it had really happened, her version of the incident told so convincingly that he wondered if she was right and he was wrong.

The more he thought about it, the more blurred the actual sequence of events became. Had she tripped? Had he stumbled? Had it been an accident? Because he couldn't believe that she would have deliberately hurt him this badly. Christ, he'd nearly lost his eye! And now... now she was looking after him so well, so lovingly. She was like a different person. The one he had fallen in love with.

He was sleeping in the spare room, where he could hear what was going on in the house if his door was open, so he still felt involved. He could hear Mel talking to the children, explaining maths to Tessa in a way that he never could have managed, talking football with Callum. Maybe they'd turned a corner, because she was trying really hard now, and even though she flared up with Luke, she had never touched the children, nor looked like she would. She might have given them the odd telling-off in the past, but it never escalated to anything physical and since his accident, there'd been no shouting at all. No, the problem wasn't them and he was sure they were safe. The problem was him.

With Mel, they were a family. Without her, he was an incompetent single parent who regularly thought that the best thing for everyone would be for him to end his life. So, surely the children were better off if he could make his marriage work? The house ran smoothly, she could do things with them that he couldn't, was there when he couldn't be and everything was so much better than when he'd tried to parent them on his own.

Maybe she was right.

Maybe he wasn't trying hard enough, running away too easily. Her comments had resonated with him and he couldn't give Ted another stick to beat him with. It wasn't that he actually wanted to go back to the farm, it was more that he had nowhere else to go. And anyway, the house was his. So why should he leave?

If it was his fault that the marriage wasn't working, then it was in his power to put things right. He had to give it another go, especially with her threat to get custody of the children. He couldn't even allow himself to contemplate that eventuality.

For the sake of all his family, and for the wellbeing of his children, he had to try harder.

CHAPTER TWENTY-FIVE

Nine weeks ago

A pattern returned to their existence, Mel taking the kids to school and usually being there to pick them up as well. Luke's shifts were still erratic, but she accommodated them without a murmur, organising her mummy friends to do pickups when she had work meetings.

The kids were behaving themselves; in fact, he hardly heard a peep from them. Mel was upbeat, having landed herself a contract with the company she'd been chasing for the last six months, and he was keeping up at work. She seemed a lot happier and he relaxed a bit, still unsure in his mind as to what had happened when he had injured his eye, time fading his memory until he was no longer certain whose version of events was correct.

He tried to forget about it and the threats that Mel had hurled at him during their argument, but his unease would not go away, gnawing at him in the night. *Have I done the right thing by staying?* But as he saw it, he had no option. If she knew about the drugs, he couldn't leave or he and the rest of his family would be in danger of being arrested. But worse than that, he might lose the right to see his own children. And if he told the truth about Mel, if anyone believed him, the kids might end up in care. It was these thoughts that really scared him, these eventualities that kept him by Mel's side, because, when he'd worked it all through, it was the safest option for his children.

He stayed in the spare bedroom, where Callum often came to share his bed when he had nightmares or wet his bed and this, in itself, became a source of friction.

'I think we should take him to the doctor,' Mel said one evening, when the kids were upstairs and they were on their own, sharing a bottle of wine. It was a routine that Mel enjoyed, although Luke hardly touched the stuff because it aggravated his acid stomach and made him feel even more melancholy. But it was Mel's daily treat, so he went along with it, pretending to drink while he kept topping up her glass.

Luke shook his head, adamant that was not going to happen. 'No, I think it's just all the changes. You've got to remember that his mum died.' He saw Mel tense and hurried the conversation on, a prickle of unease scratching at his skin. 'Then I moved them away from their friends. They're at a new school.' He shrugged. 'It's a lot for a kid to deal with.' Summarising it all for Mel gave his actions clarity in his mind, making him feel more protective of Callum. 'They were just getting settled in at the farm when I bought this place. Then you came to live with us.'

A jolt of realisation ran through him and he cursed himself for not understanding earlier. *Mel. The bed-wetting is all about Mel.* Callum had been fine at the farm. It had started when they'd moved here and Mel had started staying over. He looked up to see Mel staring at him. He swallowed, hoping she couldn't see what he was thinking. 'Too much change for the lad, that's all. It'll settle down if we just give it time.'

'But it's so much work, Luke. A set of bedcovers to wash just about every day. I'm sure it's not normal at his age.'

Luke took a deep breath to steady himself. 'Well, I do all the bed-changing and put the stuff through the wash, so…'

Her eyes narrowed. 'Are you saying I'm not pulling my weight?'

Luke tensed and shook his head, sensing the beginnings of an argument. She could get that way with a bit of wine if she was feeling tired. He rubbed her arm. 'No, love, I'm just saying that I'm doing my best to make sure it doesn't affect you.'

He smiled at her, stroked her face with the back of his fingers. She melted into him, and he breathed out his relief. Maybe she wasn't such a complicated character. More like a cat, in fact; loved attention and fuss and got narky when she was ignored. He had to learn to work with her moods, accept that she was totally different from Anna and not compare his life with Mel to the one he'd shared with his first wife. If he could be the husband she wanted him to be then there wouldn't be a problem. *Mel was right about me giving up too soon.* Marriage took time and effort, especially when there were kids involved. Everyone had to get used to putting other people first. *Teething trouble, that's all this is.*

Luke started to notice that the house was very quiet when he came home at night. So different to how it used to be at the farm, where his kids would be running round with Ceri's children, a little gang of them playing make-believe games, usually orchestrated by Tessa, who, even at ten, couldn't resist dressing up. As soon as they saw him they used to clamber all over him, telling him about their day.

Now, though, Callum was usually out at his friend's house, who lived round the corner, and Tessa seemed to live in her room.

'You okay, sweetie?' Luke said one evening, popping his head round her bedroom door. She glanced at him, startled, a frightened look in her eye, holding something behind her back. When she saw it was him, she pulled out her phone, fingers flying over the keys at a speed Luke had never mastered. He went and sat on the bed next to her, put his arm round her shoulders.

'How's school going?'

She turned off her phone and tucked it under her pillow. 'Fine,' she said, sounding the opposite, arms crossed over her chest, her body all stiff and tense.

'So, what did you do today?'

'Oh, just stuff. You know. The usual.'

'But you like school?' Luke's voice was hopeful, encouraging. Tessa always used to be such a chatterbox and having to drag information out of her was unnerving him. Had something else happened?

'Suppose so.'

'Is it better than Porthmadog?'

She nodded slowly, chewing her lip. 'Dad?'

'Yes, sweetie.'

'Can we go back to the farm?' Her voice wavered. 'Please, Dad.'

His heart contracted in his chest. That was the last thing he wanted to hear. 'But you'd have to go back to the old school then and I know you were finding it hard learning in Welsh. Isn't this school better?'

Tessa sighed and snuggled into him. 'It's not school that's the problem. It's this house, Dad. I liked it at the farm. With Ceri and the little ones and the horses. And Nana and Pops.'

'What's wrong with this house?'

'It doesn't feel like…' She scrunched his sweater in her hand, pulling herself closer to him. 'It doesn't feel like home.'

Luke's heart skipped a beat. 'Why's that, sweetie?'

Tessa let out a sigh so big it made her whole body shudder. 'Mel won't let us do anything. We can't have telly on if she's working because it annoys her. And she won't let us have friends round. And we can't have biscuits or snacks when we come in because it's not healthy. And we have to give her our phones when we come in because she doesn't like us looking at screens all the time.'

Luke frowned. 'But you've got your phone there.'

'No, this isn't mine. This is Emma's. Her old one. She just got a new one for her birthday.' She looked up at Luke, eyes beseeching. 'Mel doesn't know I've got this. You can't tell her, Dad. Promise?'

'Promise,' he said, smoothing her hair away from her face, a face that was so like her mother's it made him want to weep at times, a constant reminder of everything that he'd lost.

'She doesn't like Callum, so he has to go out all the time.'

'I'm sure that's not right, sweetie. 'Course she likes Callum. It's just he likes playing with his friends.'

'He's scared of her, Dad. She's really snappy with him when you're not here.' A shudder ran through her body. 'She freaks me out, Dad.'

Luke was silent for a long moment.

'She's never…' He swallowed, hardly daring to ask. 'She's never hurt you, though, has she?' He held his breath as his daughter chewed on her lip before answering.

'No, Dad. She doesn't hit us. I'm not scared of her hitting me. She just says nasty things. And gets all moody.' Tessa sniffed. 'And then I can't do anything right.'

Luke sighed as his daughter snuggled against his shoulder, a hollow feeling in his stomach.

'Oh sweetie, I know she can get a bit worked up, but you've got to cut her a bit of slack. She's not used to looking after children, you see. It's going to take a little while to adjust.'

Tessa started to cry. 'I want to go back to the farm, Dad. Please can I go? You can stay here, but please let me go. I hate it here. Really hate it. It's like… like I'm in prison.'

Luke's chest tightened, tears of his own pricking at his eyes. He couldn't split his family up, but his daughter was clearly miserable. There was no easy answer and as he listened to his daughter's sobs, all his energy ebbed away, his body so heavy he could hardly keep himself upright.

I've done this. I've made my kids unhappy. He was a poor excuse for a father. A poor excuse for a husband and in that moment, he wondered how he could find the energy to go on.

CHAPTER TWENTY-SIX

Six weeks ago

The days crawled by, Luke slipping further and further into a depression that threatened to swallow him up completely, painfully aware that he had failed his children in a way that would make Anna turn in her grave. Mel had spun her web and now he was trapped. It would be easy to give in to it, easy to take tablets, go to sleep and not wake up, but the thought of the children always brought him back from the brink. He had to be there for them. Had to find a way to make everything right.

He hadn't spoken to Mel about Tessa's allegations because the moment was never right and with Mel, the one thing you had to do was pick the right moment. But he believed his daughter. Why would she lie? The truth was, he didn't know what to do about it. About any of it.

He continued to sleep in the spare bedroom, something that Mel was increasingly unhappy with, but she was busy with her new contract and he had the excuse that he didn't want to disturb her sleep. She couldn't argue with that after the recent episode with Callum.

One night, when Luke walked into the master bedroom to get some clean clothes for the morning, he saw Mel stretched out on the bed, dressed in a black lacy basque, stockings and suspenders. Her head was propped on one arm. She gave him a seductive smile, batted her lashes.

'Come on, Luke, let's have a bit of fun.' She gazed at him. 'I miss you, sweetheart.'

Luke tensed. *Sex? She wants sex?* His priorities were about getting through each day without causing upsets and to be honest, sex was so far down his agenda he had forgotten about it.

'Come on, Luke. Sleep with me tonight. Come back in here. Let's connect again.' She pouted at him. 'Like we used to.'

He sat on the bed, his back to her. 'I'm sorry, Mel. My head is fit to burst. I don't think… I'm not sure I can.' He turned to her, stroked her shoulder. 'It's not that I don't want to.' He gave her an apologetic smile.

Mel sat back on her heels, grabbed his hand. 'I'm so ready for you, darling. So ready.' She gazed at him with big brown eyes. 'Please, sweetheart. It's been so long. Months.' She sighed, a tinge of impatience sharpening her voice. 'I'm forty in a few weeks. My biological clock is ticking and more than anything else in the world, I want to have a baby.' She shuffled closer to him. 'Our baby.'

He swallowed, the pressure of having to perform too scary to contemplate. Because what if he couldn't and she was disappointed and then got angry?

She put a hand up to stroke his face and he flinched. An involuntary movement that started his heart racing.

Did she notice?

Her eyes narrowed.

'What was that?' She took her hand from his cheek, put it to her chest. 'Do I repulse you now? Is that it? Is that why you won't sleep with me?' Two red spots appeared on her cheeks and a chill swept through him.

'Mel, no. You don't repulse me, don't be daft. Look at you, you're bloody gorgeous.' He tried to take her hand, but she pulled it away. He grasped at an excuse. 'It's just… it's my eye. It's not been right since my accident and I… I see things, makes me flinch. That's all. Nothing to do with you. Honestly, love.'

She frowned. 'That bloody eye.' She stroked his face, her hand roaming down his chest, undoing the buttons on his shirt, fingers reaching his skin. He tensed.

'Come on, sweetheart. Just try for me, will you?' Her eyes pleaded with him, her mouth curved into a smile of encouragement. 'Tonight's the night. Peak ovulation. You never know, just the once could be all we need.'

He took a deep breath and summoned all his courage. 'Mel, I'm not sure that a baby is what we need right now.'

Her hand stopped caressing him, her mouth hung open. 'What?' The word whipped out of her mouth.

'I just think we need to settle in as a family first. A baby... Well, a baby is such a commitment and...'

Her eyes narrowed, her fingers pulling at the hairs on his chest. He tried not to wince as she plucked at him, keenly aware that this conversation was balanced on a knife edge. 'Are you telling me that you're not committed?' Her voice was harsh now, always a danger sign, and a tremor ran down his legs. 'Is that what this is about? Is Luke planning on running home to Mummy?'

'No, Mel. No.' He tried to breathe normally, to make his voice calm. 'I just think we need a little time to learn how to live together.'

'Time? Time?' she snapped. 'I haven't got bloody time, Luke.' Her nails dug into his chest, her voice rising. 'Haven't you been listening? I'm nearly forty. Getting pregnant is going to get harder and harder for me.'

'Sweetheart. You're in such good shape and you eat well, I'm sure it won't—'

'What, so you're a fertility expert now, are you?' She slapped his face, a fast swipe that spun his head to the side. 'How dare you! How dare you go back on your word!'

He clutched at his stinging cheek and tried to talk her down from the fury that was winding up inside her. It was like facing a cobra about to strike and his heart raced so fast he struggled to keep his voice even. 'I'm not, Mel, I'm not going back. I just want to wait a few months. I'm not sure I could cope with a baby right now.'

'You won't have to cope,' she snapped. 'It'll be me coping, won't it?'

They stared at each other, his chest heaving, her face flushed. She nipped at his skin, her face getting angrier by the second.

Before he knew what he was doing, he sprang off the bed and dashed out of the room, aware that he had to get away while he had the chance. Once in the spare bedroom, he locked the door, heart pounding as he listened, expecting to hear her footsteps coming down the hallway. But all he could hear was silence, eerie in its unexpectedness. He breathed a sigh of relief, his body shaking as he got into bed.

He thought he'd had a lucky escape.

The following morning, he discovered he hadn't.

He came downstairs to find that Mel had already left for an early meeting in Manchester. He turned to make himself a coffee and realised something was wrong. Something was missing. The dog.

Bernie had been Anna's dog. He was middle-aged now and had pined for Anna after her death, always wandering around, not able to settle, as if he was looking for her. It drove Mel mad; the constant pitter-patter of his claws on the laminate floors. She hated the dog hairs, the muddy paw prints on the kitchen floor. At best she tolerated the animal but had no love for him. Normally, he would greet Luke in the morning, do a little happy dance round the kitchen and give him a couple of welcoming woofs. But today there was silence.

Luke opened the back door, wondering if Mel had let him out, and that's when he saw him, lying on the ground, his body twitching, frothing at the mouth. He gasped in horror and dashed outside, gathering the dog in his arms, as he tried to find the vet's number on his phone. But a moment later it was clear that there was no rush. The dog's body stilled. He was dead. A sob caught in Luke's throat, his heart struggling to beat, as though a part of him had died too, the part that still yearned for Anna. Gently, he laid the animal on the ground, his head on the dog's chest, feeling the warmth of his body for the last time, his heart breaking as if it was Anna dying all over again.

A shout made him sit up and he turned to see Tessa standing at the kitchen door, staring at him, eyes wide, her hand over her mouth. 'Bernie! Bernie!' she screamed as she dashed across the lawn. Luke caught her and held her to his chest as she cried, her tears soaking through his shirt.

'Quick, Dad, we need to get the vet.' She pulled at him, wanting him to do something, anything to help save her last link to her mother.

Luke stroked her hair and held her tight. 'I'm sorry, love, but he's gone. He's dead.'

'She did it! She did it!' Tessa shouted through her tears, thumping her fists on her father's shoulder.

Luke shook his head. 'I don't think so. He was having some sort of seizure.'

But he wasn't sure.

Is this Mel's way of getting back at me for not wanting a baby?

It took him a while to calm the children and get them to school, then he dropped the dog's body off at the vet's on the way to work to see if they would do an autopsy. He wanted to know for sure what had happened. Later, at the end of a difficult day, a day when his grief for the dog and for Anna filled his whole being, making it almost impossible to function, he got a phone call. He was sitting in his car about to head home.

'Sorry it's so late,' the vet said. 'But we've had a busy day.'

'No problem.' Beads of sweat bloomed on Luke's brow and he held his breath, hardly wanting to know the truth.

'So, the autopsy results… looks like it was cannabis. Capsules in a plastic bag. A lot of them. It seems he ate someone's stash.' There was silence for a moment. 'Does that sound possible?'

Luke sighed. 'Well, he did get out yesterday,' he lied. 'And it took a little while to find him. You know what cocker spaniels are like; hoovers on legs. He'll have a go at eating anything. But cannabis? Well, I've no idea where he would have found anything like that.'

'Well, I have to admit that it's not something we see a lot of.'

'So… um, do I need to tell the police? Or will you do that?' Luke tensed, waiting for the reply.

'I'll leave that up to you, shall I? And we'll cremate Bernie, like you asked. His ashes will be ready for collection at the end of the week if that's okay?'

'Fine. Yes, that's fine. And thank you.'

Luke's heart thundered in his chest. Now the vet knew that something dodgy was going on. That was all he needed. And how did Bernie get the bag in the first place? His stash was hidden in the garage and Bernie never went in there. It had to be Mel.

He knew he couldn't let this go. This was too much now, the absolute final straw. Her level of meanness appalled him and he couldn't imagine what she would do to hurt him next. Then his eyes widened. The children. Were they in danger now? Would she hurt them to hurt him? The thought seemed to press against his skull as he held his head in his hands, elbows resting on the steering wheel. He had to leave her, make her see that their relationship was never going to settle into a normal pattern. Not if she was going to be cruel and vindictive like this.

A knock on the window startled him and he looked up to see Neil, his boss, staring at him, concern in his eyes. Luke wiped a hand over his face and wound the window down.

'Everything alright, Luke?'

He nodded and cleared his throat. 'Yep, all okay. It's um… the dog died.'

Neil's frown deepened. 'Oh, that's a shame.' He rocked on his heels, gazing at Luke for a moment. 'Look, are you sure you're okay, Luke? It's just… you haven't been yourself these last few

months. There's a few mistakes creeping into your work. And...
don't take this the wrong way, but you look like shite.'

Luke gave a rueful smile. 'Don't pull your punches, hey?'

Neil shrugged. 'Look, I want you to know that my door's always
open. I know you've been through a rough time and settling into
a new... a new house and um... relationship. Well, it's all tricky
stuff when you've got kids. You come and talk to me if there's a
problem, if you need to alter your hours or anything, won't you?'

Luke looked down at his hands, the kindness in Neil's words
making his eyes sting. He bit his lip and blinked his eyes a few
times before he looked up at his boss, swallowing the lump in his
throat that made speech impossible.

'If you need a bit of time off, just let me know and I'll see
what I can do.' Neil's steady gaze made Luke shuffle in his seat,
uncomfortable, like his boss could see inside his head and read
his secrets. Could he tell how miserable he was, how close to the
edge? 'Maybe a couple of weeks rest and you'll be back firing on
all cylinders.'

Luke nodded and cleared his throat. 'You could be right, Neil.
It has been a bit full-on recently. I'll have a chat with Mel, see
what her diary is looking like.' It was what his boss wanted to
hear but, given recent events, a holiday was the last thing Luke
wanted. Then an idea grew in his mind, something he'd thought
about and dismissed many times over recent months. Maybe Neil
was right. A holiday might be just the thing.

CHAPTER TWENTY-SEVEN

Seven days ago

Luke hadn't challenged Mel about the dog. He'd told the children he'd died of natural causes – just one of those things. She hadn't mentioned it either, but it sat between them, in the silences, like an uninvited guest at a party. Every day he psyched himself up to say something and every day he couldn't face the inevitable fight. Maybe he'd asked for it by denying her a baby; that was a horrible thing to do, wasn't it? But he was clearly a horrible person. He'd got everything so wrong. Bernie dying was her way of showing him what he was doing to her; killing her hopes and dreams.

He'd been aware from the start of their relationship that she wanted a baby, but now he would never be a father again. It was a necessary act of rebellion, one that would allow him to retain an element of control, while keeping Mel happy. Something that would put his mind at ease. And she'd never know.

He'd organised the vasectomy for an afternoon appointment and was surprised by how quick the procedure had been. He was still young, at thirty-four, to be doing something so final, but he knew in his heart that he didn't need to bring another life into the world when he could hardly cope with his own. At least he could keep Mel happy in the bedroom department and take the pressure off without having to worry about her getting pregnant. It felt like a big weight off his shoulders while he worked out what he was going to do. It was time, he decided, for him to take control of the situation. It was time for him to protect his children, his family and sort out the mess he had created.

He'd moved back into their bedroom, which had delighted Mel, and for the last month or so, everything had been running pretty smoothly. At least he'd thought it had. Until he'd been reading with the kids at bedtime, a habit that had started when they were babies and he'd made sure to continue. It was their time, just the three of them. Mel had tried to discourage him in the past, but he'd stood his ground because it was something that Anna had started and he felt it kept the three of them bonded together, regardless of Mel's behaviour. Tessa was turning the page of the book they were reading when he saw something that made his skin crawl.

'What happened to your arm, sweetie?' Tessa looked up from the book and hid her arm under the covers.

She shook her head, lips pressed together as if to stop any words coming out of her mouth.

He pulled the covers back. 'Let me see.' He picked up her arm to have a closer look and could see a cluster of bruises on her forearm. Round, like fingerprints. He caught his daughter's eye, a question on his lips that he didn't want to ask. 'Was it Mel?'

Tessa chewed her lip. 'She said I mustn't tell you or she'd…'

Luke frowned, fire igniting in his belly. 'She'd what?'

'Break my phone.' She looked at Luke with big, frightened eyes. 'She found it under my pillow. I need my phone, Dad. You can't say anything. You can't.' She was crying now, pleading with him, and Luke was appalled that this was what his family had been reduced to.

'She broke my phone already.' Callum picked at the duvet cover. Luke swung round to look at him.

'Why did she do that?'

'She said I wasn't listening.' He looked up at Luke. 'But I was. I was listening. I can hear her and look at YouTube at the same time but she said I couldn't and she told me I was a rude, stupid, pathetic excuse for a boy.'

Luke's heart stuttered.

What else has gone on that the children have been sworn to secrecy about?

'Then she grabbed my phone off me and threw it across the kitchen.' He looked so defeated that Luke pulled him close. 'It hit the wall and smashed into pieces. I tried to put it back together.' His voice wavered. 'But I couldn't do it, Dad.'

Luke gathered his children to him. Callum under one arm, Tessa under the other, his heart breaking with the situation he'd put them in. His jaw clenched tight, breath pumping out of his nostrils as his anger flared. 'Look, this is not okay. You tell me if anything happens. She's not allowed to bully you like this. I'm going to sort this out, kids. Don't you worry. I'll get it all sorted.'

His stomach churned as he finished reading and tucked the children into bed before heading downstairs, knowing that he had to tackle her while he was feeling strong, before he could talk himself into backing down.

Make sure we're in the lounge, where there aren't so many things that can be used as weapons.

He caught his thought and his jaw hardened because he knew for certain now that his relationship was dead and nothing could bring it back. The kids had to come first and Mel was steadily destroying all of them.

'Darling, have you finished?' Mel looked up, a broad smile on her face. His spirits took a dive. *Christ, this isn't going to be easy. Where do I start?* She got up and wrapped her arms around him, pressed her body to his. 'I thought we could have an early night tonight.' She ran a finger down his chest, stopping at the waistband of his jeans. 'Have a bit of us time.'

He took a step back and the smile fell off her face, to be replaced with a frown.

'What? What is it now?'

'I've just seen the bruises on Tessa's arms.' His hands clenched and unclenched by his sides, the anger burning within him as fierce as anything he'd experienced in his life. *Keep cool*, he told himself, aware that he was on the edge of striking out. He took another step away from her.

Mel's hands went to her hips. 'She was being really cheeky and wouldn't listen to me.'

'But, Mel, you must have gripped her really hard to create bruises like that.' His voice was low and ominous.

She stood tall and defiant, a finger jabbing at him as she spoke. 'Your kids are spoilt rotten. They're not easy to deal with when you're not here.'

Luke took a breath, summoning all his courage.

'I'm leaving, Mel.'

Saying the words out loud, he knew it was going to happen. Without warning, she launched herself at him, scratching at his face. He grabbed her arms to stop her attack, his hands circling her wrists, and she thrashed and squirmed, trying to get free. He grasped her harder, determined that she wouldn't get away.

'Mel, stop it! Stop it now. This isn't going to solve anything.'

She glowered at him, lips pulled back from her teeth in an angry snarl. 'You can't leave me, you stupid man. You can't. Don't you remember? I know about your drugs. Didn't Bernie's death teach you anything? And you know I can take your kids from you, don't you? I have photos, remember. When I get started, you won't even have access, you stupid man.'

Luke tightened his grip around her wrists as he worried about what she might do when he let her go. He had to calm her down.

'Listen, Mel, trying to fight me isn't going to get us anywhere.' He stared at her, and she glared back, still struggling to release herself from his grasp. He clenched his teeth as he fought to keep her under control. 'Let's talk about this. Properly talk.'

She glowered at him, but stopped trying to resist and after a moment, he let her go. She stood there, chest heaving up and down, and he took a few steps back, leant against the wall, eyes scanning the room for missiles. They stared at each other for a long moment before Mel crumpled on to the sofa and closed her eyes.

'Luke, I know I can fly off the handle sometimes, but…' She sighed and opened her eyes, tears rolling down her cheeks. 'Luke, I love you so much. I want this to work.' She wiped at her tears with her hands and gave a shuddering sigh. 'You have no idea how much I want this to work. I just… I just want a baby.'

Luke sighed. He couldn't tell her. Not now, not anytime.

'Luke, I think—'

The lounge door opened and Callum stumbled in, still half asleep, a wet stain clearly visible on his pyjama bottoms. 'Dad.' He looked terrified as Mel glared at him. Then she picked up a mug from the coffee table and hurled it at him, striking him on the cheek. Callum screamed and fell to the floor, his hands over his face. Luke dashed across the room to his son, and gently prised his hands from his face so he could see the damage.

Mel stood up, shaking.

'Look what that fucking son of yours has made me do now! This is why our relationship is cracking up. It's him. And her. They don't want me. They've never wanted me.' Her hands gesticulated wildly as she spoke, her voice getting louder and louder. 'You don't know what they're like when you're not here. They wind me up on purpose.'

Luke glared at her.

'They do!'

Luke picked Callum up and took him upstairs, got him into clean pyjamas and settled him in the spare bedroom. He had a big lump on his cheek, but Luke didn't think any bones were broken. His eye was closed, though, and Luke knew that he'd have a black eye by the morning. He thought long and hard while he waited for Callum to fall asleep, then he went back down to the lounge, his face red with rage, his heart pounding.

'Mel, you need to know something. I can never give you a baby. I've had a vasectomy.'

'What?' Her mouth fell open, horror in her eyes. 'You've done what?'

'I had a vasectomy. I don't want any more children.'

The dismay on her face was a small reward for the damage she'd done. He went to the spare room and locked the door, while he considered his next move.

CHAPTER TWENTY-EIGHT

The following day, after Mel had left for work, Luke drove to the farm, his thoughts scattering like leaves in the wind.

Callum's eye was black now, the bruise a deep purple ring that covered not only his eye but the top of his cheek as well. The eyelid was firmly shut and Luke wondered how he was going to explain it to the school. They'd have to think of a story and he'd have to make sure Callum stuck to it. They could say it happened playing football, couldn't they? The last thing he needed was social services getting involved.

It's time to do something decisive, he thought, *instead of just hoping that things are going to be different.*

His mother watched them walk into the kitchen, her puzzled smile turning to a horrified frown when she saw Callum's eye and the scratches on Luke's face. She shooed Tessa and Callum into the living room, where Ceri was home-schooling her children, while Luke put the kettle on.

Luke's heart sank when his mother came back into the room with his dad and Ted behind her.

A family meeting. But then, wasn't this what he'd wanted? Some help to decide on how best to get himself out of the mess he found himself in. It was an impossible situation that had no easy solution, but hopefully, with everyone involved, they could come up with something that might work.

'It was Mel who did that to Cal, wasn't it?' His mum's eyes were wild, an expression of hatred on her face that Luke had never seen before.

He hung his head.

'How can she possibly hurt you, Luke?' The sneer in Ted's voice made Luke look up. 'You're way bigger and stronger than she is. For Christ's sake! You've got to stop being a wimp and start fighting back.'

Ted's words held barbs that pricked and pulled at what little was left of Luke's courage, taking all the strength from his legs. He pulled out a chair and slumped onto the seat.

'You have no idea,' he mumbled into his chest. 'No idea what it's like. I just seem to wind her up.' He ran a hand through his hair. 'Most of the time everything is fine, absolutely fine, and then I say something and she flares up. It's like a lightning strike.' He shook his head.

'Luke, I can't stand by and see this happening.' His mother's voice was stern. 'You've got to report her to the police.'

He looked up and caught her eye. 'I can't, Mum. She'd tell them some story, make out it was my fault. And she's threatened to take the kids off me. Because she'd tell them…' Just voicing his concerns sent his mind into a tailspin and he rubbed his hands over his face as if to scrub the thoughts away.

'Tell them what?'

This was it. He bit his lip, wondering how he could tell them. Looked around at the three pairs of eyes that were fixed on him, waiting. He took a breath and blurted it out. 'She knows about the… the cannabis business.' The betrayal of his family's trust wrapped around his chest, pulling tight until he could hardly breathe.

Ted's eyes widened. His mum leant on the back of a chair to keep herself steady. His dad rubbed his hands over the top of his head. Luke longed to be a child again. Life was simple then. No decisions to make, the only conflict being little squabbles with the other kids in the house. Nothing like this; the horror of being torn apart by conflicting priorities. Sweat dampened his shirt, making it stick to his back.

'No, Luke, you didn't,' his mum gasped. 'Why on earth did you have to tell her?' She stared at him, mouth open, and his gaze slid away. 'Goddammit! Luke, you stupid, stupid…' She grunted her annoyance at the ceiling before glaring at him. 'I thought you'd promised we'd keep this in the family? That you were happy to keep her and the kids out of it?'

'I didn't tell her, Mum. I didn't. She found my stash.'

Ted stood up, his face reddening with rage, finger pointing at Luke. 'How could you be so careless? This is an important source of income for us. Not to mention vital for Ma's health.' His voice was getting louder as he forced his words through clenched teeth. 'And you've just… you've messed everything up. We've worked on this for years. Years. And you've just ruined it!'

Luke shrivelled inside, his body hunching as Ted's onslaught pounded him.

Ted leant over the table towards him, shouting. 'You stupid bastard! You can't be trusted with anything can you, you're—'

'Enough! That's enough!'

Fay's hands gripped the back of the chair, knuckles white, looking between the two men, her jaw set. There was no doubt she was fuming, but there was something else in her expression. *Disappointment*, Luke thought, and that cut him deeply. He was at the centre of a whirlpool, drowning and pulling everyone he loved down with him.

'Right, let's sort this out.' His mum inched herself round to sit on the chair she'd been holding on to, and Luke could see the weariness etched on her face. 'So, what happened this time?'

Luke looked down at his lap, started rubbing at a stain on his jeans. 'She wants a baby. That's what we were fighting about yesterday.'

'What!' Luke jumped, startled by his mother's shout. She was staring at him open-mouthed. 'You can't bring a baby into that household. Look what she's done to the children.'

'She just gets a bit cross, that's all. Wants them to have better manners, you know, that sort of thing.' Luke wondered why he was defending Mel after everything she'd done, but every attack on her felt like an attack on him. It had been his decision to marry her, after all.

His mother looked scornful. 'You've got to open your eyes, Luke. They're kids. At that age, words are the harshest weapon. You tell a kid something negative often enough and it's in their heads forever.'

Luke couldn't look at her. 'I know, Mum. I know. Anyway, I've er… I've had a vasectomy, so a baby isn't going to happen. But I honestly don't know what to do now.'

'Just move back here.' Fay's arms were crossed over her chest, her face hard and stern. It was an order, not an option.

Ted looked at his aunt, incredulous. 'What? Weren't you listening? If he leaves her she'll tell the police, and then we're all in trouble.'

'Not just that.' Luke shook his head. 'She said she'd get custody of the kids.'

His mother's hands went to her cheeks, the thought so appalling it stole any words she was about to say.

'How much does she know?' His dad sounded tired. And old. The weight of responsibility squashed Luke a little more. His dad didn't need this sort of worry, not at his age. He should be taking life a bit easier by now, not having to mop up after his son.

'She found my stash, Dad. And she had me followed. She says she has photos of my drops all the way up the coast.'

Ted slammed a fist on the table, making them all jump.

'You stupid bastard! You're back five minutes and look at the trouble you've caused. If we didn't have this side to the business, we wouldn't be able to live here.' His arms were flying all over the place, as he spat out the words. 'The farm's only covering its costs. It brings in a little, but with just me fit enough, if we're all being honest here, it's never going to make enough money for us to live on.'

Luke looked down at his hands, picked at a hangnail. He didn't need telling. That's why he'd made such an effort to make things work with Mel.

'You weren't to know, son,' his dad said. 'Love's a funny thing, makes everyone a little blind.'

'I know you never liked her.' Luke clasped his hands tighter, remembering the way his parents had looked at Mel the first few times she'd visited. He could tell they weren't sure and yet he'd ignored any reservations he might have had.

Fay nodded. 'No, she always struck me as a bit false. I could see her looking down her nose at us while she pretended to be pleased to see us. Look how quickly she stopped coming to visit.'

'I did warn you about her,' Ted said, his finger stabbing the air in Luke's direction. 'I knew she was trouble. It was all too quick. She pushed you into marriage and you let her. You stupid, weak bastard.'

'Ted, calm down,' Fay snapped, giving him a look that would freeze water. 'In fact, why don't you go and do something useful. You're not helping here.'

Ted stared at her, mouth open.

'Go on.' She waved him away. 'Off you go.'

Ted clamped his lips together and after a moment, he stomped out of the room, slamming the door behind him.

When he'd gone, Fay let out a long sigh.

'He's getting worse, I swear. So much anger in the lad and always wants to have things his way.'

Silence settled in the room.

'So…' Phil looked round the table, worry creasing his brow. 'What are we going to do?'

The conversation went round in circles as they talked through all the possible options, but to Luke, nothing seemed realistic, because he knew how vindictive Mel could be. That was the scary thing about all this. How far would she go?

Finally, Fay brought the discussion to a close. 'Okay, well, I think we need to give our brains a bit of a rest, sleep on things tonight and see how we feel in the morning.' She looked drained and Luke knew that with her MS, stress was the worst possible thing for her, increasing the chances of a flare-up of symptoms that would leave her in bed for days. He watched his mother shuffle out of the room, holding on to furniture and the door frame to keep herself steady. As soon as she was gone, Ted came back into the kitchen and shut the door.

Luke turned to him, frowning. 'You've been listening, haven't you?'

Ted ignored him and sat next to Phil at the table. 'We can't leave things up in the air like this.'

'We've had a good run at it,' Phil said, staring at the table, where his fingers stroked a knot in the wood. 'Maybe it's time to knock it on the head. Think of something else to grow instead.'

'But Ma needs the pain relief. You know we've tried everything else and nothing worked. She turned into a complete psycho when the doctor put her on those steroid things. That's why we're doing this. It's all for Ma.'

Luke could feel his anger bubbling up inside, Ted speaking to his father as if Luke wasn't there, as if he was his son.

Phil nodded. 'Maybe we should move to America. I know a lot of states out there are giving licences to grow cannabis for medicinal use.'

Ted gave a dismissive snort. 'Come on, Da. Don't be daft. They won't let us all in, will they?'

'We could go on a visitor's visa and just stay?'

Phil looked hopeful, no doubt thinking of Californian sunshine to finish his days.

'I don't think it's that easy, Da. And if you're there illegally there'll be no healthcare. You have to have health insurance and they won't give you that now.' He pressed his lips together; a determined expression that Luke knew well. 'No. We keep on doing this and we find a way to persuade Mel to go away and keep quiet. That's what we need to do.'

Phil got to his feet and stretched. 'Well, good luck with that. My brain's addled. I'm going to catch up with your mum, get off to bed. Hope I find inspiration in the night or something.'

Luke got up as well, no intention of being left alone with Ted. 'Look, I'll go back tonight, just me, and see if I can smooth things over, buy us some time while I work out what to do.'

'It's not a solution, is it?' his dad said. 'She'll always have this hold over you and now you can't give her what she wants… who knows what she'll do.' He shook his head. 'You be careful, son. And come home if you feel threatened in any way. Your life is what's important here.'

Luke nodded, but as he was driving home he didn't feel that his life was important at all. Not when he'd ruined everybody else's. The closer he got to the house, the more certain he became of what he must do. He would take his family on holiday, as his boss had suggested, and that would be the end of this life, the end of everyone's misery.

PART THREE: NOW

CHAPTER TWENTY-NINE

Monday

Ted watched the police cars arrive at the holiday cottage. The second time today. He smiled to himself. Good, that meant they wanted to ask Mel some more questions. He wondered if they'd found his first clue yet, the phone in the forest, and wished he could be inside, listening to the conversation, watching Mel squirm. Because she must be feeling all sorts of emotions by now: scared, worried, and definitely angry. Perfect! Nothing less than she deserved, the mad cow.

He was parked in the drive of a cottage down the road a little way, another holiday home by the look of the place, so he was safe to stay there for a while, watching through his binoculars. He knew by the garden that it wasn't lived in, the overgrown lawn and tangle of shrubs giving it that uncared-for look. There were so many places like it near the farm in Wales, he could spot them a mile off.

He waited.

Luke had insisted that he was going to sort things out, but Ted couldn't trust him to do it properly. As usual, it was up to him to take control, before Mel ruined all their lives.

CHAPTER THIRTY

Mel needed the police officers to go away now and get on with the job of looking for her family. She was exhausted by all the questions and really needed some time to think.

'Please find my children. Please,' she said from behind her hands, which were hiding her face.

'Come on,' Inspector Stevens said to his sergeant as he stood. 'We've got work to do.' Mel glanced up and saw something in his eyes. Something that she didn't like. Suspicion maybe? Her pulse quickened. The muscles in the inspector's jaw tightened. 'Don't you worry, Mrs Roberts, we'll find them.'

He headed for the door, Sergeant Lockett on his heels. Mel stayed in her seat and held her breath, hardly daring to believe they were going at last. She waited for the sound of the front door opening, but instead she heard the murmur of voices from the hallway. Then the sound of footsteps coming back into the kitchen. *Dammit!*

She dabbed at her eyes with a tissue.

'Do you mind if we have one more look around?' Stevens said. 'See if there's anything we didn't spot earlier? Now that we've got more information, well, we need to be looking for different things.'

'Yes, yes,' Mel said with a sniff, not looking at them as her whole body tensed. 'Help yourselves.' She blew her nose on what was left of her tissue while the officers headed upstairs, wondering what they might be looking for. *How much do I tell them?* she asked herself as she listened to the clump of footsteps above her head, the sound of doors opening and closing. There was no doubt that they had questions she couldn't fully answer. *Oh, what a mess!* Tears of frustration trickled down her face and she swiped them away with the back of her hand, forcing herself to sit up straight. This was no time for self-pity. No, this was a time to take control. She pulled up her sleeves, making sure her bruises were clearly visible. *Now what else can I do to make sure they believe me?*

Her nerves were in tatters; in fact, she could feel her body shaking and she still hadn't come to a decision about what she should do next, her brain working so hard that she'd developed a splitting headache.

Finally, she heard the police officers coming back downstairs and she really hoped they'd go now. She looked up when they came into the kitchen, tears glistening on her cheeks, hoping she presented the right image; the desperate wife and mother.

'It's all very tidy up there,' Stevens said. 'Is that how you found it?'

'Oh no,' Mel shook her head. 'No, it was a tip. How you could make such a mess in such a short time is beyond me, but those kids… well, I have to say they were semi-feral. Never trained to look after their possessions and keep their bedrooms tidy. To be honest, it's been a bone of…' She stopped and looked down at her hands, which were clasping a mess of damp tissues, cursing her mouth for running away with itself. *You know better than that*, she told herself, and nipped at her bottom lip to stop herself from saying any more.

'So, Mrs Roberts, can I ask what your relationship with the children was like?' Mel looked at the sergeant, annoyed with herself for getting it wrong and opening up a whole new line of questions. 'Did you get on with them? It's not easy with stepchildren, is it?'

Mel looked away, dabbed at her eyes and softened the tone of her voice. 'Oh yes. Lovely kids, don't get me wrong. Just…' She sighed. 'I think they were finding it a little hard to accept me.

The death of their mother hit them really hard. It was so sudden, you see. And, to be honest, they're still grieving, poor little mites.'

'Must have been hard for them.'

Mel nodded and chanced a look at the sergeant, but her face was blank, giving nothing away. 'I think Luke was a bit soft on them sometimes, because of… you know, the circumstances.'

'And you were trying to correct that?'

Mel knew Lockett was leading her onto a path that she didn't want to go down and her headache thudded at the base of her skull. She willed the muscles in her neck to relax and gave the sergeant a sad smile. 'Trying. But not succeeding. They were a tight little unit. The kids and Luke. They played us off against each other to get their own way.' She sighed again. 'Luke couldn't see it.'

The police officers were silent for a moment before Stevens spoke.

'So, what did the place look like when you arrived? Can you describe it?'

Mel frowned and put a hand to the ache that now circled her head, pulsing behind her eyes. 'Well, it looked like they got out of bed and had something to eat. Then went out.' She visualised the mess in her mind, wishing her heartbeat would slow down. 'There were plates and pans all over the place in here. And then their clothes were all over the bedroom floors. Books and DVDs and all sorts of bits and pieces in the lounge. Shoes just kicked off.' She looked at them, eyes wide. 'I'm sorry, I didn't think. I automatically tidied up, while I was waiting.' She pressed her lips together, chin quivering. 'To make it nice for when they got back, you see?'

'Did you hoover round?' Lockett asked.

Mel frowned, not sure where this conversation was going. 'No. No, I haven't even found the hoover yet. But it didn't need it. I think Luke must have done a bit. It was just messy. Not dirty.'

The police officers nodded in unison, before Lockett pulled a make-up bag from behind her back. Mel felt her mouth twitch in recognition, her mind exploding with questions that ratcheted up her headache by another notch.

'We found this in the bathroom, Mrs Roberts. Is it yours?'

Mel stared at the bag, rubbing her temples, as if that might tease out the jumble of her thoughts. 'It's an old one. Spares.' She frowned. 'I'm not even sure why it's here. I suppose Luke must have thought I'd forgotten it, but I've got a new one that I take when I go away to work.'

The sergeant unzipped the bag and pulled out a little bag of powder, held it up.

Mel's eyes widened, a shiver of unease running down her spine.

'Can you tell us what this is?'

She was silent for a long moment, the blood draining from her face. 'I've no idea. But whatever it is, it's not mine. I didn't even pack that make-up bag.'

'I'm afraid we're going to have to take it away,' Stevens said. 'For analysis.'

The officers stared at her, silence filling the room as her headache squeezed and squeezed, until all her thoughts were gone, wrung out of her like water from a wet cloth.

'It's not mine,' Mel repeated. She sounded panicky. 'Luke must have put it in there.'

Stevens nodded. 'Well, we'll check for fingerprints, so if it is yours it would be better if you told us now.' His stare was uncompromising, his suspicions obvious.

'We were wondering if you could give us the name of the hotel you stayed at, Mrs Roberts,' Lockett said. 'You'll appreciate that we have to check everyone's movements. Nothing to worry about.'

Mel nipped her lip so hard that she tasted the sharp tang of blood. *Christ!* She was cornered, trapped in her bending of the truth, and the look on the police officer's faces showed they knew it too.

CHAPTER THIRTY-ONE

Mel's hands dropped to her lap, her body slumped in defeat. The silence thickened, pressing down on her. Stevens cleared his throat, a reminder that they were waiting for an answer, and she knew there was only one course of action open to her. *I'm going to have to tell them.*

Her hands tangled together, fingers clutching at each other for support. 'Um… I've had a bit of time to think and… well, I might have got a bit muddled with times. I was… I didn't…' She flicked her gaze from the inspector to the sergeant and back again, her heart hammering, as she fought against the words she had to say. *Go on, tell them the truth.* She took a deep breath, her words coming out in a long sigh of defeat. 'I stayed with somebody on Saturday night. A work colleague. We left the hotel together on Sunday. Then we went to a pub for lunch. A long lunch. And then we went our separate ways.'

There, I've said it. She felt so weak it took all her energy to keep herself sitting upright.

'Do you mean you were having an affair?' Lockett laid it out, stark and bare.

Mel blushed. 'No, no, not an affair as such.' She stopped herself. *Is that a lie? Would they know?* 'I just… slept with a client. One night. That's all it was.' Perspiration beaded on her forehead and she pointed at Lockett, who had that look on her face again. 'Don't you go judging me. Luke was hell to live with. Absolute hell. This was a make-or-break week away, but to be honest, I was coming to the conclusion that our marriage was over. As much as I love him and the children, it was…' She stopped herself and selected her words more carefully. 'It was a mistake that couldn't be rectified.' She took a moment before she carried on, sorting out her best line of defence. 'I was upset. My client was concerned. We had a few drinks and well, one thing led to another.' Her gaze was defiant now. 'Luke was horrible to me. I wanted a baby and do you know what the man did?' She looked at Stevens, then Lockett, as if they could possibly know the answer. 'He had a vasectomy! Just to spite me.' She nodded when she registered the shock in Lockett's eyes.

Yes, she thought, *he did that to me. Denied me the hope of a child of my own.* And that was surely the worst kind of betrayal.

'I have to ask again,' Stevens said. 'Is it possible he's left you? Is that what this is all about?'

Mel shook her head, adamant. 'I told you before – he wouldn't do that.' She sounded certain because she was. Luke knew she didn't make idle threats. 'It would leave too many loose ends. Hurt his family.'

'And suicide wouldn't? Weren't you suggesting before that suicide was a possibility, or have we misunderstood?' Stevens asked.

Mel looked at the inspector, her mouth opening to speak, but no words came out. *Shut up!* she warned herself, deciding that it would be better if she didn't say too much more. She decided that she really didn't like the way this was going, the spotlight being shone on her movements. Not to mention the cocaine. How had she not found that when she'd cleaned up?

She got up and started clearing the mugs away, putting them in the dishwasher.

'We'll just have another look down here, if that's okay,' Stevens said. It wasn't a question.

She nodded, unable to look at the man. He was trying to trick her. Trying to get her to say things that would catch her out. He thought he was so clever, but she'd been trained in manipulation,

trained in neurolinguistic programming and body language. Oh
yes, it was clear as day to her what he was trying to do, and it
wasn't going to work. She puffed out a breath as she switched on
the dishwasher, glad of the noise to break the silence. This was
about damage limitation now, making sure she came out of this
in the best way possible.

She scowled. *The little bag of powder. What was that all about?*
Her heart started racing at the thought. If that was cocaine, then
she was in trouble, that was for sure. *But how did it get in there?*
It could only be Luke.

Her head was so full of worries, she felt it might crack open. She
put a hand to her forehead as she gazed through the kitchen window
into the garden, felt the dampness of sweat and wiped it away. *Stay
strong*, she told herself as she gripped the edge of the worktop.

As far as she could see, there were two potential scenarios.
There'd been an accident of some sort and her family were dead,
or Luke had done a runner. Of course she'd be sad if they'd died,
but if this was the second option being played out, she would be
properly livid. It was a possibility she hadn't considered before, but
now the police officer had mentioned it again, she had to give it
some serious thought. *No way is he going to leave me!* She'd loved
him completely up until the vasectomy incident, had trusted their
wedding vows and now, if he'd run away, and made trouble for
her, well he was going to face consequences. Oh yes, she'd make
sure of that. *No way is he keeping his children. No way on this earth.*

Lockett and Stevens came back into the kitchen and started
opening cupboards, then got the bag out of the bin and started
sorting through it. Mel's eyes narrowed, her nose wrinkling at the
mess. But that wasn't her main concern. *What are they thinking?*

'When's bin day?' Stevens asked.

'Wednesday, I think,' Lockett answered. She headed outside
before returning a few moments later, shaking her head. 'Nothing
in the wheelie bin. Completely empty.'

Stevens looked at Mel and she tensed when she saw the glint of suspicion in his eyes. 'That's a bit strange, isn't it? Everyone produces rubbish. Especially when you've got kids.'

Mel stared at him, not knowing what to say. There was no explanation. Then a thought crept into her mind that made her legs weaken. *Do they think there was some sort of incriminating evidence in there?*

'We need to ask you to come down to the station with us,' Stevens said. 'So we can have a more thorough chat.'

'Am I under arrest?' The inspector's gaze was unnerving and Mel leaned against the worktop, her hands behind her back so they couldn't see them shaking.

'No, we just need to ask you some more questions.'

'Well, ask them here.' Mel swallowed, panic crushing her chest. She knew all about being interviewed by the police and how they twisted your words, made you flustered, catching it all on tape. No, she wasn't going anywhere if she didn't have to.

'I need to get my colleagues involved, and we need to test this powder. So I'm afraid we can't do it here.' He gave her a look that she didn't like, the sort of look you give to someone when you know things they don't.

Mel swallowed.

Now it really begins.

CHAPTER THIRTY-TWO

Ted watched with interest as the police car headed out of the drive. *Is that Mel in the back seat?* Well, well, well. He wondered what she'd said, what they'd found, why they were suspicious. He smiled to himself. It looked like the plan was working.

He knew they'd let her go. It may take a while, but they would. And in the meantime, his family in Wales was in danger. He rang Phil on his mobile number, having given him his own personal phone before he came away so they could talk without Fay and Ceri knowing. This was a job for the men, no need to worry Ma with anything, not with her mind being so fragile at the moment.

'Have you done it?' Ted asked.

'Just finished, son. If the police turn up it'll be fine now. Everything sorted.'

'I don't think it'll be a thorough search or anything, so as long as everything has been moved, we should be fine. I know that Idris is on duty tonight and he's not going to want to see us closed down. Not when his dad is so dependent on our products. So, no panic. But you never know. He might have to bring someone with him.'

'Okay, son. You take care now.'

Phil sounded quite perky, Ted thought. More upbeat than he had for some time, which was odd, given the seriousness of the situation. He wondered if he really knew what was going on and hoped for all their sakes that he'd followed instructions.

Ted's blood pressure was building, making his heart pound, and his ears ring. *Calm down*, he told himself. *Getting worked up isn't going to help you think straight, is it? There's still work to be done.*

CHAPTER THIRTY-THREE

Stevens opened the car door and guided Mel into the police station in Windermere, which looked like it might once have been a house, built of local slate and set back from the road. He showed her into a small, windowless interview room located at the back of the building, just big enough to fit a table and four plastic chairs. Mel wrinkled her nose as she sat, the smell of damp hanging in the air, a large patch of cream paint peeling off the wall in one corner.

'I'll just go and see if there's any news, then I'll be right back,' Stevens said and left her, the door closing behind him with a heavy thunk, suggesting it was self-locking. *Keep your cool*, she counselled herself as her hands found each other and clasped themselves together. She looked round to see if there was a two-way mirror or CCTV, but there was nothing. Nobody was watching her and she allowed herself to relax a little and take some calming breaths.

It was a good few years since she'd been interviewed in a police station, but those memories had been refreshed and now sent adrenaline racing round her body. She had to keep sharp, even though it had been an incredibly long day and all she wanted to do was succumb to sleep; wake up and find it had all been a dream. *This is really happening*, she told herself. *You have to concentrate.*

She started by trying to work out what the police did and didn't know. What else might they uncover that would show her in a bad light? She was just beginning to answer that question in her mind when the door opened and Stevens and Lockett walked in. Their faces were grim and Mel tensed, preparing herself for the worst.

The sergeant was first to speak. 'You're not under arrest, Mrs Roberts. This is an... exchange of information, not a formal interview. Okay?'

Mel nodded, relieved, because she'd been about to ask for her solicitor and that would have made her look guilty. She felt a little calmer, aware that if they'd had any evidence against her, she would have been cautioned. There was still the matter of the cocaine, but if she kept on denying any knowledge of it, she'd be fine. She steeled herself, told herself to be careful, just in case they tried to trick her.

'I'll just give you an update first,' Stevens said. 'We've had a few calls tonight and a couple of them have piqued our interest. The first one is a sighting of your family in a service station outside Dumfries on Friday.' They both looked at her and she knew they were checking her body language, checking for little tells that this news would mean something to her.

She frowned. 'Dumfries? Are they sure it was them? I don't see how they could be at a service station in Dumfries if the car is still in the drive? And it was Aberdeen where Luke lived before, nowhere near Dumfries. Aberdeen is where his contacts are.' She shook her head. 'I don't... It doesn't seem very likely, does it?'

'Well, we're following it up and we'll let you know if anything definite comes of it.' The inspector paused for a moment before his next question and Mel made herself sit still, although her hands fidgeted under the table. There was something else, she could sense it, an uncomfortable feeling creeping up the back of her neck.

'Mrs Roberts, some other information has come to light that we need to talk to you about.' Mel met the inspector's even gaze. 'A former colleague of yours rang the helpline. One who worked with you at a nursing home in Leeds. A Mrs Eva Harding?'

Mel gasped, her hands covering her mouth, unable to stop her body from responding. *That bitch! That utter bitch!*

'Eva Harding?' She looked at the police officers in turn, unable to keep the scorn from her voice. 'You're kidding me! You're going to listen to her?' Mel leant forwards. 'That woman was nothing but trouble, always causing problems between the residents.' She huffed in disgust. 'Oh yes, she did it for fun. And you're going to listen to what she has to say?' Mel folded her arms across her chest and sat back in her chair, her mouth set in a tight line.

Silence settled around them for a moment, before Lockett spoke. 'We're just trying to check out what we've been told. Perhaps you could tell us why you were let go from your job at the nursing home? We'd like to hear your version of events.'

Both officers watched Mel's every move. *Truth or lie? They're testing me.* She swallowed as she prepared to speak, knew she had to tell the truth.

'I was a manager at the nursing home for over ten years and there was never any trouble until I gave Eva Harding that job. She always had it in for me, trying to undermine me at every turn. In all honesty, I think it was a case of attack being the best form of defence for her, because she was not a good worker.' Mel shook her head, lips pursed. 'But it was hard to get staff, so I kept letting her off. Then there was a complaint about me, which got sent to the authorities. Who investigated.' Mel wrapped a strand of hair round her finger and tugged, welcoming the discomfort as tears sprang to her eyes. 'It was the worst time of my life and it was all down to that woman. A whistleblower. That's what she called herself. A liar, I say, bending the truth to get herself out of trouble. I was about to sack her, but then her lies got me suspended and the new manager disregarded anything I ever did. Ten years of work unravelled in weeks and a year later the home went into administration.'

'And what were her allegations?'

'Oh, she claimed I was bullying patients.' Mel threw up her hands. 'They had dementia, for God's sake. Weren't even sure what planet they were on half the time. Of course I was firm with them. I had to be to keep them safe!'

Lockett gave her that look again. 'Mrs Harding said you were fired for trying to get terminally ill residents to leave money to the nursing home in their will. She didn't mention bullying people with dementia.'

Mel's eyes widened before she caught hold of her shock and used it to her advantage. She sat back in her chair. 'Where's the proof? You can't make allegations like that without proof.' She tapped the table with a finger. 'And I can tell you that there wasn't any. Or there would have been a police investigation. And there wasn't.' Her chest was heaving as she worked herself up into a state of righteous indignation.

'But you moved away?'

'Well, I couldn't stay in the area, could I? Not with accusations like that hanging over me. And I couldn't get a reference. No, I decided I'd draw a line under the whole thing and start again. Do something a bit different. We always went to North Wales on family holidays, so it had a special place in my heart, and I'd had enough of living in a city, so I decided to go and live in Bangor.'

'And that was six years ago.'

Mel nodded. 'Yes. It's in the past and I really don't see what it's got to do with my family going missing.'

The police officers looked at each other.

'Right, Mrs Roberts, let's move on to the matter of the powder we found in your make-up bag. It's been tested and it's definitely cocaine.'

'It's not mine.' Mel enunciated every word and glared at them, eyes narrowed. 'I told you. My husband has been dealing drugs. He must have put it there.' She banged a fist on the table, her voice cracking. 'Why aren't you looking for my family instead of asking me these stupid questions? Why is nobody trying to find them?'

Stevens glared back. 'We are trying to find them. Our colleagues are working hard, following up leads. We just need to take your fingerprints for elimination purposes. And we'd ask you to stay locally for the time being. You may be interviewed again under caution about the cocaine when we have investigated further, so you might want to organise legal representation.' He nodded to his sergeant. 'Would you do the honours, please?'

Mel sagged with relief in the knowledge that she'd done it. She'd got through the ordeal without anything negative happening and she was free to go. Her hands were shaking as the sergeant took her fingerprints, her emotions battered and bruised. But she was determined now to make the most of the opportunities that freedom gave her, determined to make sure that she came out of this with the upper hand.

CHAPTER THIRTY-FOUR

Forty minutes later, Mel was dropped off at the house with a reminder that she should go nowhere because they would want to speak to her again. Her mind was numb after the turn of events. *I might be charged with possession of cocaine!* That would be her business ruined. She sniffed back furious tears as she dug the key out of her handbag and let herself into the house.

It was chilly and unwelcoming, because she'd forgotten to stoke up the fire before she went to the police station, distracted by everything that was going on. She pressed her fingers to her temples, a headache pulsing behind her eyes.

How has everything got so out of control?

Is Luke playing games with me?

He must have planted the cocaine. It was all so obvious now. He'd wanted her in prison so he could be free of her. She scowled, annoyed with herself for not finding the stuff before the house had been searched. *So much for a new start.* There she was thinking she'd got everything sorted out, and now this.

She stomped into the kitchen and opened the fridge, got out a bottle of wine and popped the cork. She hesitated for a moment as she remembered the possibility of a child in her belly, then decided that the last thing she wanted to be was a single parent, told herself that it had been wishful thinking anyway and there was no point denying herself. Her life had gone to shit and what she needed right now was a drink. She poured herself a large one and gulped it down, quickly filling the glass again. She leant against the worktop, her glass hugged to her chest, and shivered.

It's a nightmare. A fucking nightmare.

She thought about the note.

When did Luke leave? That was the question. Had he gone on Friday, the last time he was seen? Then she remembered the phone in the forest. Or Saturday, then?

That's when she'd originally been planning to get to the holiday cottage. Saturday night. But the event had finished late, she'd stayed behind for drinks and Chris, her client, had been very persuasive.

She closed her eyes and pictured Chris, his dark hair, attractively speckled with grey, high cheekbones, straight nose and those beautiful grey eyes. He was suave and charming, and as a senior manager in her client's company, was off limits in so many ways.

'Go on, Mel,' he'd said after their first drink at the end-of-day gathering. 'Let's have a bottle of champagne, celebrate success. You did brilliantly, getting everyone on board.'

Mel was on a high, the event having gone so much better than she'd hoped – the tricky managers were now fully committed to the proposed restructuring. It had taken all her wiles, all her neurolinguistic programming skills to get them thinking straight, but now they were she was so happy she thought she might burst into song. *Champagne?* It was so tempting, but she had to get to the Lake District, having told Luke she'd be there that night. A feeling of dread had built in her chest as she imagined a grotty little cottage somewhere, and compared it to the comfort of the hotel.

'I'm sorry, Chris. But I really should go.' She hadn't sounded very convincing, even to her own ears.

'One little glass.' He'd flagged down a passing waiter. 'Go on. Please? You're not going to make me drink it on my own, are you?' He'd given her a gorgeous smile which lit up his face, his eyes twinkling a promise that she hardly dared to believe. He was a very persuasive man and every time she'd tried to say no to him, she ended up saying yes. In fact, over the three months that she'd known him, she'd said yes quite a lot. Which had been immensely enjoyable and not something she could bring herself to regret.

She'd grinned at him. 'Go on then. Just the one.'

But there's no such thing as just the one glass of champagne, is there? Well, there wasn't that night. They'd finished the bottle and ordered another one, while the rest of the management team gradually drifted off to their homes, leaving the two of them alone.

She hadn't intended to, she told herself, but she'd ended up staying the night with him. It wasn't the first time they'd slept together; in fact, it had become a regular occurrence over the last three months, even though each time she told herself it wouldn't happen again. She'd justified it as being Luke's fault for denying her and anyway, it was only sex. That night it was a delaying tactic as much as anything. Truth be told, she'd been dreading the holiday, because it was so far removed from the one she would have liked. In terms of sparking the relationship back to life, the flicker of hope had started to fizzle out as soon as Luke had described where they were going and what he had planned for them. She'd sent him a text message, telling him she'd been delayed, but if he'd lost his phone, he wouldn't have received it.

The police had that phone now, though, and would be reading everything on it. Her chest tightened. They'd find her messages, and then start asking all sorts of questions she didn't want to answer. She took a big gulp of wine, enjoying the warmth that it spread down her throat and into her stomach. She wanted to be numb. Wanted this mess to go away.

The jangling of her ringtone made her jump, and she snatched up her phone, checked the caller and let out a big sigh of relief.

'Chris.' Just the mention of his name made her hand gravitate towards her belly. She put her glass down and walked into the lounge.

'Can you speak?' His voice was rich and warm and wrapped itself around her like a cosy blanket.

She sighed and settled herself in a chair, a hand to her forehead. 'Oh, Chris, you wouldn't believe what's going on here.'

'Is he playing up again? I can come and get you. You know that, don't you? If he lays a finger—'

'Calm down... sweetheart.' The word felt right now, not presumptuous at all. He'd rung her, hadn't he? And he'd called her that just yesterday. 'He's not going to hurt me. And anyway, I'm not sure your wife would approve if you dashed up here.'

'She wouldn't know.' There was a heavy lacing of scorn in his voice. 'She takes absolutely no notice of me, off playing tennis and bridge and whatever else she does with her time. Honestly, we hardly see each other.'

Mel nodded to herself, a warm glow enveloping her heart and spreading through her body. Chris was a passionate man, like her in so many ways; it would kill him to be with a cold woman. An idea of an alternative future, a new beginning, started to build itself in her mind, brick by brick, faster and faster, like a time-lapse video.

'I don't like you being with him. You know that.'

Mel smiled and wrapped her hair round her finger.

'Look, Mel. I've been thinking. I know this is sudden, but we've known each other for a while now. I've always admired you and now we've... now that...' He sighed. 'I'm making a right hash of this. What I'm trying to say is... I don't want you to think I'm using you in any way. Any way at all. Mel, I want it... us, to be real.'

Mel's heart started to race, his words fuelling its rapid beat.

'Oh, Chris. I know you're not using me. I know that.'

She could hardly believe it. He'd been thinking along the same lines as her. He had! Soulmates, that's what they were. Bloody identical. She allowed herself to fantasise for a moment, wonder what it might be like to share her life with someone who thought the same way. How much easier than constantly having to stand her ground and fight for what she thought was right. All the bloody time. Her body felt weary just thinking about it, the muscles in her shoulders a little more tense.

He sighed and she could visualise him stalking around, his hand pulling at his earlobe, a little tic of his that she found adorable. 'I worry about you.'

'I know, sweetheart. I know.' Mel sighed, thinking how easily that word came out of her mouth. Sweetheart. It felt so right. 'But things seem to have changed.' She paused. *Should I tell him? Involve him?* 'Luke's gone.'

There, it was out in the open, and it was a relief. *Can he help me?* she wondered. *Will he want to? Or will he run a mile at the thought of trouble?*

'Gone? What do you mean?'

'Well, he's disappeared. With the kids. Didn't you see the news? I did an appeal for information.'

'What? No, I never really watch the news. You're kidding?'

'When I got here, the place was empty, deserted, all the lights on. Honestly, it was weird. His car's here, but they went out and haven't come back.'

'Christ!' There was silence for a moment. 'So where do *you* think they are?'

She hesitated for a moment, wondering if she'd said too much. 'I don't know. The police are involved now, though. In fact, I shouldn't be talking to you.'

'Let me come and get you. Please, Mel.'

She dithered for a minute, uncertain. *Run away? Leave this mess behind?* It was tempting, so very tempting. She rubbed at her forehead as she thought it through for a moment.

'No, Chris. That wouldn't look good, would it? No, I've got to stay here.' She could hear his breath rattling down the phone, and a part of her wondered whether she should just let him take control. *Wouldn't that be easier? Jesus, this needs some careful thought.*

She swallowed. 'Look, I've got to go.'

'I love you, Mel.'

Her breath stuck in her throat. *He loves me?* She closed her eyes, embracing the passion embodied in those three words and the promise they contained. The possibility of a different life.

'Oh, Chris. I don't want to drag you into this. Really. Look, I can't talk now. It's probably better if you wait for me to contact you.'

'Oh, Mel.' Her heart dissolved at the emotion in his voice and she had to fight not to contradict herself, tell him to come and get her. 'Are you sure? I don't mind. I really want—'

'I know, sweetheart. I know. I'll call you. It might be a day or two. But I've got to sit it out.' She clenched her jaw, telling herself she was doing the right thing. What would the police think if she ran away? No, she had to stay. For now, anyway.

'Well, give me your address, just in case you change your mind.'

She thought for a moment and decided that having a contingency plan wasn't a bad idea. She delved into her handbag and brought out the map that Luke had printed off and read out the postcode, gave him the name of the cottage.

'Take care,' Chris said. 'And ring me. Promise you'll ring me.'

'I will. I will.' She hung up, the phone grasped so tightly in her hand that her knuckles were white. She sat for a moment, staring at the fire as she worked things through. Then she found a pen and the little notebook in her bag where she kept clients' contact details, wrote down his personal mobile number and deleted all evidence of Chris from her phone, along with all the messages she'd sent to Luke. Hopefully the police wouldn't be able to get into his phone and they'd never know what had passed between them. That thought made her feel much better.

CHAPTER THIRTY-FIVE

Later that evening, Inspector John Stevens sat at his desk, waiting for his constable, Jackson, to finish his summary report of their investigation so far. Then he'd be ready to discuss with his superior whether he should hand over the investigation to a team of detectives at HQ. He still wasn't sure of the rules these days, where his responsibilities stopped and those of other teams started, given all the changes that were still bedding in.

His team of uniformed officers based in the Windermere office were officially called Problem Solvers, because that was essentially what they did. *But when does a problem become a criminal investigation?* That was the grey area in his mind, because apart from Mel's cocaine possession there was still no evidence of a crime. *So, is it still just a problem? Our problem?* He'd have to let his boss at HQ decide on that one, because he really hadn't a clue.

He was impressed with his officers. Everyone had stayed late to see the case through, and make sure they showed the higher-ups that they could be relied on to do a good job. Even his newest recruit, George, had stayed, and he came into the office now, holding a bin bag at arm's length.

'Some guy just dropped this off. Guy on a bike. Said he found it in a layby. He was taking a pee and he saw the bag stuffed behind some bushes.'

Stevens stared at the bag, wondering why he should be involved.

'Stick it in the bin, George. I honestly haven't got the energy to deal with fly tippers tonight.'

'No, guv. You're missing the point.' George looked more animated than he had in weeks. 'It's got clothes in it. I opened it to see if there were any papers in there with addresses on and that. Look –' he held up a pink T-shirt with red splodges on it and stared at his boss – 'does that look like a bloodstain to you?'

Stevens got to his feet, trepidation sending familiar pains across his chest.

'Put it down, George.' His voice was sharper than he'd intended and George did as he was told, some of the contents spilling onto the floor. More clothing. Children's clothing. 'That could be evidence. Get some gloves, will you, then we can have a proper look.' He put a hand to his forehead. 'What about the guy who brought it in?'

'Oh, he went. Had to get back to Glasgow, he said.'

Stevens cursed under his breath and George blushed. 'Did he tell you exactly where he found it?'

George went over to the map of their area that was stuck on the wall. 'From what he said –' he jabbed a finger at the map – 'I'd say about there, I think.'

Stevens made a note of the map coordinates and scratched at the fuzz of hair on top of his head. They wouldn't be able to do anything until the morning now. You can't search an area by torchlight, he reasoned, not without trampling potential evidence into the mud.

His gut told him things had taken a turn for the worse. *No bodies yet*, he reminded himself. *There may be an innocent explanation for the clothes.* A nose bleed. A kid who fell off her bike. There were many scenarios, and most of them bore no relation to criminal activity. And, when he thought about it, this bag of clothes might have nothing to do with this case. Could have been there for weeks.

George came back with the box of gloves and they both put on a pair, George holding the bag open while John pulled out items of clothing. As well as the girl's T-shirt there was a boy's hoodie and a man's fleece. That was it. Three items of clothing, all with what looked like bloodstains on them. Not sinister enough to immediately think three people had been murdered, Stevens decided, but enough blood to start asking questions.

His hand rasped over the stubble on his chin.

'Okay, let's put them back in the bag, George, and we'll get them over to HQ tomorrow, get some DNA tests done.' Until then, he wouldn't be sure if this was relevant evidence or not, but it did seem like a strange coincidence, that the bag had been handed to them.

Jackson popped his head round the door.

'New information. The Welsh guys can't do anything until tomorrow. They've got a major RTC to clear up and I've tried ringing the number Mrs Roberts gave us for the farm but I can't get an answer.'

Stevens tutted, frustrated that they couldn't make more progress. There were so many possibilities with this case. He swivelled in his chair, letting his mind work through them while he waited for Jackson to finish his report.

With the family still not being found, he decided it was unlikely they were on the hill somewhere. The paths would have been crawling with people at the weekend and he felt that the lost-out-walking scenario had run its course. Grizedale Forest had been well and truly searched and nothing had been found, so they weren't there. And now this bag of bloodstained clothes.

Of course, they could have just scarpered.

That was an option that he'd been too blind to consider before, given Mel's assertions that her husband wouldn't think of doing such a thing. The possibility that he'd taken his chance to leave her had to be put on the list, given the comments from Mr Roberts' work colleagues. In fact, he felt stupid now that he'd taken Mel's word for it. Too stupid to pass the case on to his boss without checking a few more things first.

He went into the office to speak to his sergeant. 'Ailsa, will you give the guy in Scotland a ring, please? Just to tie up loose ends. And Jackson, have you called the hotel Mrs Roberts was staying at yet? We need confirmation of arrival and departure times.'

Jackson nodded. 'Will do. I've finished the report, it's in your inbox.'

Stevens checked his watch. Nine thirty. Half an hour max, then they'd wrap it all up. They'd put in a long day and it looked like tomorrow could be just as demanding.

He read through Jackson's report, adding his own comments and clarifying points so they didn't sound quite so blinkered. He'd just finished when Jackson walked in, frowning, looking at a piece of paper in his hand.

'Apparently Mrs Roberts checked out on Saturday evening.'

Stevens thought for a moment, tapping his pen against his chin.

'She said she slept with a client on Saturday night. Ailsa wrote his name down, I think. I suppose if she stayed with him she wouldn't have needed her room. Call her client, will you?'

After a few minutes, he followed Jackson back into the main office and saw that his sergeant had finished her call.

'The Scottish guy who rang in earlier thought he saw a man and two children in a Fiat Punto. Little lad had the remains of a black eye, he thought. But they were all wearing baseball caps, so he says now that he might have been mistaken.'

Stevens nodded. 'Okay, good. There might be CCTV if it was a service station. Will you ask?'

He saw Jackson put the phone down and called to him, 'Jackson, what you got?'

'Seems she was telling the truth about timings in terms of leaving the hotel. The man was a bit reluctant to talk at first, and when I told him that Mel had given us his details, he wasn't too pleased. In fact, I'd have to say he was pretty pissed off. I have a feeling that his wife might have been there. Anyway, he confirmed that she stayed with him and they left at lunchtime the following day.'

'Eight hours to get from Manchester to here is still a very long time,' Lockett said.

'They had a leisurely lunch together.' Jackson wiggled his eyebrows. 'Not sure if that's a euphemism for "had sex for several hours"?'

'Hmm. Well, I suppose that's a possibility.' Stevens looked at the weary faces of his team. 'Okay, let's call it a day. Thanks for staying late and good work everyone. We'll see what tomorrow brings.'

He went back into his office, made a couple of final tweaks to add in the new information, and sent the report. Then he picked up the phone and asked to speak to the boss on the night shift.

'I'm sorry, John,' the supervising officer said, after he'd had time to assess the situation. 'We've a major situation going on here. From what you've said, even with the bloodstained clothes, which we don't know are theirs yet, there's no compelling evidence that anything has happened to the family and I'd say you've done everything you can at this stage. It'll have to wait until morning, then we can see how resources are shaping up, but if you could keep the case for now, chase up the remaining leads tomorrow and we'll take it from there, okay?'

When Stevens put the phone down, he knew that this was one of those cases that wasn't going to let him go. He just hoped for a happy ending.

CHAPTER THIRTY-SIX

Mel made herself some food, tidied up and wandered round the house, sipping her wine, restless and unsure what to do. It was late but her brain was too busy for sleep. She didn't have much time to work out her next move. In her mind, she played through all her conversations with the police and she nodded to herself. They knew enough. But not everything.

Maybe there's a way I can get through this and start again?

Her life as she knew it was over. Luke, who she'd given herself to completely, was gone. Along with her ready-made family. And her career, that she'd so carefully built up, could topple at any moment if she was charged with possession of cocaine. She stifled an angry scream and stomped back into the kitchen to top up her wine glass.

What else is going to happen? Her eyes stung with tears, but she gave herself a mental shake. *This is no time for self-pity. You've been through it before and came out the other side.*

That time she'd hadn't been convicted of a crime, but she had been fired without a reference, so couldn't get a job very easily. She'd lost her home as a consequence and the rumours made sure she was disgraced in her community. So much so that she'd had to move away and start again. She'd lost her family that time too; her parents had disowned her. She took a big glug of wine. If she'd done it once, she was sure she could do it again, but my goodness it had been a hard and lonely slog.

She poured the rest of the wine into her glass, gulped it down and found another bottle.

Her thoughts went to Chris and his offer to come and get her. Maybe…

A sound from outside made her stop and listen. Was that footsteps crunching up the drive? She scowled. *Not the police again?* Surely it was too late for them to be bothering her now? Couldn't they just leave her alone for tonight? Let her get a bit of rest and work out what to do. She needed a solicitor, that was for sure. *Maybe Chris will sort that out for me?* She decided she wouldn't say anything to them this time. Not a thing, except for 'no comment', until she had proper legal representation. Her jaw tightened and she swallowed down the rest of her wine.

The knock at the door, a firm rat-tat-tat, made her body tense. Part of her wanted to ignore it, but another part was furious that they were bothering her at this time of night. She marched into the hallway, cheeks flushed, and threw open the door.

But it wasn't the police.

CHAPTER THIRTY-SEVEN

Perched on the edge of the settee, Mel gulped down her third glass of wine, from the second bottle, completely unnerved by the events of the day and the sudden presence of the man who was now inside the house. She had calmed down after her initial shock at his arrival. And eventually, when she'd actually listened, he'd made a lot of sense. Still, though, there were things about the situation that were bothering her. If only she could get her mind to think. She appreciated the fact that he'd thought to supply wine, but she realised she may have consumed it a little too enthusiastically. Now, she was feeling quite dizzy and she frowned as she tried to focus. The man paced in front of the fire as he spoke. He seemed to be growing bigger, then shrinking again.

Weird.

Her chest felt tight. And was getting tighter.

She couldn't really hear what he was saying for the buzzing in her ears. But she was sure that he'd said he'd take her to safety. Yes, that's definitely what he'd said. And that little word, safety, had blossomed in her chest, creating a feeling of warmth that had spread through her body and persuaded her to go along with his suggestion. She squinted to sharpen the blur that was his face, but it was moving about, making her feel even more disorientated and woozy. She closed her eyes, her head spinning like she was on a fairground ride.

Mel thought about his plan for a moment. He wanted her to go with him, start again in a new place, with a new name. And as he laid out the details of the impossible situation she found herself in, it seemed the best option. Exciting even. She knew how to be careful, knew how to be somebody else. And after everything that had happened, his suggestion flowered in her mind into a glorious idea.

He shook her arm and her eyes flickered open, reminding her that she was supposed to be writing. She strained to focus on the words written on the paper in her hand, struggling to hold the pen. She scrawled her name, and her eyelids drooped, her body overwhelmed by tiredness, the pen and paper falling from her hands.

CHAPTER THIRTY-EIGHT

Tuesday

Ted arrived back at the farm in the early hours of the morning, exhausted but exhilarated, adrenaline still pumping round his body. It had all been surprisingly easy, he thought as he pulled up in the yard. But then he'd planned it properly, because he could always be depended upon to do whatever was needed to look after his family. Unlike Luke, but at least he was out of the way for good now; Ted had made certain of that.

He crept upstairs to bed, careful to be quiet so as not to wake Ceri's children, and quickly fell asleep.

When he woke, groggy and thick-headed, the day was far too bright for it to be his usual getting up time and he sat up, in a rush, grasping for his watch. He jumped out of bed when he saw that it was already after eight, a couple of hours later than he normally rose. Sleep fogged his brain and it was only when he got out of the shower that he realised something wasn't right. He stopped towelling his hair dry and listened.

He cocked his head. Nothing.

None of the usual banging and clattering that signalled his mother was in the kitchen. No squeaks and squeals from the children, the patter of their feet as they scurried around, or the putter of the tractor engine, signalling that Phil was pottering outside, moving things from here to there. All he could hear was the dogs barking from their pen, faint but frantic, wanting their breakfast, no doubt. They didn't normally bark in the morning, but then he didn't normally go away. Ever. So their routine would be all messed up. He hoped Ceri had remembered his feeding instructions. He'd had to rely on her because his uncle's memory wasn't wholly reliable these days and he didn't want to burden his aunt with an additional task when she struggled through every day as it was.

He dressed quickly and ran downstairs. The kitchen was empty. So was the living room, children's toys scattered over the carpet where they'd been left. He scowled. He'd told Ceri about this a million times. You could tread on all sorts and go flying. Little bits of Lego, cars, trains; they were all dangerous when they were left lying on the floor like this.

Where are they all?

He rubbed at his chin, then his eyes widened. *Christ, has Ma had a fall?* Her legs weren't good with her MS and it would be so easy for her to trip. *Or is it Da?* Maybe he'd had an accident on the tractor. In which case, they could be at the hospital.

He ran round the farm, checking all the outbuildings, but there was still no sign of anyone. And the bungalow, where his aunt and uncle lived these days, was empty. He went back to the yard, let the dogs out and fed them, then did his rounds, feeding the rest of the livestock, all of them starving hungry, almost knocking him over in their haste to get to the feed troughs. Unease swilled around his stomach.

It was a long time since his parents, or Ceri for that matter, had been away from the farm. All their groceries and clothes were bought online and delivered. Ella and Finn were home-schooled for now, so there was no school run to be done. Ceri had been a bit reticent about that at first, but she'd seen sense in the end and Ted knew it was the right thing because he'd hated school with a passion and didn't want his nephew and niece to go through the horrors he'd been through.

He tried to think when his aunt and uncle had last been out on their own. It was years ago. Years. There was no need, and Ted took them to hospital appointments and to the doctor's because they required a bit of supervision and an interpreter, as it were, to make sure whichever health professional they were seeing got the proper story. Otherwise they were likely to ramble on about all sorts of things that they really shouldn't be talking about.

They've got to be at the hospital.

An emergency. It was the only answer. His heart started to race and he stopped pouring sheep nuts into the troughs, oblivious to the animals hustling around him, pushing past him to get at the food. *Maybe one of the children has been hurt?* He blew out a breath, couldn't bear to think about it, and went back to pouring feed to stop himself dwelling on all the possibilities. He'd been so careful with the children, ever since they were born, making sure Ceri kept them away from all the dangers present on a farm. He would never forgive himself for not being here, if anything had happened to them.

A sense of urgency speeded up his movements as he hurried to finish his jobs. He put the dogs away again and headed to the hospital in Bangor. They had to be there. There was no other possible scenario.

It took him almost an hour to get to the hospital, with one hold-up after another on the journey; tractors and lorries and road works all slowing him down. By the time he got there he was in a foul mood, frustrated and annoyed, a headache pounding at the base of his skull. But when he went to reception, they could find no record of any of them being admitted. So he went round to the A & E department to double-check, but they weren't there either. He walked back to his car, completely flummoxed. It made no sense. No sense at all.

By the time he got back to the farm, he thought his head was going to burst. All the energy he'd put into looking after his family and he went away for a couple of days and… this happened, whatever this was. They were gone and he had no idea where they might be. Or even how they'd gone anywhere given that the spare car was still there in the yard. His heart was hammering in his chest, panic rising up to form a lump up his throat.

What if I never see them again?

What if I'm alone?

That was his worst nightmare, ever since his parents had died so suddenly; just him alone with his thoughts. It didn't bear thinking about. What purpose would he have without his family? He'd built his life around looking after them all, and was the only one who knew how everything worked, how the mechanics of their lives fitted together. He kept everything running sweetly, kept the money flowing and decided which direction to take the business in. All down to him. If he didn't have them, then he'd be nothing. His life would be nothing.

Where the fuck are they?

A sudden realisation stopped him in his tracks, a thought so horrible it rooted him to the spot.

Maybe Mel said something and the police have arrested them.

CHAPTER THIRTY-NINE

Stevens woke up to a bright morning and, even though he'd had a late night, he was more energised than he had been for a while, determined to get to the bottom of the missing family case. He arrived at work to find the station quiet, only Jackson in the office. He looked around, frowning. 'Where is everyone?'

Jackson looked up from his computer. 'I've sent George up to HQ with all the evidence. Thought you'd want the fingerprints done and DNA checks on those bloodstains ASAP, and then there's the phone to get unlocked and the laptop. Ailsa's in your office, just trying to get hold of the guy in Dumfries again, to see if she can get more information.'

Stevens raised an eyebrow, impressed by the keenness of his team.

'The ANPR has been checked for timings,' Jackson continued, 'but there's no sign of Mrs Roberts on the motorways when she said she travelled up here. So she must have used the A roads, if her timings are right. Oh, and I've tried getting hold of Mr Roberts' family at the farm again but there's still nobody answering.' Jackson grinned at his boss, clearly pleased with the progress they'd made. 'And that's where we're up to.'

Stevens rubbed his chin while he thought. 'Okay, well why don't you come with me and we'll go and check out the witness at the café, who responded to the appeal. Get that loose end tidied up.'

The café was only a short walk from the police station and the two officers strode down the pavement together, lost in their thoughts. The day was chilly but bright, snow capping the mountains, a slight breeze ruffling the surface of the lake, and it seemed far too cheerful given the possibilities they were investigating.

The café was only small, tucked round a corner, but every table was full. It probably wasn't a good time to speak to the owner, Stevens realised. She came to the counter looking red-faced and flustered, wiping her hands on a tea towel. Her blue apron was speckled with chocolate powder and the sweet smell wafted around her like an invisible cloak.

'I can see you're busy,' Stevens said. 'We won't take up too much of your time. We're just following up a sighting of the missing family. I think they were seen in here on Friday. Someone rang after the social media appeal.'

'Oh yes. That was Lucy.' She nodded to a waitress who was serving a table by the door. 'I'm sorry to ask you this, but there's not much space in here. Would you mind having a chat with her outside?'

'No, no that's fine,' Stevens said, turning to walk over to the waitress, Jackson right behind him.

The girl frowned, looking worried, her brow creased into delicate waves. She was only young, a school leaver by the looks of her, and as they stepped outside, she crossed her arms across her chest, shivering in the strengthening breeze.

'I don't think I can really tell you much,' she said. 'The man in the cap was sitting at the table by the window there.' She indicated with her head. 'When the family came in all the other tables were full and they went and sat with him. I'm not even sure they knew him.'

'But they were chatting?' Jackson took over the questions and Stevens let him, happy to watch the waitress's reactions and listen.

'Not for long. The man had been there for half an hour or so, and I think he was ready to go when they came in. To be honest, he looked a bit annoyed when they sat down.'

'So how long were they sitting together for?'

'Oh, it can't have been more than five or ten minutes really. I was busy, honestly time just flies in here.' She shrugged and looked apologetic. 'I can't be definite.'

'Then he went and the family stayed?'

'That's right. The kids had milkshakes. That cheered them up a bit. They didn't look very happy when they came in.'

'What about the father?'

'Hmm, well, he looked a bit rough.'

The girl's mouth twisted from side to side, as if she was chewing over her words before speaking them. 'There was something about them, though. The man in the cap seemed a bit… tense, I suppose. Jittery. He kept looking around. And –' she screwed up her face as if she wasn't sure – 'I thought he passed something over the table. I just caught it out of the corner of my eye. But… I've been thinking about it and I can't shake the feeling that's what I saw.'

Stevens glanced at his constable, who raised an eyebrow. *Drugs*? That was Stevens' first thought. This was surely evidence that would back up their theory of third-party involvement in the case.

'Would you be able to give us a description of him? The man in the cap?'

She slowly shook her head. 'Nothing that would help, I don't think. He was big, well over six feet, broad, like he worked out. He had a beard, dark brown, but to be honest, that's all I noticed.' She shrugged. 'I was so busy and his cap shaded his face, so I didn't get a good look.'

Stevens gave her his card. 'If you think of anything that would help us identify him, then give us a ring, would you?' He smiled at her. 'You've been a big help. Thank you.'

The girl gave him a nervous grin and went back into the café.

'So, what do you make of that?' Stevens asked Jackson, as he worked through the main points of the conversation in his mind.

'My first thought is a drugs deal. Given what the wife told us.'

'Hmm,' Stevens scratched at the stubble on his chin. 'I can't help thinking we've been making a lot of assumptions based on what people have told us. People who've also lied.' He turned and they started walking back to the station. 'Let's see if there's anything from the Welsh police yet, then we'll catch up with Ailsa and see where we're up to.'

Jackson glanced at him. 'Is it just me, or are we going round in circles with this one?'

CHAPTER FORTY

Ted stood in the yard, looking around him, a tingle of fear fizzing in his head. He just couldn't work it out. He'd rung Idris, his policeman friend, so he knew that his family hadn't been arrested. *So, where are they?* This was their home, their livelihood, everything they owned. They didn't have any money, for God's sake – he was in charge of all the finances and they didn't have debit or credit cards, so they couldn't have gone far. And they hadn't taken the car, so someone must have come to collect them. *But who?*

A movement made him turn his head and his heart leapt when he saw a police car, followed by a police van, heading up the track towards him.

His breath stuck in his throat, refusing to go in or out as he watched the vehicles come to a halt. Two policemen got out, his dogs running up to them, barking and snarling, as if they were going to bite. Ted knew they wouldn't, but it was quite scary when they were like that around people, baring their teeth, and had proved an effective deterrent to uninvited guests.

'Can you take control of your dogs, please?' the driver said, using the car door as a shield while three dogs launched themselves towards him, claws clattering and scratching at the paintwork. He was a stern-looking man, with a square face, short grey hair and dark eyes, who didn't look like he was the life and soul of the party.

Ted forced a tight smile. 'Sorry, we don't have many visitors. They get a bit excited.' He whistled and the dogs slunk back to him, cowering on the ground by his legs, their eyes still on the police officers.

'Can you put them away somewhere, sir?' the man said. 'We need to have a chat.'

A chat. That didn't sound good. That sounded like there was something to discuss, which suggested knowledge, which— Ted told himself to stop, to focus and not do anything that could be viewed as suspicious. He forced a smile. 'Of course, just hold on a minute while I get them in the shed.'

Ted's heart pounded in his chest as he walked across the yard, over to the outbuilding where they manufactured and stored the cannabis capsules. He glanced over his shoulder and saw two springer spaniels being unloaded from the second van, which he could see was labelled 'North Wales Police Dog Section'.

Sniffer dogs! His jaw tightened, teeth grinding together. *This is trouble. Big, big trouble.* He hadn't had time to check how well everything had been hidden and he'd only been able to speak to Phil on the phone, so there was no saying what had actually been done. Sweat beaded on his brow and stuck his T-shirt to his back as he closed the dogs in their pen. He wiped his face with his sleeve and made his expression as noncommittal as he could before walking back towards the officers. He didn't know these men. They must be from police HQ up the coast, not the local officers he knew and supplied with capsules. These two didn't know him from Adam.

There were four officers huddled together, studying a map, pointing and looking around at the layout of the farm. A couple more were waiting by the car. Ted ran his tongue round dry lips, his mind a blank, rubbed clean by panic as he struggled to work out how to keep them away from the hiding places.

He gave them a friendly smile as he approached, trying to look unconcerned. 'How can I help you, gentlemen?'

They turned to look at him. 'Are you Mr Edward Roberts?' the stern man asked.

'Ted.' He stuck out his hand for a handshake and dropped it when he realised it wasn't going to happen. He puffed up his chest. 'This is my farm.'

'I'm DS Davies,' the stern man said. 'And this is my colleague, DC Jones.' He indicated the tall thin man who'd been in the passenger seat of the car. 'Then we've got PCs Pritchard and Jeffries with the dogs, and PCs Evans and Dean assisting.'

Ted widened his smile. 'Nice to meet you all.'

The men all stared at him, the silence filling Ted's head until it felt like it was stuffed with cotton wool.

'We've had a tip-off that cannabis is being grown here,' DS Davies said eventually.

Ted swallowed, raised his eyebrows. 'Cannabis?' He laughed, wanting to sound incredulous, but it came out as a strange bark of a sound. He cleared his throat and made himself meet the man's stony gaze. 'No, well, you've got that wrong. The only thing we grow here is sheep and cows. And a bit of veg in the polytunnel.'

'Well, we have a warrant to do a search.' DS Davies handed him a piece of paper, which Ted pretended to study, his eyes skimming over the words as his mind exploded with expletives. There was nothing he could do. Nothing. He just had to hope that all the precautions he'd taken actually worked.

He shrugged as though he didn't mind, wondering if they could tell how hard his heart was hammering in his chest, whether they could see his body juddering with the force of it. 'I honestly can't think why you'd believe I'd be growing cannabis. Who told you that?'

The man stared at him and Ted struggled to maintain eye contact. 'Anonymous tip- off.'

Ted huffed. 'That's nice. People causing trouble.' He spread his arms wide. 'Help yourselves. Just be careful of the livestock. Not everything is friendly.'

He stood in the yard, shivering in the cold wind that blew up the valley while he watched the officers at work. He winced as the sniffer dogs got closer and closer to the outbuilding where the stash of capsules was stored up in the crog-loft. He was confident it was not somewhere a dog would be able to reach, given that he'd hidden the ladder in the barn before he'd gone up to the Lake District. He'd stacked a pile of straw on top of it, so he was pretty sure it wouldn't be found. Anyway, his dogs were in there now. That would help mask the scent.

The next problem, of course, was the plants. They were all over the place, the main growing area being behind padlocked doors in a small stone barn that sat in a field opposite the house. It looked disused, slates sliding off the roof, but a new shell had been built inside, rows and rows of growing lights installed. That's where their main crop was. Another outbuilding housed a germination area, but fortunately nothing was sprouting yet and the plant pots could contain anything.

One of the loft spaces in the house contained a second growing area. It was where it had all started, but Ted was pretty sure the dogs wouldn't smell anything up there, given the layers of insulation and the fact that the hatch was hidden behind a false ceiling panel.

He had talked himself into a state of calm when he heard a whirring sound overhead and looked up to see a helicopter flying up the valley towards the farm. His chest clenched so tight he thought he was having a heart attack. *The police helicopter!* Probably with thermal imaging equipment on board that would detect the heat profile coming from the lamps in the barn and the house and would know instantly what was going on.

His legs felt weak, his whole body threatening to crumple to the ground. There was no denying any of this now. He gritted his teeth and watched one of the dog handlers turn and look at him as he listened to something on his radio.

Ted glanced round, wondering if there was a way out, but the police car and the dog handlers' van had been parked across his exit route, and the helicopter would be able to follow him if he ran. He let out a desperate groan. There was no escape.

His hands clenched so hard his nails dug into his skin. *Goddammit, this is all Luke's fault. If he hadn't come back none of this would have happened.*

PART FOUR: EARLIER

CHAPTER FORTY-ONE

Friday

The holiday cottage in the Lake District was ideal, Luke thought, as he drove up the gravelled driveway. Tucked away in a sleepy little village, behind tall privet hedges, nobody would notice what they were doing. In fact, a lot of the other properties they'd passed looked like they were holiday cottages and it could well be there weren't any neighbours at all. Which would be perfect.

'Here we are then.' Luke looked in the mirror to see Tessa gazing back at him, uncertain. 'Help me get the stuff in, will you?'

Callum sat in the passenger seat, arms crossed over his chest, not looking like he was going anywhere.

Luke ruffled his hair and Callum hunched away from him, out of reach. 'I know it's going to be hard leaving your friends, son. But it won't be for ever. When all this is sorted out, things will be very different. And anyway, you'll make new friends.'

Callum scowled at him.

'Tell me again,' Tessa said. 'Where are we going?'

'You remember Granny Eileen and Grandpa Bob who live in Ireland, don't you? Your Mum's grandparents, who we visited a couple of times when you were little? Well, they've just moved into a retirement home and we're going to stay in their old house for a bit.'

Tessa screwed up her nose. 'I sort of remember. Did they have a donkey? Is that them?'

Luke turned and smiled at her. 'Yes, that's them. You remember now?'

'Do they have a tractor?' A note of curiosity had crept into Callum's voice.

'Oh, I would think so. I think every farm has a tractor. Although it's not really a farm. It's just a big house with a few acres.'

'Didn't they have chickens?' Tessa said. 'I seem to remember collecting eggs.'

Luke nodded. 'That's right.' He looked at his son who was still frowning. 'Come on, Cal. I know it's a lot to take in. But we've got to get away from Mel, haven't we? And this is the only way we're going to do it.'

'I don't understand why we can't just move back to the farm,' Callum muttered. 'I liked it there.'

'Well, there's some things that need sorting out, which means that's not going to be possible.'

Callum sighed, one of the big heaving sighs that children do so well, and gazed at his dad. 'I'm just so fed up of moving. First we left my friends in Scotland and then we had to go to that school that just spoke Welsh and then we went to Bangor and I found the best friend I'll ever have and now we've got to move again.'

There were tears in his voice and his eyes shone. He was a tough kid, but Luke realised he'd been pushed to his limit. He desperately wanted to tell him that everything would be alright, but he couldn't because he didn't know himself what was going to happen. There was no doubt that his plan was risky, so many things that could go wrong. He rubbed his hands on his jeans.

'Look, I'm trying to keep you safe, son. That's what this is all about. Like I said, it's not for ever. And the best bit is, you won't have to go to school for a while.'

Callum's eyes widened. 'For real? No school?'

Luke nodded.

Callum's face cracked into a grin.

'Not sounding quite so bad now, is it?' Luke laughed, although his insides were a mass of nerves, like having a whole bunch of snakes writhing in his stomach. He clapped his hands.

'Right guys, bags out of the boot, let's get this show on the road.'

It took them a little while, but eventually he was satisfied that everything looked right. They'd all put on their pyjamas and got into to bed, ruffled up the sheets to make it look like they'd slept there, spread out their possessions in as messy a way as possible, all to give the impression they'd been there a couple of days. He put crockery in the dishwasher and turned it on, coats on hooks, shoes in a pile by the door, opened his laptop and pulled up a page on Grizedale Forest. Then he lit a fire, to leave evidence that the wood burner had been used. In the master bedroom, he unpacked his bags, put on latex gloves and placed the old make-up bag of Mel's in the bathroom cabinet.

Back downstairs, he made sure the kids were ready, their rucksacks with everything they'd need for the journey already packed and waiting for them to grab from the car.

'Why can't I bring my tablet, though?' Tessa whined when he made her put it back in her bedroom. They were almost ready to leave when, out of the corner of his eye, he'd caught her trying to sneak it out.

'Because it's got to look like we just went out for a walk and expected to come back. It would look suspicious if we took it.'

She stomped back upstairs and Luke promised himself there would be lots of treats over the next few weeks. It was a heck of a thing he was expecting from them, but having talked it over with his family, it was the only solution they could come up with. *If it works.* By the time they were ready to leave, Luke was hot and flustered, so many things to check to make sure they'd left the house looking just right.

He'd tried to make it into a game, especially when he'd needed to get some blood to smear on their old clothes. So now they were all blood brothers, something the kids had submitted themselves to with curiosity rather than fear. They'd made a pact, to protect each other, whatever happened, which all sounded very melodramatic, but the kids were at an age where they loved that stuff. He wanted to make them feel they were going on an adventure rather than make it an ordeal, and once he'd convinced them that it was a Native American tradition, they didn't mind a quick nick on their hands. Blood spots and smears. He hoped they would be enough to plant a seed of doubt. Make life uncomfortable enough for Mel to make her willing to go into hiding.

He scribbled a note, propped it on the mantelpiece and did one final check round. *Yes,* he nodded to himself, *that should do it.* He glanced at his watch and picked up his bag.

'Come on, Tess,' he shouted up the stairs. 'We'll miss the bus if you don't get a move on.' Then they were out of the door, leaving the place unlocked and all the lights on.

Once in Windermere, they made their way to the café. Luke saw Ted sitting in a window seat, a cap shading his face as he scrolled through his phone, and he took a deep breath to prepare himself. They would pretend to be strangers, people who just happened to share a table, and Luke hoped that Ted could pull it off. Truth was, he hadn't wanted Ted in the plan, in any shape or form. But then his mum had come up with another idea, one which, he'd had to admit, had shocked him at the time, and getting Ted involved was central to making things work. The more he'd talked it through with her, the more adamant she'd become and, in the end, he'd given in, rather than see her getting all worked up about it. Thankfully, Ted had been cooperative, *but can I trust him?* He still wasn't sure.

Luke's face settled into a worried frown, as he thought about the finality of what he was about to do. Could he really end this life of his, leave it behind, permanently? It was such a risk. His father was getting a bit frail now and definitely not functioning

well, his mother so prone to those awful mood swings, her grasp
on reality coming apart at the seams as the degenerative effects
of her MS started to become more obvious. And then there was
poor Ceri, stuck as a dogsbody looking after them all with Ted
lording it over her, as though her children were his and she was
just the skivvy.

He shook his head to dislodge his concerns and concentrated
on guiding the kids through the menu, placing their order for
drinks and cakes while ignoring Ted, who was scrolling through
his phone messages. Luke chatted to the children until the waitress
had brought everything over and when nobody seemed to be
paying them any attention, Luke took the keys that Ted pushed
across the table and slipped them in his pocket. The café was busy
and he was confident nobody had seen anything.

'So, remember the deal,' Ted murmured, hardly moving his
lips. 'You take your kids and you go away.' His voice was laced
with annoyance, the only tone he seemed to be able to use in a
conversation with Luke these days. 'I don't want to know where
you're going. In fact, it's better if I don't know. Then if the police
ask, they'll know I'm not lying when I tell them I have no idea
where you are.'

Luke didn't reply, just gave a curt nod.

Ted turned his back to the children, who were busy munching
their way through enormous chocolate muffins. 'You've put Ma
and Da's future at risk, put us all in danger, including the kids. So,
the price for me sorting out your mess is, you stay away. Okay?
For ever.'

Luke glared at him, happy that today was the last time he would
have to share the air that Ted breathed. There was a look in Ted's
eye, a tone to his voice that didn't used to be there, and the way
that he dominated the farm and everyone who lived there stirred
a fury in Luke that he didn't want to feel. His chest ached with
the effort of keeping his emotions in check, silently cursing as a

means of letting off steam. He didn't feel quite so bad now about the risks that Ted was unknowingly taking. He was the fall guy, the backstop if things didn't work out how they were supposed to. His mum had persuaded him that it was for the best, for the collective good of the family and anyway, she'd said, Ted needed to learn a lesson.

Her words ran through Luke's mind as he watched Ted pick up the rucksack, which contained the blood-spattered clothes and Luke's phone, slinging it on his back as though it belonged to him. Luke let out a long breath, relieved that Ted was gone, that part of the plan completed, his hands shaking as he unpeeled the paper from his cake.

'Why's Uncle Ted so mad with us, Dad?'

Luke forced himself to smile at Tessa, always the one with the emotional barometer firmly switched on.

'Oh, that's just the way he is, I guess, sweetie. An angry sort of a man. Nothing for you to worry about.' He ruffled her hair and she smacked his hand away, but she was smiling. The first smile he'd had from her in weeks.

This is the right thing, he told himself. *This is best for all of us.*

They finished their drinks and headed off to the car park next to the train station, where it had been arranged that Ted would leave the hire car. Luke looked around for a moment and then spotted it parked at the back. A little blue Fiat. He checked the registration plate against the number printed on his keyring.

'Come on, kids.' He pointed to the car. 'This is ours.'

There was an envelope in the glove compartment and he tipped the contents out onto his lap, his pulse whooshing in his ears, hands still shaking a little as he checked that everything was there. You never knew with Ted; he could just as easily be leading him into trouble as helping him to get away from it.

The new passports looked completely legitimate, provided by some dodgy bloke that Ted was mixed up with. A friend of a friend of a friend, he'd said. There was a thick wad of cash, enough to keep them going for a little while until he found some work. And the ferry tickets were there for the late sailing at half past eleven from Cairnryan, a ferry port just north of Stranraer in Dumfries and Galloway, over to Larne in Northern Ireland, booked in their new names. From there they would drive south to Cork, in the Irish Republic, and on to the smallholding a little further down the coast. Satisfied that everything was present and correct, Luke fumbled all the documents into the envelope and put it back in the glove compartment.

He looked at Callum, who was sitting next to him, carefully watching what he was doing. He gave his son a quick grin, glanced in the rear-view mirror and caught Tessa's eye. 'All set? Ready for an adventure?'

Neither of them said anything and he couldn't blame them. The last time he'd said those very words, he'd landed them in Mel's web of madness. *This has got to work*, he told himself as he set off, clear in his mind that he had no choice. *It's the only way we'll ever be at peace.*

The M6 north of the Lake District was quite empty and they made good time, stopping at Dumfries to refuel. With hours to spare before they had to be at the port, they found a supermarket to stock up on food for the rest of the journey. They all had new baseball hats as a bit of a disguise, and Luke had bought them all new pay-as-you-go phones, so the kids could keep themselves busy with games. It was the least he could do after all the disruption and it gave him some quiet time to think as they drove.

Ted's words filled his mind, the warning that he wouldn't be able to see his family again and something inside him snapped, tears welling in his eyes, his chest aching with the sense of loss. He had to hope now that his parents and Ceri could summon up the courage to play their part, but he was keenly aware that he'd put everyone in an impossible situation, given them dilemmas that they shouldn't have to face. Nobody was going to be a winner here; in reality they would all lose something.

He couldn't blame Ted for his situation. He'd done it to himself, hadn't he? By getting involved with Mel. He clasped the steering wheel tighter and told himself to stop being pathetic, because this was all about the children and they needed him to be strong. So that's what he was going to be. *Strong.* He repeated the word in his mind until the lump in his throat dissolved and his tears dried. He used to be strong. He could be again; he would be because his children deserved nothing less. Anna deserved nothing less. And this was the only solution.

Once they got out of Dumfries itself, the vast stretches of the Dumfries and Galloway forest rolled out for miles on either side of the road, the silhouettes of the mountains rising up in the distance against the night sky. They found a parking area, hidden from the road, with picnic benches and they sat there, eating their sandwiches by the light of the moon, listening to the sounds of birds and animals rustling and squawking and screeching around them.

Luke felt safe here, hidden in the forest. He wondered if anyone had seen them, and ran through their journey in his mind. They'd only stopped a couple of times and there was only one person who might remember him, he thought. The guy at the petrol station who'd been getting himself a drink and heating up a burger while Luke had been waiting for the kids to use the loo. He'd tried to get Luke into conversation, had commented on his bonny kids, and Luke had given a cursory nod before hurrying Tessa and Callum out to the car.

It's okay, he told himself. *It's all okay.*

CHAPTER FORTY-TWO

Saturday

A pale winter sun was climbing into the sky as Luke drove out of Cork and towards their final destination. He was hyped-up on coffee, which he'd been drinking all night to keep him awake on the long and tedious drive, and he could feel his body trembling with the caffeine shakes. Night-driving was never pleasant but when you were in a strange place and nothing was familiar, it was even worse. He could have stopped, but he knew he wouldn't rest if he did, because he had to know that everything was going to work out as he'd hoped.

The children were still asleep when he pulled into the driveway; no more than a potholed track leading to a square yard in front of the house, which was separated from the road by a narrow field. His eyes were dry and sore, lack of sleep making him feel floaty and disconnected from his surroundings, and when he finally pulled to a halt he just sat for a while, hardly believing that he'd done it. He was here. Safe. He stared through the windscreen without seeing, numb with exhaustion, and it was a few minutes before he realised there was a light on in a downstairs window, a gentle glow behind the kitchen blinds.

It took a moment for him to register what that meant. Then his eyes widened, a grin spreading across his face. *They made it!* As he stared at the door, it opened, and his mum stood in the doorway, apron on, looking as if she'd lived there all her life.

'Luke!' she screamed, and hobbled towards him.

She was laughing, tears rolling down her cheeks as he clambered out of the car and ran to meet her, wrapping her in a hug.

'Mum, you're here!'

His mum pushed away and beamed at him. 'Yes, love, we're all here. All present and correct, thanks to you. We couldn't have done it without you, sweetheart. We really couldn't.'

'Nana!' Tessa called as she climbed out of the car, eyes still bleary in the early morning light. 'I didn't know you'd be here.' She clung to Fay's waist, and Fay stroked her hair, smoothing it away from the girl's face.

'I couldn't let you leave us,' Fay said. 'Not when I've just got to know you. We're all here now, anyway. One big family.'

Tessa frowned and looked a little wary. 'Even Uncle Ted?'

Fay gave a tight smile. 'No, love. Uncle Ted's still at the farm.' Fay glanced at Luke. 'Plenty of time to talk about that later. Come on, let's get you inside. Sort out some breakfast for everyone.'

Luke watched his daughter slide her hand into his mother's, then he turned and lifted a sleeping Callum out of the car. The boy mumbled, still drowsy. 'Are we there, Dad?'

'Yes, we are. And Nana and Pops are here. And Ceri and your cousins. This is going to be our home, for a while, all together.'

Callum's eyelashes fluttered, then his eyes opened, his face crumpled into a frown. 'Mel's not here, is she?'

'No, son. Mel's not going to be part of our lives anymore.'

Callum sighed and his head relaxed against Luke's chest. His black eye was starting to fade now, the edges a faint blur of green and yellow. It was a mercy, Luke thought, that black eye. Because if it hadn't happened, he didn't think he would have been able to shake himself out of his fear and denial. He'd wanted his relationship with Mel to work so much he'd become a different person, someone who hadn't seen what was happening to his children. He'd wanted to have what he'd had with Anna, but he realised now that it would never have been the same. Mel wasn't Anna. She was a chameleon, an actress, an expert manipulator. Worse. An abuser. Unable to control her anger, which flared up in an instant. It was her source of power, making everyone around her afraid, making them tiptoe around her emotions; a state of affairs that had suited her very well. And he'd been too ashamed of his situation to tell anyone what was really happening for far too long.

He shook thoughts of Mel from his mind. It would be a few days before he'd know if the plan was going to be a success and, in the meantime, he had to think very carefully about what happened next.

He'd hoped that his family was going to be able to follow him to Ireland, so they would be out of the way if Mel mentioned the drugs business, which she'd threatened to do if he left her, but it had all hinged on Ted being cooperative. Because if Ted hadn't agreed to go up to the Lake District to help, then it wouldn't have been possible for his parents and Ceri to get away. Of course, there was a Plan B, which involved hiding all the plants and turning the power off for the heat lamps so thermal imaging wouldn't pick them up. But it was risky and there'd always been a chance that the drugs would be found and the family arrested. Then who knew what the outcome would have been.

After the initial family meeting, he'd rung his mum and talked it through without Ted being able to eavesdrop on their discussions. His parents and Ceri had been fully aware of the risks and implications but had still urged him to go ahead, promising him that whatever happened it would be worth it to get Mel out of their lives.

So now they were all safe.

Except for Ted.

After breakfast, Luke was alone in the kitchen with his mother.

'I can't believe you're all here, Mum.' He reached over and held her hand. 'I'm so sorry I got you wrapped up in my mess.'

She gazed at him and sighed as she stirred sugar into her tea. 'Well, Luke, we were wrapped up in our own mess, weren't we? You got a taste of how things were with Ted. But for us, that's been going on for many years. And when we thought about it, we realised that your situation gave us an opportunity to get away. So don't think we've done all this for you, love. We've done this for ourselves as well, you know.'

'I didn't think you'd come, Mum. I didn't think you'd want to leave the farm. Or drop Ted in it.' Luke frowned. It was the one bit of the plan he felt uncomfortable about. 'However much we don't get on, he's still family and it doesn't seem right, leaving him to face the music on his own.'

His mum nodded, sadness dragging at the corners of her mouth. 'I know. I feel bad about it too, but I couldn't see another way and, to be honest, Luke, that lad needs to come to his senses. Over the years he's become more and more controlling and –' she looked down at her tea as it swirled in her mug – 'I just haven't the energy to stand up to him anymore. None of us have. Honestly, he's worn us down, got us frightened to disagree with him. Even me.' She scowled. 'And he's moving away from therapeutic cannabis now. He wants to sell the strong stuff, and add cocaine into the product line.'

His mum swallowed and he could see her eyes shining, her voice wavering.

'We don't want any of that. We just want to have a quiet life. My health's getting worse and your dad's feeling the strain. We want some quality time together now, time with our children and grandchildren. And Ceri needs a bit of freedom, a life for herself and the chance to make it up with Dylan. She still loves him, you know, but with Ted in the way they have no chance of getting back together.'

She squeezed Luke's hand. 'We've given Ted a good life. Looked after him since his parents died. We've done our best for him.

And in the long run, I think this is what he needs.' She stared through the window and shook her head, sadly. 'He scares me. You know, he gets in such a temper if things don't go his way, and he's so strict with Ella and Finn, I worry what he'll be like when they get older. How he'll cope with the backchat that's bound to come.' She nodded to herself. 'No, although this seems harsh and believe me, I feel terrible about it, we're stuck between a rock and a hard place and whatever we do, there'll be consequences we don't like. He needs some professional help and given the waiting list for NHS counselling...' She pursed her lips and looked at Luke. 'I honestly believe prison is going to be the best place for him. They'll sort him out.'

Her shoulders slumped, and she gave him a rueful smile. 'Nothing fair or easy about life, is there? But your troubles, son, honestly... you know how they say that every cloud has a silver lining?'

Once again, Luke realised how much he hadn't seen, how much he'd been wrapped up in himself. He hadn't thought for one moment what life must be like for his family under Ted's regime. For the months that he was living there, they'd all seemed happy to give him the leadership role. And in his heart, Luke had thought it was just his mum humouring Ted, while she was still organising everything in the background, trying to smooth over the disruption caused by Luke coming home. He hadn't realised they were all virtual prisoners, caught in Ted's protective net.

He frowned, trying to imagine what Ted's reaction was going to be when he found out he was alone on the farm. 'When will he know you're not there? What if he rings and nobody answers before he's done everything in the Lake District? What will he think?'

'You don't need to worry about that. He's given your dad a mobile. He won't know where we are if he rings on that, will he?' She looked unsure for a moment.

Luke gave her a reassuring smile. 'No, that's perfect. So, have you heard from him?'

'He rang last night to say you'd got away. He's camping out somewhere, waiting for Mel to turn up. Then once she's there, he's got to give the phone in to the Grizedale Information Centre and then he's going to wait a bit to hand in the bag of clothes to the police. That's right, isn't it?'

Luke nodded, his mind going over all the possibilities, all the things that could go wrong. Would he ever really be free of Mel? That was the niggling doubt gnawing at the back of his mind. Even over here, would he ever really be free?

'Does he really think it's your idea, Mum?'

Fay nodded, a sad look on her face. 'Yes, he does. He wouldn't have done it for you, would he?'

'If he thought he was going to rid of me for ever, he would. That's what he said to me in the café. He told me it was the price to pay.'

Fay frowned. 'It was never going to be that, love, was it? How could I let you go that easily?' She squeezed his hand again and Luke felt a lump in his throat, preventing him from answering. He squeezed back instead, hoping that she knew how much her actions meant to him. 'I know this seems a cruel way to teach someone a lesson,' she continued, 'but Ted needs to learn one way or another that love isn't a weapon you can use against people. He needs some help to understand what he's been doing.' She sighed. 'Anyway, we're talking as though it's a given that he'll be arrested. There's a good chance that he won't be, not with our local police contacts.' She took a sip of her tea, put her mug down carefully, her hand shaking. 'No, chances are he'll be fine. And if that's the case, we'll have to decide how to bring him round to our way of thinking.'

They sat in silence, sipping their tea. He could hear the children screaming and laughing, playing some game out of sight. Through the kitchen window, he could see Ceri tying a washing line between the house and the outbuilding and his father sitting on a log in the yard, sharpening an axe, a pile of logs waiting to be chopped at his side. Already, they were settling in.

Still, Luke's mind was restless. There were a lot of things that had to happen before he could believe they were really safe. And he was relying on Ted playing his part. Could they really trust him?

The rest of the day was spent sorting out the house, Fay keeping Luke busy with a long list of jobs, while the children played and explored their new surroundings until it was supper time.

Luke was about to follow Ceri upstairs to put the children to bed when his mother called to him from the lounge, where a fire now glowed in the hearth. She closed the door and turned to him, looking worried. 'We've got a slight problem. Mel hasn't turned up. But she sent a text to your phone to say she was going to be delayed and will be there tomorrow evening.'

Luke winced and frowned. 'Yeah, her events do sometimes go on longer than she thought. It's the networking afterwards, she says.' He sighed. 'She's probably had too much to drink. You know how she likes her wine. Is Ted okay with staying an extra day?'

Fay nodded. 'He was a bit annoyed, because he's camping out and he says it's freezing, but I managed to talk him round. It's okay.'

Luke wrapped her in a hug that he hoped conveyed the depth of his gratitude. 'Love you, Mum. You know I couldn't have done this without you.'

His mum clung to him and the fragility of her made him more determined than ever to get everything right this time. In that moment, in the silence of their embrace, all the events of the past couple of years played out in his mind and he could see all the trouble he had caused for his family, first with Ted and then with Mel. He could sense the burden of worry he had placed on his parents and his resolve hardened. There could be no wavering, no backing down or taking the easy way out. It was up to him to do everything in his power to right the wrongs and make sure their lives could be lived out in peace.

CHAPTER FORTY-THREE

Sunday

Luke woke on Sunday feeling jittery and unsettled, able to do nothing but wait while the events he'd set in motion in the Lake District played themselves out. Was Mel going to show up? Would Ted bother to stay around to play his part?

He kept himself busy, moving furniture and cleaning up the house. He'd kept in touch with Anna's grandparents since her death and had received a letter a few months ago, telling him they'd moved into a residential home, giving him their new contact details. The house was going up for sale, but when he'd phoned them a few days ago, they'd said they were waiting for the spring to put it on the market and it was fine for him to use the place while he got himself sorted out. Better, they'd said, that it was lived in and kept aired and it would be a great help to them if he could tidy it up a bit. His shoulders ached, not just with all the lifting and carrying he'd been doing, but because his muscles were so tense, the waiting an excruciating form of torture. Conversation in the house was sparse, all of them on tenterhooks, listening for the call to tell them that Mel had arrived and when it finally came, there was a collective sigh of relief.

Stage one was complete. But would the rest of it work?

Later, when everyone had gone to bed, Luke lay in the dark, listening to the noises of the house and its inhabitants as they settled, unable to relax for the flow of thoughts that sped through his mind, all the what ifs and maybes queuing up to be inspected and sent on their way, only to be replaced by another batch of worries. He was distracted by the sound of his mother's voice coming from the next room, the gap under the door big enough to let the sound through. He listened, puzzled because he knew his father was in the bathroom, so she wasn't talking to him. She had to be on the phone.

'Mountain Rescue?' his mother said. Then there was a silence. 'Good, good. Thank goodness… Yes… yes. Well done, Ted.' Silence for a few minutes. 'Okay, well we're all going to bed now… What's that? Yes… Keep up the good work, Ted. See you in a couple of days then.'

Luke tensed, his heart stuttering in his chest.

Ted's coming here?

Had he misunderstood, or had she gone back on her word, not able now to let Ted be the scapegoat? Ted's involvement in the plan was something he'd had to grudgingly accept, and, in truth, he wasn't totally convinced it would work, but when he voiced his concerns earlier in the day, his mother had said he had to trust Ted to do whatever was required to solve the problem that was Mel.

'He's not like you, Luke. That's what you've got to remember. He doesn't mind using brute force to get what he wants. Man or woman, there's no difference to him, because she is a threat to our safety. He has a loyalty to this family that means he will do whatever it takes to make her go away.'

There'd been a curious look on her face and he hadn't been sure how to take her comments. *What on earth has she told him to do?* And was she proud of Ted's lack of morals, his loyalty at all costs? Was she telling Luke that he'd fallen short in that department? It had puzzled him for the rest of the day as he'd debated with himself whether there was anything else he could do to make amends for all the trouble he'd caused.

Now, all he could hear in his mind were her last words. 'See you in a couple of days.'

Ted's coming.

He tried to ignore the rattle of annoyance that reverberated round his brain, frustrated that his mother had insisted on her plans instead of letting him sort things out his own way, without any involvement from his cousin. He didn't understand the logic. *Probably because there isn't any*, he told himself, his mother's mind seeming to flit between reality and fantasy, the past and the present. It was becoming a worry and he wasn't sure what he could do about it. He wondered if she was taking her medication, if that was perhaps the problem, and he resolved to talk to Ceri about it in the morning.

He was too agitated for sleep now, so he sat up and scrolled through his new phone, checking to see if there was any news about their disappearance, but there was nothing and he knew it was probably too soon. They'd have to wait for the Mountain Rescue to draw a blank before the police got involved.

More waiting.

It was unbearable.

He sat staring into the darkness and finally he realised that Ted wasn't coming at all. He was getting himself all worked up about nothing. Ted had no idea where they were, had no idea his family had gone; his mother was just playing him along so he'd stick to the plan, but Luke's panicked brain had taken her words at face value. However, a connection had been made in his mind, a joining of dots to create a picture of what needed to happen. And as it unfolded, he was clear that it was the exactly what he had to do to give his family the biggest gift of all. Peace.

CHAPTER FORTY-FOUR

Tuesday

Ted sat in the stuffy, windowless room, anger burning up his throat. The police were about to interview him and they'd left him to stew while he waited for his solicitor to arrive. His brain had been working so hard, his thoughts bashing around, bumping against each other as he tried to sort out what he was going to say and what he should keep to himself, that he now had the mother of all headaches. He rubbed at his temples.

Who grassed us up?

That was question number one and the only answer he could come up with for that one was Mel. He obviously hadn't got to her in time. His hands tightened into fists and he cursed himself, because in his mind, he'd known that Mel was a sneaky bitch who'd tell the police anything to save herself. But his mum had been so sure it would be okay he hadn't taken all the necessary precautions.

Question number two was harder to answer. *Where's my family?*

He hoped they'd been warned and had escaped. That made sense, because surely Idris down at the Porthmadog station would have been told that the drugs squad were planning a raid. It must be protocol to let the local force know you were doing an operation on their patch, mustn't it? So, the most likely explanation was that he'd got them out. *Yes*, he reassured himself. *Idris put them somewhere safe.* Better that he didn't know where. He nodded to himself. Much better.

He sat back in his chair, clear now about his way forward. He would be helpful to the police. Because there was no escaping the fact that he'd been caught red-handed growing a lot of cannabis. He'd take the rap for his family. Of course he would. But he wouldn't take the rap for Luke. No way. A smile twitched on his lips. That guy was going down. He'd tell the police about the hire car. He'd tell them about the false names and he'd tell them about Luke's delivery route, the one he'd set up with his ex-forces contacts. Because this situation was all Luke's fault. His fault for marrying that woman, his fault for not being man enough to stand up to her, his fault for letting her find out about the drugs, and his fault she'd told the police.

None of this would have happened if Luke hadn't come home.

Ted nodded to himself, sure of his reasoning. If he was to be punished, then it was only fair that Luke should be too.

CHAPTER FORTY-FIVE

Tuesday

It was almost evening by the time George had returned from HQ and Inspector Stevens got his team together for an update.

'Let's start with the family, shall we? Jackson, what you got?'

'Well, I've just had a very interesting conversation with the drug squad in Colwyn Bay. The local force put me on to them. Apparently, they've been to the farm after an anonymous tip-off. Found a whole cannabis growing operation up there and they arrested a guy called Edward Roberts.' He held up a printed mug shot for everyone to see. 'He's Luke Roberts' cousin, apparently. They're waiting for his solicitor to turn up, then they'll be interviewing him.'

Stevens took the picture and looked more closely, glanced at Jackson.

'I'm just wondering… the description the girl at the café gave us. Could this be the man she saw with Luke Roberts?'

Jackson smiled. 'Way ahead of you. The Welsh drugs team have done an ANPR check on his car over the last week, to see if they could spot drop-offs or associates who might be involved. Because there's obviously a network of people selling the stuff. Anyway…' He paused for effect.

'He's been up here, hasn't he?' Lockett was too impatient for the punchline.

Jackson nodded. 'ANPR caught him coming up the M6 on Friday and going back again late last night. Well, technically it was very early this morning.'

'We've got to put him on the persons of interest list then.' Stevens wrote himself a note on the board. 'Well done, Jackson.'

'I've not finished yet.' Jackson's eyes were shining, clearly delighted with what he'd managed to find out. 'The other thing you need to know is that the local police didn't have time to get to the farm before the raid. But the drugs guys said that only Edward Roberts was there. No sign of anyone else.'

Stevens frowned. 'So where did the rest of the family go? Isn't there Mr Roberts' parents and his sister and her couple of kids living there?'

Jackson shrugged. 'Nobody knows where they are. And if Edward Roberts knows, he isn't saying. Maybe they had a tip-off that the raid was coming? That's the only thing I can think of. The guy I was speaking to had only just started working on the case, but he knows our investigation is connected now, so he's going to keep us up to speed.'

Stevens nodded and turned to Lockett. 'So, how did you get on?'

'The guy in Dumfries thought it was probably Mr Roberts and the children that he saw, especially when I sent him more pictures. But the more I pressed him for details, the less sure he became.' She pulled a face. 'To be honest, he sounded pissed when I spoke to him last night and not much better this lunchtime. I don't think we can rely on him as a witness.'

'But we also can't discount that he may be right,' Stevens said. She nodded.

'I've found something,' George said, eager to have his turn. 'I've looked through the contacts on Mr Roberts's phone and then I went through birth and marriage records and all that stuff. And I've found another couple of relatives. In Ireland. Seems they're his first wife's grandparents. Her only living relatives. She lived with them for a time when she was growing up and used their address as her home address when she and Mr Roberts got married. Their marriage certificate is from a parish near Cork.'

Lockett got up and went to her computer, started tapping on the keyboard. 'Just had a thought,' she said as she typed, then leant back as she waited. She nodded, looking pleased with herself. 'So, let's suppose Mr Roberts was going to see his only other living relatives. If he was in the Lake District, where would he sail from?'

The men looked at her, frowning.

'Cairnryan, that's where! It's in Dumfries and Galloway, north of where the guy thought he spotted them at a petrol station.' Her eyes were bright. 'It was them, wasn't it? I bet it bloody was.' She picked up her phone. 'I'll check the passenger list.'

A couple of hours later, Lockett and George were on their way to Ireland, retracing the steps they now believed Mr Roberts and his family had taken. They were working on their own time now, the trip outside their brief, but having started the case, the whole team was keen to see it through to the end and this lead was too strong not to follow up.

George had managed to locate Anna Roberts' grandparents in the residential home where they both lived, and having spoken to the manager, Lockett was feeling hopeful – it seemed they both had bright minds, even if their bodies were failing them. Maybe Luke still kept in touch with them? That's what they hoped to find out. It was their last lead to follow up and if it didn't go anywhere, then at least she'd know that she'd done a proper job on the case before HQ took it over.

Although Luke and his family hadn't appeared on the passenger list for the ferry on the Friday, Lockett had worked out the journey times up to Cairnryan and found that it was perfectly possible they were aboard, if the sighting of them in Dumfries had been genuine. Jackson had scrutinised the passenger list and although there was no Luke Roberts among all the families travelling that night, there was only one male passenger with two children in tow. A Mr Lucas Bright, with his children Tilly and Cai. And on that basis, Lockett and George had set out.

CHAPTER FORTY-SIX

Wednesday

After an early start from their hotel and some time spent getting the necessary clearance for their enquiries from the Garda, it was almost one by the time Lockett and George completed their drive through Ireland.

'We're getting close now,' Lockett said as the sign welcomed them to the city of Cork. 'You'd better help me with directions. I'm rubbish in busy traffic, always end up in the wrong lane.'

The residential home where the grandparents now lived was a modern two-storey building on the outskirts of Cork, set in lovely landscaped gardens – all gravel and grasses, rockeries and shapely trees, which looked good even in winter. They were shown into a spacious lounge where an elderly couple sat together in a large bay window. They seemed a little confused as to who the British cops were, and after half an hour of cryptic answers to straightforward questions, Lockett decided they should leave them in peace.

George looked a bit downcast as they got into the car, because it was his research that had led them to the home. 'I hope I haven't wasted our time.' He looked anxiously at Lockett.

She gave him a smile. 'Well, we know all about the lovely holiday our elderly couple had in the Lake District in 1964, but that's about it. Couldn't get a straight answer to anything, could we? They wouldn't even confirm if they still owned their previous address. I know it's still registered to them, but property sales take a while to get updated on the land register sometimes. And I suppose if they have moved into a home, they might be renting it out.'

They mulled over the different scenarios.

'Right,' Lockett said as they set off. 'Now we're here, let's visit the address where the old folks used to live. It's as good a starting point as any.'

The property was easy to find, standing on its own on the outskirts of a village, surrounded by fields. There was a car outside, washing on the line and four children of assorted ages playing in a field next to the house.

George frowned and checked the address again, to make sure he'd got it right. 'This is it. Is there somewhere we can pull over?'

Lockett parked a little way up the road next to a derelict cottage and they got out, walking back towards the house, George using binoculars to get a better look. He watched the children, a smile growing on his face. He recognised two of those faces, faces he thought he'd never see in person after he'd found the bloodstained clothes in the binbag. He passed the binoculars to Lockett. 'Have a look.'

She adjusted the focus and scanned the field where the children were kicking a football. 'It's them, isn't it?' She was grinning. 'We've only bloody found them, haven't we?'

'I don't know who the other kids are. Friends, maybe?'

Lockett thought for a moment. 'Didn't the Welsh force say that the rest of the family had disappeared? Maybe they all decided to do a runner? Anyway, looks like everyone's home. Let's pay them a visit.'

When they rapped on the door a young woman opened it, wiping her hands on her apron. Her face fell when she saw them.

'Oh, hello,' Lockett said, all jolly. 'Um, I was wanting to see Luke Roberts. Is he home?'

'No, he's…' The woman stopped herself, her eyes widening before her face hardened into a deep frown. 'I don't know who you're talking about.' She gave them a tight smile. 'I'm sorry, you must have the wrong address.' And with that, she shut the door in their faces.

After a moment's silence, Lockett signalled to George that they should go back to the car.

'Well, that says it all,' she said, getting back in the driver's seat. 'Look no further. The missing family are here.' She ran her hands through her hair, unsure what to think. Relief that they were alive, or annoyance that they'd wasted so much police time?

George turned to her. 'So, what shall we do now?'

She was just working out what the correct procedure would be when her phone rang. It was Jackson.

'Ailsa, just thought you'd like to know, the Welsh police have been on with some information they were given by Edward Roberts when he was interviewed. Apparently, he's told them everything, including the fact that his cousin was involved in the drugs business. He also said something else, something very interesting…' Ailsa waited, wondering why he always had to do this. Why couldn't he just spit the bloody information out?

'Go on, put me out of my misery.'

'You were on the money, Ailsa. Those names on the passenger list were indeed our Mr Roberts and his children. His cousin arranged false IDs for them so they could escape his marriage.'

Ailsa laughed. 'Way ahead of you. We've found them.' A swell of satisfaction grew in her chest. It was nice to be right. But then her boss had been right as well, when he'd suggested that they had just run away. Were they running from the drugs business, or Luke's wife? She thought it was a bit of an extreme way to get out of a marriage when all was said and done. Especially when he was an abuser. But there was so much they didn't know and a lot that didn't make sense. He was running away from something, that was for sure, and her job was to keep those children safe until they knew exactly what was going on.

'I better speak to the boss, see what our next move is.'

She was very much looking forward to meeting Mr Roberts now. It would be interesting to hear his version of events. His justification for all the resources that had been used in the search for him, and the bruises he'd given his wife and children. She nodded to herself as she talked to Stevens, then said her goodbyes and disconnected.

'Right, our mission, should we wish to accept it, is to watch and wait. The boss is going through whatever channels he has to go through to get them picked up and shipped back to Cumbria for questioning.'

CHAPTER FORTY-SEVEN

Wednesday

After his conversation with Lockett, Stevens walked out of his office, a satisfied smile on his face.

'Okay, Jackson, I guess this is the happy bit. Let's go and tell Mrs Roberts that we've found her family, shall we?'

They arrived at the holiday cottage to find everything was still the same, the two cars still in the drive, which was a relief, Stevens thought, because there was always a chance people might try to do a runner in these cases. Vulnerable, was how he would describe Mrs Roberts, but then, as he knew from experience, appearances could be so deceptive.

The curtains were still closed and he wondered if she was asleep. He checked his watch to find it was just after four o'clock. Late for an afternoon nap, he thought. He gave the door knocker a few hard whacks, and they waited.

He banged the knocker again, waited a bit longer, but there was still no reply. When he tried the door, it was locked. They walked round the back of the cottage but the back door was locked too. He sighed, went round to the front and knocked again.

Unease prickled his skin. Nobody could have slept through the racket he'd been making, and he wondered if he'd been wrong and she had done a runner after all. There was the man she'd been having an affair with. She could have got him to come and pick her up. He pursed his lips as he thought, his heart beating a little faster.

'Right, Jackson, we're going to have to break the lock. Give it a go, will you?'

Jackson's eyes lit up and he hurled himself at the door. A few minutes later they were in. Straight away, Stevens could feel the absence of life in the house. It was so still, so quiet. And very cold.

'Feels empty, doesn't it?' Jackson said, eyes scanning the hallway, wary.

'I'm afraid so,' Stevens sighed. He'd obviously got it wrong, his character antennae letting him down. 'Let's have a quick check round, get those DNA samples, then we'll call it in.'

'Right.' Jackson went outside to get the gloves and evidence bags, then they checked downstairs, but everything was neat and tidy, only a couple of empty wine bottles on the worktop. Apart from that there was no washing up, no mess of any sort. Stevens noticed that Mel's coat was still on the hook by the door. And underneath sat a pair of her shoes; the ones she'd been wearing yesterday. His stomach griped. This wasn't feeling good now.

'I'll go first,' he said to Jackson, as he led the way up the stairs. He peered into the master bedroom but there was nothing there. He let out a long breath. 'Go and get the DNA samples from the kids' rooms, will you? Or there may be toothbrushes in the bathroom down the corridor.'

He took the two bags that Jackson held out to him and headed into the en suite off the master bedroom.

And stopped, his heart thumping so hard he'd swear he could hear it.

Mel Roberts was lying in the bath, motionless, her face underneath the water, eyes closed as if she was asleep. A glass was perched at the end of the tub, an empty bottle next to it. And folded into the glass was a scrap of paper.

She was very obviously dead.

A sadness wove itself into his heart as he gazed at her lifeless form. The bruises round her wrists looked darker, more livid in the water, where her arms floated on the surface. Or was that his imagination? Maybe the action of the water or the start of decomposition? He was no expert.

An accident or suicide?

He picked the scrap of paper out of the glass and unfolded it, looked at the scruffy writing, which straggled all over the place and it took him a minute to understand what it said.

I'm sorry, I can't go on.

He looked at her peaceful face, unable to move for a few moments. Then his brain kicked into gear and his training took over. He called to Jackson, who came dashing into the bathroom, stopping when he saw the body in the bath. Stevens noticed the lad's face go pale and he realised it was probably the first dead body he'd ever seen.

'We're going to need an autopsy. Can you call it in?' Jackson didn't move, his eyes glued to the body. Stevens turned away, his hand on Jackson's arm as he steered him out of the bathroom. 'I think we've done everything we can here. Come on, we better wait outside.'

CHAPTER FORTY-EIGHT

Wednesday

Luke rubbed at his eyes and slapped his cheek. He'd covered too many miles over the last week, with too little sleep, and the last thing he wanted was to fall asleep and come off the road so close to home.

'I've got to take the hire car back to England,' Luke had said to his mother on Monday morning, having come to some clear decisions during the previous night, when sleep had eluded him. 'Then I'll get us a bigger car. There's an MPV for sale near Dublin – a private cash sale, so I think we'll be safe enough. We can all fit in that. It means a couple of days away though. Are you okay to keep an eye on the kids?'

His mum had smiled at him, so much more relaxed now they were settling in to the new house, and that in itself made everything he had put his family through worth it.

'Okay, love. That's not a bad idea. The kids will be fine here, in fact, I think you'd have trouble tearing them away.'

Luke knew she was right; his children were having a wonderful time with their cousins, the four of them running around like a little herd of wild animals after the restrictions of the journey and the stress they'd been under for so long. After all, it wasn't just the adults in the family who'd had to abide by Ted's rules, it was the children too, and although Luke knew Ted loved his nephews and nieces, his love was so oppressive they hardly dared to speak out of turn. Now he could hear them all laughing and shrieking as they ran round the field outside, playing a game of chase.

The noise of them, that innocent laughter, was enough to fire up his resolve. He knew what he had to do, and even though his mother wouldn't approve, it was the only solution.

Late on Monday night, he rang his mother to check that everything was okay with the children and to find out what Ted had been up to.

'It's nearly done,' she confirmed, relief in her voice. 'Mel has been taken away by the police. Ted's just got to hand in the bag of clothes, then he's more or less finished.'

'Great, Mum. Well, I'm going to turn in for the night, I'll let you know when I'm on my way back, okay?'

He said his goodbyes and hung up, but didn't go straight to bed. He had one more call to make that night, while his nerve held. He rang the Crimestoppers number he'd found online.

'I've got some information,' he said when the operator answered. His dilemma formed a hard knot in his stomach. *Am I doing the right thing?* He remembered his mother's words, her tales of how Ted had controlled every aspect of their lives, not letting them have their own money, or even leave the farm. Isolating them from friends and cutting off contact from all their local connections. He remembered how he'd been moved to tears by the fact that his family had uprooted themselves for him, to help him resolve his problems.

They did that for him.

Now he had to do this for them.

'It's about a cannabis farm in Gwynedd, North Wales. It's run by a man called Edward Roberts.' He took a deep breath and answered all the questions and when he disconnected he sat for a long time, letting the enormity of what he'd done sink in.

*

By Wednesday lunchtime, Luke had managed to pick up the car in Dublin and was on his way back south when his phone started to ring. He answered straight away – there was only one person who had this number, and that was his mum. His gut twisted, unsure why she'd need to contact him.

'Hey, Mum, everything okay?'

'Oh, Luke. Where are you?' Her voice was shaking, panicky, and he knew there was a problem. 'I thought you'd be back by now.'

The tone of her voice grabbed the back of his neck like an icy hand. 'I'm on my way. What's wrong?'

'They've found us. The police. They were at the door. A man and a woman.' He could hear the short gasps of her breath, as if she'd been running. 'What are we going to do?'

Luke's pulse quickened, his mind searching for an answer that might calm her down. 'What? Are you sure?'

'Well, it was Ceri who opened the door. The woman asked for you and Ceri realised that nobody knew you were here. So, she denied any knowledge and shut the door.'

Christ! How did they track me down so quickly? A flush of heat surged through his body, sweat gathering on his brow. 'And they were definitely police?' He pulled into a layby, wanting to focus on the conversation. This was the worst news. The very worst.

'Well, she didn't give them time to say. They weren't in uniform or anything and not Irish. But who else would be asking for you here?'

Luke had to admit that the logic was sound. He couldn't think of anyone else who'd be knocking on their door. *The police. Already?* He closed his eyes, telling himself not to panic as adrenaline coursed round his body. Maybe it wasn't as bad as he thought. Maybe Ceri had got it wrong. Misheard or something, her worry about them being found making her hear things that hadn't been said. That was possible, wasn't it?

'Mum, I'm almost at Cork. I'll be there as fast as I can.' He gathered his breath, a whole herd of thoughts galloping through his mind as he tried to decide what he should do to keep his family safe. 'Don't worry, just keep an eye out and don't open the door to anyone.'

'Okay, Luke. You take care now.' There was a tremor in her voice and he knew he'd done little to ease her panic. 'Don't go driving too fast. I couldn't cope if you had an accident.'

Luke thought the possibility of an accident was probably the least of his worries. 'I'm sure it's all okay, Mum. See you soon.'

He ended the call and screeched away from the kerb.

They found me. How the hell did that happen?

His heart was racing, panic searing through his body as he ran through everything in his head, trying to work it out. His plan was in pieces, the risks he'd taken all for nothing. *How has it all gone wrong?*

Ted. That was the obvious answer. He was always the weakest link and his mother's insistence that he should be involved, that the timings wouldn't work without him, had proved to be their undoing. He was pretty sure Ted would have had an uncomfortable encounter with the police by now after the call to Crimestoppers. Maybe Ted had told the police that they'd escaped, told them about their new identities. *He'd do that, wouldn't he?* And once the police knew they were alive, well, it was simple to check through family connections and that would lead them to the house.

Luke clenched his teeth and snarled at the naivety of them all. Ted had known too much. And now he'd put them all in danger. *Or did I do that myself?* It had been Luke's decision to get the drug squad involved. Had that been his downfall? *What goes around comes around*, he reminded himself, and he knew that none of them were blameless. All of them had made decisions that had led them down this dead-end. There had never been an easy solution, no miracle cure to ease their desperation.

As he approached the suburbs of Cork, he knew what he had to do. There was only one way to keep his family safe and he had to be brave and just do it. He stopped the car, checked the map on his phone, and found the place he was looking for. Easy enough to get there, he realised, memorising the directions. With his jaw set, he ticked off the left turns and the right turns in his head until the building he was looking for was there, in front of him. He parked in a visitor's space, took a deep breath and walked through the doors.

The person at the desk looked up, his Garda uniform crisp and tidy, an enquiring expression on his face.

'I'm Luke Roberts. I'm visiting relatives and I've just been told that the police in Cumbria are looking for me.'

CHAPTER FORTY-NINE

Ten months later

Nine months and twenty-three days after he'd been taken into police custody, Luke walked free from Wrexham Prison. There was a car waiting for him, his children standing beside it, along with Ceri, who'd been looking after them while he was inside. He'd admitted to everything relating to the drugs business, told the police everything he knew and was rewarded for his cooperation with a more lenient sentence. He'd never known time go so slowly, each day inching to its conclusion, but he'd made sure that he was a model prisoner and now he was out on parole.

'Dad! Dad!' The children jumped up and down and ran to greet him, throwing their arms around him as he crouched down. He held them to him and savoured the precious moment, the feel of his children, his flesh and blood. The people he would do anything for to ensure their safety.

'I've missed you both so much.' He buried his head in Tessa's hair, Callum clasped to his chest, unable to say more for the lump in his throat.

He'd had a lot of time to think in prison. Time to understand his priorities and come to terms with the decisions that he'd made. As luck would have it, he was put on the same wing as Ted and with the help of a mediator, over the space of several months, they'd managed to talk through what had happened, and why the family had needed to get away from him. How his over-protectiveness had become oppressive and abusive.

Counselling had helped Ted's view of the world to become more balanced and he and Luke had come to an understanding. Ted would be inside for at least another year, having admitted to being the mastermind behind the cannabis operation, and Luke had promised to visit him on a regular basis, hoping that, over time, they could work out how he could become part of the family again.

The children pulled Luke towards the car, where Ceri was standing waiting, a wide grin on her face. He'd never seen her looking so happy and he wrapped her in a big hug.

'Thank you so much for looking after these two.' He let out a shuddering sigh as the realisation hit him that he was really free. 'My God, it was…' He could feel the emotions swelling up in his chest and he turned to look back at the place that had been his home for almost ten months, clear in his mind that he would never do anything that might risk a return visit.

'No problem,' Ceri said. 'They've been great. No problem at all. We've all settled in to that big house of yours just fine.'

'I can go for sleepovers with Sion still, can't I, Dad? It's only round the corner.'

''Course you can, Cal. When you're invited.'

'And Tessa comes swimming with me on Thursdays,' Ceri said, throwing an arm round her niece's shoulder. 'It's okay if we keep that up, isn't it?'

'We have to go,' Tessa piped up, ''cos Auntie Ceri fancies the lifeguard.' She giggled as Ceri pulled a horrified face.

Luke laughed and nodded. 'Of course it is.' Swimming. He was glad Tessa had found something she enjoyed and if it was allowing his sister to have a more normal life again, then all the better. 'Swimming sounds great.'

'It's such fun, Dad. We do life-saving and dive for bricks and I can swim a mile now.'

Luke looked at Ceri, who was hiding a smile. 'A mile. Well, that's pretty impressive.'

'And I want to go on Tuesdays as well, Dad. Then I can train to be in the team.'

Luke blinked harder. 'Yep, yep, I'm sure that'll be fine.'

'Hey, let's give your dad a bit of space,' Ceri said with a laugh, bundling the children into the car, while Luke got into the passenger seat.

Luke watched the prison fade into the distance as the car moved away from the kerb and they started on their way home to Bangor, where his parents would be waiting for him, having sold the farm and bought a bungalow on the same estate as Luke's house.

It's over. It's really over.

Ceri had been given a suspended sentence for her part in the drugs business. Luke had testified that she had nothing to do with it and the court believed him for the most part, because it corroborated what Ted had said. His parents had also been exonerated of any blame, all their children having testified that they'd had nothing to do with the business.

'Sion's dog has just had puppies, Dad.' Tessa's voice was wheedling.

'They're so cool,' Callum chipped in. 'Just little balls of white fluff. And there's two left that nobody wants.' Luke looked over his shoulder and caught Tessa giving Callum the thumbs up.

'Yes,' Luke said, not having to be asked. 'Yes, we can. It would be mean not to give them a home, wouldn't it?'

'Really?' He turned and looked at the joy on his children's faces, his heart swelling with love for the two people he cared most about in the world.

He nodded. 'Yes, really.'

A couple of puppies would be a great focus for them all, and he didn't even need to know what breed they were. What did it matter? It would get them out on walks and they could all get involved in training them.

It was going to be tricky to find work now with his criminal record, but he'd got a volunteer placement working at a home in Llandudno for blind ex-servicemen. Selling the cannabis had been wrong, and he accepted that, but he still wanted to help his former colleagues. This placement sounded perfect and he'd been told that if it worked out, then come the summer, there would be seasonal work. And who knew what might happen after that.

They turned onto the A55 and headed home, and the chatter faded for a while. Left with his own thoughts, Luke nodded to himself. He'd done the right thing, he was sure of that now. It had been a hard choice to make and a big risk, but looking at his children and his sister, seeing how they'd blossomed, he knew that he'd make the same choice again because it had been the only way to set them all free. Free to be themselves and escape their life of fear and abuse.

Luke smiled and let out a whoop of joy that set the children off laughing; a sound that was music to his ears. It was the sound of his future.

EPILOGUE

It was almost nine in the evening and dark by the time he got to the Lake District and the house. He parked down the road a little way, in an entrance to a field where his car wouldn't be seen, then walked, glad to see that the lights were on, the cars were in the drive and Mel was home.

He tried the door, but it was locked. He knocked, his heart pounding in his chest, no idea how his arrival was going to be received.

She stood in the doorway, swaying slightly, and stared at him, her mouth hanging open, before throwing her glass of wine into his face. He didn't flinch, but instead moulded his expression into a mask of regret and apology, letting the wine drip from his chin, stifling his instinct to wipe it off, smothering the curses that ran up his throat, threating to burst from his mouth. He had to take care. *Baby steps*, he told himself. *Little baby steps until I've got this done.*

'I'm so sorry, Mel. We need to talk.' He put his hands together as if in prayer. 'Please let me explain. Then you'll know I've got your best interests at heart. Please?'

Her eyes were wild, fury twisting her mouth from side to side. 'Damn right you need to explain!' she yelled. He kept his distance, letting the anger work through her system.

'Will you let me in, Mel. Please?' He kept his voice soft. 'Let's talk this through, then you'll understand.'

She stood on the doorstep, her breath puffing out of her mouth, making white clouds in the icy air as her hand reached for the door handle as if to slam it shut. She frowned at him for a long moment. He could almost see her thinking. Then she went back inside, throwing a look over her shoulder. 'You better come in.'

The tension tightened in his shoulders. That was the first obstacle dealt with. Now he had to focus on the next. *Be nice*, he told himself. *Persuasive.*

He followed her to the lounge, where she stood in front of the fire, glaring at him.

'So, go on then, tell me why you're here.' She looked him up and down as if he was the most repulsive thing she'd ever seen and he reminded himself that it didn't matter.

Grovel, he told himself, his fists clenching with the desire to smack that derisive expression off her face

'Look, Mel. I'm pretty shaken up myself.' He put a hand to his forehead. 'Let's be civil about this.'

'Civil?' She spat the word at him, fury reddening her cheeks. 'You are going to pay for this. You and your shitty kids. You think you can do something like this to someone? Do you?' She shook her head, advancing towards him, her empty wine glass stabbing at his face. 'I told you what would happen if you tried to leave me, didn't I? I'll have those kids off you in the blink of an eye.' She nodded. 'And then they'll know what proper discipline is.' A sneer twisted her face. 'The police think you've been abusing them. Oh yes, and the teacher at school rang in to say she thought you were hitting them and I showed the police these bruises on my wrists.' She laughed then. 'So who's going to believe you, eh?'

Luke staggered backwards, shaken to the core by her words, and knew then what he had to do, what he had to say. He'd hoped with all his heart that it wouldn't come to this, but her words had narrowed it down to one option and one option only.

'No, no, you've got it wrong. I'm not leaving you. There was an emergency. Let me explain.' He grabbed her glass, keen to neutralise the only lethal weapon he had spotted in the room. 'I'll fill this up, shall I? I could do with a drink, my nerves are shattered after what's happened.'

His heart was hammering so fast he thought it was going to burst out of his chest. *Will she go for it? Will she?* He held his breath, watching her, getting ready to take evasive action if needed. The tic jumped by his eyebrow as he waited for his wife to strike. Her mouth screwed into a scowl, bringing back memories of all those times she'd hit and scratched and thumped and thrown things at him. All the words of derision, the constant chipping away at his self-esteem. The fear they'd all felt in her presence.

That's when any doubts evaporated.

Later, he watched her, lying there in the bathwater, looking so peaceful, and he wished with all his heart that things had been different. But he'd tried, hadn't he? He'd tried until he himself was on the point of suicide. His children deserved to be free of her. As did his family. Imagine if she'd got custody of his kids. Imagine what torture that would have been for all of them.

Bubbles of air floated to the surface.

Then they stopped.

A LETTER FROM RONA

I want to say a huge thank you for choosing to read *Love You Gone*. If you did enjoy it, and want to keep up to date with all my latest releases, just sign up at the following link. Your email address will never be shared and you can unsubscribe at any time.

www.bookouture.com/rona-halsall

The inspiration for this story came from a discussion with my husband during one of our long dog walks, when I was throwing story ideas about. It struck me – when do we ever hear news stories about men as the victims of domestic abuse? Clearly, it happens, but seems to be one of society's taboo subjects, something that isn't acknowledged and therefore makes it so hard for victims to find any sort of support or even recognition that it is happening to them.

In writing this novel, I wanted to look at impossible situations and explore what lengths someone might go to in order to free themselves, especially if the safety of their children was involved – this element is told through both Luke and his mother's perspectives. Abuse comes in many different forms, and possessiveness can be just as damaging to a person, especially when they become a virtual prisoner in their own home.

I hope you loved *Love You Gone* and if you did I would be very grateful if you could write a review. I'd really like to hear what you think, and it makes such a difference helping new readers to discover one of my books for the first time.

I love hearing from my readers – you can get in touch on my Facebook page, through Twitter or Goodreads.

Thanks,
Rona Halsall

f @RonaHalsallAuthor

🐦 @RonaHalsallAuth

ACKNOWLEDGEMENTS

Firstly, I would like to thank you, the reader, for choosing my book, and I hope you have enjoyed the reading experience as much as I enjoyed the writing.

As always, I have to thank my agent, Hayley Steed of Madeleine Milburn Literary, TV and Film Agency for her enthusiasm, and Bookouture for giving me such a warm welcome to their family of authors and amazing support team.

Massive thanks have to go to my fantastic editor, Isobel Akenhead, for seeing the story within and showing me how to turn things inside out and upside down until it all fitted together properly. Amazing clarity, as always! And then there's Noelle Holten and Kim Nash, Bookouture's publicity magicians, who seem to work wonders with only twenty-four hours in the day. Love you guys, for all your wizardry and motivational kicks up the bum.

Talking about motivation and support, I'd be nowhere without the backup given by my fellow Bookouture authors – thanks for the pep talks, answers to research questions and the laughs. The author's lounge has got to be my favourite place to procrastinate! And then there's the Savvy Authors – what a generous, lovely bunch you are – and especially Tracy Buchanan, who set up the Snug, made it the best place to be and taught me so much about the nuts and bolts of being a published author. Quite an education!

And then we come to those closest to me. I have to give a shout out to my friend and first reader of early drafts, Kerry-Ann Mitchell, whose perceptive comments have helped to shape this book. I need to thank my family for understanding that they should not try and talk to me on certain days and at certain times. All I have to say is 'edits' and they slink off into a quiet corner, embracing their neglect. And while we're talking about neglect, none of this would be possible without my husband, David, who has been ignored for long periods of time during the writing of this book, but has been unfailingly enthusiastic and tolerant.

Finally, there's the dogs, Freddie and Molly, who drag me out when I don't feel like it and give me space to think. Without them I'd be a shapeless blob with a brain like custard.

Made in the USA
Columbia, SC
27 September 2020